Danger in the

Bahamas

Cathy Zelenka

First published in 2015
Cathy Zelenka has asserted her right under the Copyright, Designs and patents Act 1988 to be identified as the author of this work.
@2015 Cathy Zelenka
ISBN – 13:978- 1512330533

This book is dedicated to my encouraging and immensely patient husband Bob, in memory of my mum Eileen and to my inspiration Sue Johnson (author).

Best Wishes,

Cathy Zelaka

Prologue

This is Radio Grand Bahama, Hurricane Bertha has been upgraded to category three. We repeat, Hurricane Bertha has been upgraded to category three. It will hit Grand Bahama in the next twelve hours. We expect winds in the region of one hundred and eleven to one hundred and thirty miles per hour and extensive damage. You are urged to go to a place of safety immediately. Don't forget to keep your radio dial tuned to Radio Grand Bahama - your sunshine station.

Becky slid down onto the solid earth floor crying tears of frustration, her voice hoarse from screaming for help. It was pitch dark in the wooden hut and she knew all too well that it contained nothing to aid her escape.

Dragging herself up and onto her feet, she winced as pain shot through her left knee. "Have to do something... There must be a way..." she muttered to herself. She couldn't remember how many times she'd made her way around the walls, but she started again. Whenever her feet encountered an object she crouched down and felt it with her hands behind her. "Yuk!" she should have remembered that the plastic bag contained only a mess of what felt and smelt like decaying food. She stumbled over a collection of large tins and careered into a pile of stacked up plastic seats. They crashed onto the ground, she almost fell over them in the darkness and grazed her arm on them. "Damn! Damn!" She bit her lip and tried not to cry.

She felt down for one of the tins with her hands which were tied behind her back. Scrabbling with her fingernails she located the plastic handle. Her wrists were sore and she could feel that they were bleeding, where they'd chafed against the rope in her efforts to free herself. She gritted her teeth and holding the handle tried to hit the tin against the wall. It hardly swung and did nothing. *This is hopeless, I can't even wipe my tears away,* she thought.

She tried to swallow but her throat was dry. *Stop feeling sorry for yourself it's not helping!* Her stomach lurched when she wondered how long she'd been there - *it must be over an hour now. An hour - how much longer have I got?*

When she stopped her efforts she could hear the wind howling and the sea pounding the nearby shore. Somewhere the rigging of a boat was metallically clanging, plastic was blowing around, some of it rustled against the side of the hut as a can rattled its way past. The noises made her feel lonely, as though she was the only living being. Alone. Waiting for disaster, in the middle of the maelstrom happening all around outside.

Suddenly there was a huge crash. Becky screamed. The tin roof and wooden walls of the hut vibrated, she guessed that a large branch of a palm tree must have landed on the roof. She knew that soon the trees themselves would be torn down in the coming hurricane's fury.

Her blonde hair fell over her face and she shook it away impatiently. Clad only in jeans and a T-shirt she shivered with cold and fear. She hurled herself against the frame of the door, but she was no match for it and only succeeded in hurting her shoulder.

Getting herself down onto the floor she lay on her back and grimacing at the discomfort banged her feet against the wood of the wall. "Damn!" her knee hurt like hell.

It was dark and claustrophobic in the confines of the small hut. Her heart raced and she could hear her breathing, ragged and fast. Her terror felt as though it was consuming her. Panic was taking her over. She slid down onto the floor shaking from head to foot, moaning, "Oh my God. What can I do? What can I do?"

She was alone, locked in a hut, on a deserted beach, with a hurricane on its way. However, it wasn't the coming hurricane that was terrifying Becky. It was much worse than that.

Making a desperate effort to regain control she sat upright against a wall and drew her legs up to her chest as far as she could. Rocking to and fro she tried to calm herself. Closing her eyes she forced herself to remember how beautiful it was when she first arrived in the country of seven hundred islands - in Freeport, Grand Bahama.

Chapter 1

This is Radio Grand Bahama your sunshine station. A beautiful day is forecast on this fifteenth July 1975, clear skies, and a high of eighty four degrees Fahrenheit with humidity at seventy five per cent. Now here's 'Mr Smooth,' himself, it's Barry White, with, 'Can't Get Enough Of Your Love Babe...

Becky fell deeply in love before she ever got off the 747 that flew her from Heathrow's overcast skies to the azure of the Caribbean.

Looking out of the cabin window she glimpsed tiny palm tree laden islands. They seemed to float in a tranquil sea that changed from deepest violet and ultra-marine over the reefs, to jade and turquoise as it lapped crystal white beaches.

Howard a balding retired English bank manager inclined towards Becky and said, "You know the space astronauts marvelled and remarked on these colours from way up in space."

"They're incredible. It's so beautiful," Becky agreed. She thought it was like a scene from a travel brochure. She could hardly believe she was there, that it actually existed.

Howard had been admiring Becky's slim jean clad legs and figure for twelve hours now. She had a habit of twirling her long blonde hair around a finger and Howard kept finding himself thinking how great her hair would look spread out across a pillow. He'd also had plenty of time to indulge himself in thinking how great she'd look - spread out on his bed. A dreamy smile crossed his face. He felt a sharp dig in his ribs.

"Howard! The seat belts sign's on - you're daydreaming."
Howard's plump middle-aged wife Celia gave Becky a chilling
smile, her grey eyes cold beneath her winged bi-focal glasses. Her
rigid permed hair matched the usual expression on her face.

Becky forced herself to smile back. She was only too happy
that she wouldn't have to listen to the everyday life of a bank
manager in Littlehampton for much longer and excited at the
prospect of her new life in the sunshine of Freeeport, Grand
Bahama.

*This is Radio Grand Bahama your sunshine station. It's three a.m.
on the fifteenth of July, we have a warm moonlit night and a low
of seventy five degrees Fahrenheit.*

Earlier on the same day that Becky arrived other people
were making their way towards their new life in The Bahamas.

At three a.m. the skipper of the 'New Dawn' was cursing
the moonlit night. A quietly groaning mass of people were silently
cursing the skipper himself, who'd taken so much from them for
this never ending journey in the leaking rust bucket that was the
'New Dawn'. Ostensibly a fishing vessel, the real money was to be
made transporting human cargo to a new life. Whatever its
uncertainty, it held out more hope than Port Au Prince - the
capital of the most corrupt and impoverished island of the
Caribbean, the hell hole that was Haiti.

The passengers spoke mainly in Creole.

"How much longer, Maman?" the little girl Mari asked.

"Not long, ma petite," her mother Eugenie replied. She
held Mari close to her and wrapped her blue shawl around them
both a little more tightly. It didn't warm them. They wore thin
cotton dresses which had clung damply, since the evening of the
previous day, when they'd waded out to the boat. Josef, Mari's

father, had held Mari as high up as he could but they'd all been splashed by the sea. The floor of the boat was now soaking. Water sloshed around as the boat crested small waves.

"Teddy's, cold," said Mari, clutching a patched and worn teddy with one ear missing.

"Tell him he'll be fine. We'll be in the sunshine soon and he'll have lots of new friends to play with. He'll be warm and happy always" Eugenie shifted her position, her back ached and the new life growing inside her stirred. "You too," she whispered, "a good life, a happy one for all of us."

"How are you both?" Josef said in English with a heavy Haitian accent.

"Bien. OK. Husband."

Josef tried to use English whenever he could. He'd spent long hours poring over old school books by the light of the kerosene lamp in their hut in Haiti. He'd practised speaking it whilst working clearing tables at one of the smart hotels for foreign tourists. Like all the passengers on the boat, he'd never left Haiti before. They'd sold everything they possessed and promised much more to get out of Port Au Prince and start a new life in the Bahamas, with maybe the chance of reaching the 'Promised Land' of America in the future.

They'd been chugging along for hours when the moon suddenly came out from behind a cloud and illuminated the shore some five hundred metres off. At that same moment a little distance away, another much stronger light shone out on the surface of the water. The sound of fast approaching engines could be heard.

"Bloody hell! Dowse all the lights!" exploded the skipper.

"Oh Christ! Customs!" said the mate.

"Get them off!"

"What?"

"You heard! Get them off! We get caught with this lot we'll both be in Fox Hill Jail for the next twenty years. Not that you'll last five minutes in there with your white skin. Now move!"

"How?"

The skipper cut the engines and pulled out a gun. "Damn fool, just do it!" He ran to the people huddled in the hold of the boat and started wrenching them to their feet, gesturing with his gun. His black eyes were menacing seen above the scarf which was tightly wrapped around his face. Obviously Bahamian from his accent, he was fit, strong and determined.

"Out! Out! Look it's not far. Out! Out now or I shoot!"

"Non! Non! Que Dieu nous aide! - God help us!" came from all sides.

The sound of the other boat was coming closer. Several of the younger Haitian men slipped over the side of 'The New Dawn' and struck out for the shore. The skipper and the mate started dragging and pushing the others out into the water.

"Now! Or I swear I'll shoot the lot of you!"

"Don't piss us about! Bloody jump!" said the mate, to Josef and Eugenie. He grabbed Josef who was slightly built and bundled him to the side. In the struggle a scarf came off the mate's face momentarily and almost without realising it, Josef saw the man's white face and blond hair. The mate hastily pulled it up again and grabbed Josef by the shoulders. The light from the approaching customs boat illuminated a large gold signet ring on the middle finger of his right hand.

"My wife and child they cannot to swim!"

The skipper moved in. Pushed his gun into Josef's face, "I ain't got time for this shit! Customs be here any minute, man. They'll pick you all up."

The Haitians were both confused and frightened. They ran from side to side, not knowing what to do. The skipper pushed

Josef hard and at that same moment, the boat rocked violently with the uneven weight of the people rushing about. Both Eugenie and Mari fell into the water screaming, along with some of the men and several other women and children.

Josef jumped in after them. Luckily the water was warm but he went under momentarily, his clothes and the weight of his sandals pulled him down. He came up spluttering and frantically looked around. People were floundering and grabbing each other, yelling and going under. Others tried to hold to the slippery barnacled sides of the boat but couldn't get a grip. The mate hit at their frantically flailing hands with a heavy stick. They cried out and vanished under the waves. The high pitched cries of children and the cursing of the men filled the air.

"Mari! Mari! Eugenie!Eugenie!"

"Papa! Papa!"

He heard Mari's voice close by, and as the moon came out again, he clearly saw her. Her arms were stretched high above her head. Then she went under. He swam to where he'd seen her and dived beneath the water, frantically trying to find her. He could see nothing. He was forced to surface, gulp in air and dive again. He reached out with his hands and touched something. A handful of clothes. Heavy. He grabbed at the bundle and with his breath bursting, he tried to swim back up to the surface dragging it in his arms. It seemed as though hours went by in that strange dark quietness. Somehow his feet propelled him upwards. He exploded through the surface some distance away from the boat, carried by the current. He gasped and spluttered his chest burning. He looked at the bundle, "Mon Dieu!" it was Mari that he held.

She was choking and crying. She started to frantically claw at him whilst screaming, "Maman! Maman!"

"Mari! C'est Papa! Lie still and let me take you. You're going to drown us both! Lie still!" It was as though suddenly all the strength went out of her and she lay in his arms shivering and whimpering. Her huge brown eyes fixed on his face.

The sound of the throbbing engines of the approaching customs boat grew louder. A search light strobed the sea. The fishing vessel erupted into life, its engines churning the waters up, leaving people floundering in its wake.

The customs boat lights were coming closer and the sound of the engines filled the air, urgent and menacing. Josef yelled twice more, "Eugenie! Eugenie!" but there was no answer. He struck out for the shore dragging Mari with him. When he got a little distance away he looked back. The lights illuminated a scene from hell. People were still thrashing around in the water. Their screams floated back to him on the still night air.

"Maman! Maman!"

"Au secours! Au secours! - Help! Help!"

"Je ne sais pas nader! - I can't swim!"

"Tomas! Tomas!"

"Annette! Beatriz!"

"I'm drowning!"

As he watched helpless, the sounds were diminishing all the time. He saw people and children simply disappear in the wake. Little children and even babies were handed up into the customs boat, other people were dragged on board, some of them protesting and cursing, fighting the men pulling them from the water.

It was quiet then except for the sound of the engine turning over and the customs men shouting to one another. Josef had got to know some of the other passengers on their long journey. Under the bright lights on board he could just glimpse them. He felt their agony, imagined them sitting shivering silently, or quietly crying. All hope of a new life gone.

In the beam of the customs boat's lights Josef thought he saw something else in the water. He screwed up his eyes. He wasn't certain for a moment. But then he saw it clearly. *God no!* It was a dorsal fin. A shark was circling the boat.

"Jesus nous aide!" he struck out for the shore with Mari half on his back her arms around his neck. His heart was pounding, his whole body aching with the effort. He kicked out as hard as he could with his legs to propel them forwards, the panic giving him a strength he didn't know he possessed. At last, swallowing sea water, retching and sobbing he hit his knees on a rock. "Jesus!"

Mari was crying, "Maman, Maman."

Josef unclenched Mari's hands from around his neck and carrying her he staggered to his feet and onto the beach. He put her down for a moment. Aged only five she looked tiny and vulnerable, her hair clinging to her face, water streaming from her dress. She was shivering and her teeth chattered with cold. Josef sighed and stroked her head.

"What's happening Papa? Where's Maman?"

"Hush, baby, hush. Bad people are looking for us. We'll find Maman later, right now we need to get away, or they'll make us go all the way back. We'll be forced back into a boat. We need to be really quiet."

"I've lost teddy, Papa," she sobbed.

"I'll find him I promise, but for now you must be quiet. Can you be quiet for me?"

"OK, Papa. I'll try," she said little gasps still escaping her.

"That's, my baby. I'll carry you. It'll be like a game, we can warm each other up." He took off his T-shirt and quickly wrung it out and replaced it and did the same with Mari's dress. He rubbed her cold arms and body with his hands and picking her up hugged her to his chest.

Josef looked around him, the beach seemed deserted, but he had no idea where they were exactly. The moon illuminating the beach increased his anxiety that they could be discovered at any moment. At the back of the beach was a large area of scrub and trees. He carried Mari through it, his legs and arms scratched by thorns and branches. Eventually he reached a dirt road and he started to run as best he could with the weight of Mari in his arms. Water squelched from his thin sandals.

Out of the darkness he heard the sound of a siren and saw lights approaching in the distance. He scrambled back into the scrub and bushes at the side of the road, and pushed Mari under a large bush before diving in after her.

"Papa, it scratched me!"

"Tais-toi!-Hush child. Let's pretend we're playing Hide and Seek like at home. Be quiet for me."

The car headlights approached and Josef tried to control his shaking body. It was travelling slowly now and men were holding torches from the windows.

"Tais-toi-quiet," Josef whispered. "Bad people want to find us. Stay quiet, cherie."

The light raked the bushes where they hid.

"Heh! I've found something!" one of the men shouted.

Josef felt sick. He stifled a moan. He could feel Mari shaking in his arms. Then he heard them laughing. He held his breath. The bushes moved.

Josef suddenly heard snuffling and panting very close.

"Damn wild dog, you idiot! Come on! We're losing time! Let's go!"

They accelerated away. The distinctive smell of wet dog drifted in to Josef and Mari and they could hear it, very close by, scuffing up the sandy soil. A huge filthy brown dog, its ribs sticking out, its breath foul, suddenly stuck its head right into the bush where they were hiding.

Josef was shaking from head to foot now. "Clear off!" he yelled.

The dog stopped dead still for a moment and then started to growl menacingly, its fangs emerged and its teeth shone white in the darkness.

"Papa!" screamed Mari.

Josef stood up and quickly looking around him grabbed a nearby stick and raised it. He yelled, "Fous le camp batard! - Fuck off you bastard!"

The dog seemed to understand the sentiment if not the language and turned and ran off, its tail between his legs.

"Papa, I was frightened."

"Don't worry, cherie. I'm never going to let anything happen to you"

"But, Papa where are we going? Where's Maman?"

"We're going to see Uncle Peter. He will look after us. Maman's going to join us in a few days. It'll be OK. You'll see everything will be OK." Josef's voice cracked and he hugged Mari to him, glad of the dark so that she couldn't see the tears running down his face.

The 747 touched down smoothly. The cabin doors opened and warmth and light flooded in. The scent of jasmine and the heady perfume of hundreds of other exotic flowers wafted through the cabin.

At the top of the steps Becky stopped and looked around her. She screwed up her eyes against the dazzling tropical light, the intensity of the heat combined with the humidity already causing the sweat to run down her body. Scarlet and shocking pink bougainvillea covered the airport buildings and from the foot of the steps, she heard the tinkling Caribbean rhythms of a small steel band playing the classic Harry Belafonte number, 'Island In the Sun.' A nudge from the person behind and smiling broadly Becky went down the steps to her new life.

When she arrived at the bottom of the steps she saw a small low concrete building in front of her, the sign grandly announced, 'Freeport International Airport.' Once inside she found herself in a cool air conditioned and white painted concourse, with a customs desk and two 'check-ins'.

Eventually Becky's large brown leather case emerged onto the carousel. She lugged it off and looked around her. Howard and his wife, along with all the other tourists, were being shepherded away by their tour operators. She felt uneasy and more out of place than she ever had in all her twenty three years. She suddenly realised with an almost physical sense of shock that she was the only white person left. It wasn't that she was a racist, it was just that in 1975 the only black person to be found in Dorset where she came from was the occasional foreign doctor. Her holidays abroad had been spent with her family in a 'gite' in Brittany, where again virtually everyone was white. It felt strange that upon stepping into the airport building the status quo had been reversed in an instant. Here it was the norm to be black and she was the outsider. She felt conspicuous as though she was an intruder.

At her interview on a grey March day in windswept England, a free ticket to the Bahamas in exchange for being a nurse there for two years had seemed almost too good to be true. She realised with a start that she hadn't thought it through. She'd been told that she'd be met. The airport was emptying fast and she felt foolish standing there on her own in a foreign country, not knowing what to do.

An immensely tall and large black man with a scar running down the left side of his face was leaning on a counter. Aged about thirty he was smoking a huge cigar whilst chatting and laughing with a beautiful Bahamian girl sitting behind the counter. He whispered something in the girl's ear and she smirked. After a few minutes she got up giggling, carrying a clipboard in one hand. She blew him a kiss with the other and wiggled off in a uniform that left little to the imagination.

The man looked at Becky for several minutes and then started walking casually towards her. She gripped her handbag a little tighter and looked around her but very few people were now to be seen. When he reached where she stood he took his cigar out of his mouth, looked down at her from his great height and said in a heavy Caribbean accent, "You must be the new nurse."

Becky laughed in relief, "Yes, that's right, I'm Becky Lewis."

"Clifford, ma'am. At your service," he said with a big smile and stretched out and shook her hand with a strong grip. He picked up her heavy case as though it was a bag of sugar. "Let's go," he said and strolled out through the doors with Becky trotting beside him, to a waiting ancient and battered, small ambulance.

He gestured to the front seat, "Welcome to the Bahamas, Nurse, you're gonna love it here. Ain't no better place to be." She could have sworn he winked at her. As she clambered in she glimpsed him appraising her bottom with a practiced eye, and he seemed to hold her arm for a fraction longer than was necessary.

Becky wasn't sure if she'd imagined it. She pushed her hair off her sweating forehead and looking around her at the profusion of greenery and brightly coloured flowers.

"It's certainly beautiful, Clifford."

Clifford's bulk occupied most of the front seat which was in the style of a couch. Becky tried to ignore the embarrassing sensation of his thigh wedged up against her own. She tried very gently, to ease herself away a fraction.

"Are we going to the hospital, Clifford?"

"No. Matron ain't there jus' now. I's taking you to an apartment where you can stay 'til you get something permanent settled."

"An apartment! Isn't there a nurses' home?"

"Ain't no home for nurses here, Becky," he chuckled. "Less you count mine of course." He slapped his leg and enjoyed the joke for some minutes. "Nurses home! Lordy!"

Becky forced a smile onto her face. She wanted nothing more than to stop travelling - after fourteen hours she was exhausted.

They drove along almost completely empty tarmac roads before pulling up outside a small white, two storey modern apartment block. In front of the building were waist high hibiscus bushes, covered in saucer sized flowers in an array of yellows and pinks, whilst purple bougainvillea cascaded over the entrance. Becky and Clifford got out and he fetched a small cardboard box of food out of the back of the ambulance.

"The hospital send you this to keep you going," he said as they walked up to the first floor.

Becky looked and saw a loaf of bread, margarine, eggs, bacon, coffee and milk.
"Great, how much do I owe them?"

"Notin' its free."

Becky was astounded, she couldn't imagine the N.H.S. being so thoughtful to foreign nurses arriving in Britain. "That's lovely, thanks a lot, Clifford."

"I'll be round tomorrow 'bout nine, take yous across to The Royal." He gave her the apartment key and a tatty piece of paper with a phone number on it. They arrived at a white door, the entrance to number seven.

"You be wantin' any little t'ing afore then, you just ring Clifford," he said with a big grin, his eyes lingering on her T-shirt.

"Thanks, Clifford. I'm sure I'll be just fine. I'll see you in the morning," Becky said firmly.

"Bye, Nurse, see ya soon."

Becky turned the key in the lock, picked up her case, went in and closed the door behind her with a sigh of relief.

She gasped when she went through the small hall and entered the lounge. The air conditioning was on full - a cold physical shock after the sweat-trickling heat outside. She looked around her open-mouthed. It bore no resemblance to the dreary tiny room in the nurse's home in Dorset that she'd just left.

A fully equipped kitchen led off a large modern lounge decorated in vibrant shades of blue. Opening another door she found the bedroom. It was painted in shades of cream and lemon, the crisp white sheets on the double bed looked inviting. She couldn't resist sitting on it and bouncing up and down for a moment. "Amazing!" she muttered smiling to herself. An en suite immaculate bathroom led off the bedroom. Going back into the lounge she pulled back white curtains and a mosquito screen to reveal French windows opening onto a small balcony, overlooking a large swimming pool.

"Wow," she said. *If the girls back home could see her now.* She walked out onto the balcony and again the heat encased her. Fading in the sky were the remnants of a beautiful sunset - a pastel reflection of the colours of the hibiscus that she'd seen earlier. Dusk was rapidly falling. She leant on the balcony and yawned. Looking below her she saw that the pool and surrounding gardens were completely deserted, one or two apartments had their blinds drawn and she could just glimpse light seeping out, the others seemed to be empty. The shadows were lengthening and she suddenly felt uneasy.

Suddenly a sound rose up all around her like nothing she'd ever heard before. It was a vibrating, throbbing, almost metallic noise, she was startled and grasped the balcony railing. It was the sound of the cicadas - the large grasshoppers of the Caribbean settling down for the night. It sounded completely alien to her and the noise filled the gardens.

The perfume of the flowers increased in its intensity, the humidity and the heat were overwhelming. She jumped as another noise cut through the still evening air. It was an emergency vehicle trumping even the cicadas with its high pitched undulating screeching, very unlike ambulances or police cars back in England.

A chill ran down her spine. Becky fumbled with the door catch and stumbled back inside. Looking around the apartment she felt very alone, a long way from home and for the first time she wondered what she'd done.

Across the island May Lee was also wondering what she'd done. She tried not to look at the filthy kitchen table that she was lying on. What light there was struggled through a dirty locked window, its dingy and tattered net curtains held together with a large safety pin. She found that she was breathing quickly and the cloying smell of sweat and stale blood in the air was making her feel nauseated. It was claustrophobic and hot in the kitchen of the tiny wooden house. She tried to swallow but found her mouth was too dry. She licked her lips.

Filtering through the thin walls she could hear that someone out in the street had their radio tuned into a gospel channel. The sweet sound of the choir, the chants of "hallelujah," and the loud cries of "Jesus" from the congregation interspersed with the pastor's rhetoric, all reinforced her feelings of guilt and the certain knowledge that she would be going to hell.

Her back ached and her head swam. She was uncomfortable on the hard table. Maybe she could still back out. Maybe she should say something. Maybe...Before she could open her mouth to say, "I've changed my mind," a bright light at the foot of the table was switched on. It dazzled her, as it danced off the stainless steel instruments lying on a grubby tray.

"Legs wide apart!" came a woman's voice.

May Lee bit her lip. *I really don't have a choice*, she thought. She'd already taken off her underclothes. She was glad she couldn't see the woman behind the light, she knew it was better that way for both of them. Even if the light hadn't blinded May Lee, the woman was indistinguishable wearing a surgical face mask and a woollen hat pulled down tightly over her hair. She did as the woman said. Suddenly she felt the kiss of cold steel between her legs.

"Keep your legs apart, girl!" said the woman as she shoved a stainless steel speculum in, and opened it wide.

May Lee scrabbled for the fabric wedge in her hand and put it in her mouth as the pain went through her. She felt as though she would be split apart.

"Keep them apart, girl! Jesus you must have spread them four months ago!"

May Lee tried not to moan, her fingernails dug deep into her palms as silent tears streamed down her face. She knew she deserved to be punished for her previous foolishness and the sin she was now committing.

The preacher's voice rose up from the radio, "Those that don't observe The Lord's laws will surely go to purgatory and everlasting damnation!"

"Amen," cried out the congregation. "Praise the Lord! Hallelujah!"

"Oh! It's hurting!"

"For Christ's sake keep still, child!"

She felt an unendurable pain - sharp and twisting like a claw. May Lee fell into blissful oblivion.

Chapter 2

This is Radio Grand Bahama your sunshine station. It's the sixteenth of July and another beautiful day in our land of seven hundred beautiful islands. We have an expected high of eighty seven degrees Fahrenheit with ninety two percent humidity. You may get a heavy shower this afternoon. Have a nice day.

Becky woke early the next day feeling both tired and excited. Pulling back the curtains she said, "Incredible!" The sun was already high in the sky, birds were singing and in the gardens the hibiscus blazed in their vibrant shades of scarlet, tangerine, yellow and pink.

Becky showered and got ready for work her stomach churning, as she wondered what the day would hold. She put her blonde hair up and looked at her reflection in the mirror. She'd bought a white uniform and she was surprised by how different she looked. At home she wore a royal blue dress with a starched white apron. She made herself a strong cup of coffee and picked at some toast from the supplies she'd been given.

She was ready by eight thirty. She tried reading a book whilst she waited for Clifford but she couldn't concentrate. Then she turned on the TV. She flicked through several channels - a quiz show, an old movie, yet another quiz show, cartoons, and adverts every few minutes. She sighed and turned it off. Eventually she decided she'd just wait outside and enjoy the sunshine.

Even at that time of the morning the heat startled her as she opened the door. It was very quiet, no-one else was up, the only movement was that of the birds flying overhead and the little khaki coloured lizards darting about in the bushes. The time dragged and she started to sweat.

The door of the apartment underneath her own opened and a woman in her forties with blonde dishevelled hair emerged. She pulled her blue floral dressing gown around her and yawned. She looked as if she'd had a very late night. Looking over she saw Becky, "Hiya, honey. How ya doin? Are you OK?"

"Yes, thanks, I'm fine."

"What ya doing out here at this time of day?"

Becky introduced herself and explained that she was waiting to go to work. She was growing impatient now and the woman's American accent grated on her.

"Well, sugar, I'm Margaret and my husband he's Max. You know where we live now, so don't be a stranger. Any time you want anything just come down and see us all. We can have a little drink together."

"Thanks." Becky was relieved when at this point the ambulance pulled up, as by now it was almost half past nine.

"Bye, Margaret."

"Bye, honey."

Clifford leant over and opened the cab. "Mornin', Nurse. Wow! You sure look different in uniform," he said.

"Good-morning, Clifford. Did you have some sort of emergency to go to first thing?"

"Hell no. Everyone sleeping this time of day," he said with a big grin.

"We're a bit late aren't we?"

"This is the Bahamas. You'll get used to it." He put the radio on and a calypso filled the cab. He drove in no particular hurry, swaying from side to side in time to the music, one hand on the wheel, a cigarette in the other. Every now and again he slowed down to shout out of the window at someone he knew. His thigh was again pressed up against Becky's in the confines of the cab. The ten minute journey to the hospital felt like ten hours to Becky.

The hospital was a low white building with a corrugated roof. The Royal Freeport Hospital was proudly emblazoned on the front. Becky got out and hitched down her dress under Clifford's approving gaze. They walked from the car park with Becky shading her eyes. Everyone they passed gave them big smiles and spoke to them.

"Hi, Clifford. How you doin'?"

"Good morning, Nurse," came from all sides. They walked through a massive entrance hall, with plain plastered walls, two or three brown plastic chairs and a few rickety tables dotted about. There was a strange absence of the distinctive disinfectant hospital smell so familiar to Becky in England. Later she was to discover that that was because there was no disinfectant.

Two Bahamian nurses were giggling and whispering together and Bahamians some fully dressed and some in nightwear were chatting, smoking, lounging around or walking in a leisurely fashion. The switchboard was behind the front desk, manned by two girls filing their nails and giggling.

Clifford showed Becky to the office on the ward. The desk was in total disarray, covered in laboratory reports, patient details, X-rays, notes and half empty plastic coffee cups. A cockroach hastily scuttled underneath a cupboard.

"This is the new nurse, Sister Carey."

A black woman aged about forty, turned around from putting drugs into medicine pots on a tray. She was a big woman. A white uniform struggled to contain her generous bosom and clung to her rolling hips. Her straightened and glossy ebony hair hung to just above her shoulders.

"So I see," she said unsmiling, her brown eyes appraising Becky and, from her sour expression, finding her lacking.

"I'm Becky Lewis," said Becky holding out her hand.

There was a pause when Sister Carey just looked at Becky and her outstretched hand before taking it for the briefest of handshakes. Becky was surprised to see that the sister's nails were manicured and she wore bright red nail varnish. She turned back to putting drugs into pots.

"Clifford, ain't you got no work to do?" she said glancing over her shoulder.

"Sure thing, Sister Carey," said Clifford shooting Becky a wink before quickly leaving.

Without turning to face Becky she said, "Lewis - go find O'Hara. She's taking her break in the coffee room. She'll show you round."

"OK," said Becky all too pleased to leave Sister Carey's presence. *Great - she looks like she's going to be a lot of fun to work with,* she thought to herself.

Becky walked down a brown linoleum-floored corridor with white walls. A lot of cramped rooms held two patients and there also seemed to be larger ones holding about fifteen. She only glimpsed one other nurse. Eventually she opened a wooden door marked Staff Room. It opened into a small room with walls that were once white. There were three or four scruffy plastic tables with chairs around them. Sitting at one was a nurse in a white uniform with her back to Becky.

She turned around and Becky saw an attractive, slim, red haired girl aged about twenty-five. A huge grin broke across the girl's face.

"Well what have we here?" the girl said in an Irish accent. "You must be the latest lamb to the slaughter! I'm Teresa, welcome to the Royal. Jesus, Mary and Joseph! What are you wearing?" She looked at Becky's uniform in open amusement and shook her head. "Too long, too loose, too English. Don't worry I'll get you kitted out in the local shop. What's your name?"

"It's Becky. I'm..."

"Come on. I'll show you round, Becky. Do you want a coffee first? Where are you from? How old are you?"

Becky laughed as Teresa paused for breath just long enough to take a drag from her cigarette. Teresa crossed her long brown legs and tugged ineffectually at her skimpy white open necked uniform. Two pockets on her hips bulged with an assortment of scissors, tape and surgical dressings.

"I'm from Dorset. I trained in Poole and I'm twenty-three. Anything else you need to know?" said Becky.

Teresa tried to speak through the pins she'd now got in her mouth, she was jabbing them through her long red hair which was falling out of an elastic band.

"Come and sit down," she mumbled.

As Becky sat down she couldn't help but notice Teresa's heavy black eye shadow and eye liner worn in the style of Dusty Springfield. She had the most startling and beautiful blue eyes underneath.

"Sorry, it's just that it's so long since we've had a new English nurse here. The last one only stayed two weeks and that was about nine months ago. I want to know all about you."

They chatted for about fifteen minutes. Becky warmed to Teresa, she was fun, she made her laugh and she seemed genuinely pleased to meet her.

After a while Teresa said, "I'll show you round. I warn you it's not like home."

Becky was already sweating profusely, it was about ninety degrees and the humidity was high. There was no sign of any air conditioning.

"How do you cope with this heat?"

"Don't worry you'll get used to it and there's no rushing about like at home."

Becky looked around her and wondered if she'd ever get used to anything at the Royal. She realised with a start that Teresa was still talking.

"OK, so this is the room where we put the children. Most often it's diarrhoea and vomiting they come in with." The sound of a child wailing emerged from the room. Becky walked in and saw children of all ages, in small beds and cots, in an airless, stiflingly hot room. The walls were painted white and there were no pictures or toys of any description. Many of the children were under a year old their faces shrunken like old men, their eyes huge and staring. Some were crying. There was no sign of a nurse.

"Of course their parents are so scared that they'll get a big bill, they don't bring them in until they're half dead." She looked at Becky's face. "Luckily kids are pretty resilient so once we get a drip up they usually do great."

"Yes, yes that's true, they are resilient," said Becky faintly.

"We'll find one of the aides on our way round to go and sort out the ones that are crying," said Teresa looking at Becky's face.

Teresa moved on and opened the door of a small room with two beds in it. "Hello, ladies. I've got a new nurse for you to meet, this is, Nurse Lewis.

"Nice to meet you, Nurse," said a white woman her face swathed in bandages.

"Yes, nice to meet you," said a black woman lying propped up with an infusion running into her arm.

"And, you too."

"How are you both today?" asked Teresa.

"Oh I'm really excited, Nurse. I get to see the results of Mr Silver's work this morning," said the white woman

"I'm sure you're going to look a million dollars. But you know you'll look a wee bit bruised at first don't you?"

"Oh, yes, he's warned me about that."

Teresa turned to the patient next to her, "And how are you doing, Lucy?"

"Tryin' to make it, Nurse. I feels a lot better than yesterday."

"Great. I'll be back to see if you both need anything a bit later, when I've shown Nurse Lewis around."

"What are they in for?" Becky asked as they walked on down the corridor.

"Mrs Clinton-Smythe she's had a face lift and Mrs Ward's had a cholecystectomy. She came in, in agony about four days ago, with gall stones.

In the next room one patient had had a heart attack and another had pneumonia. "So, you get all types of patients here in the one ward, Teresa?"

"Yeah, sure. This is the only hospital on the island and there's just this one ward."

"Oh... Right...Yes, of course."

Teresa explained that patient's with health insurance or those who could pay were admitted to the rooms with two beds, if there was one available. Everyone else was put into either the Men's or the Women's rooms.

. "This is the Women's room."

Becky walked in and saw about thirty five patients lying in beds; one or two were chatting to each other, the rest were mostly sleeping, a couple of them were moaning softly, many had infusions running. A nurses' aide was moving a rickety fabric screen around a woman who wanted a bed pan. When the aide took the bedpan away Becky noticed that it was uncovered. At the far end of the room there was a chipped wash basin with one tap, there were no signs of soap or paper towels. A ceiling fan moved the hot, humid air around.

Becky was astonished. *The patients however*, she thought, *were like patients everywhere - stoic.* All greeted them with affection and respect.

"Morning, Nurse, how you doin'?"

"You new, Nurse? That's real nice. Hope, you likes it here."

They moved next door to the Men's ward. One man turned to the one in the next bed, "You wanna use this, man?"

"Sure thing. Thanks."

The first man handed the second a urine bottle that was already a third full. Teresa didn't appear to notice. There was a crunch under Becky's foot. She looked down. A dead cockroach lay under her shoe.

"My God, Teresa!"

"Yep. I'm sorry, Becky, but it's the real Bahamas we've got here. Not the one you see in the ad's. back home."

"Yes...I had no idea...still...the patients seem lovely."

"Yeah, they are. In fact I find some of the older patients almost embarrassingly polite and respectful. It's because these islands were British for many years, they only became self-governing in sixty five and independent two years ago, so people still remember white rule. Originally they were brought here as slaves to pick cotton. Then, you Brit's kept them down just like you did us."

"Us?"

"Yes. Us Irish. You must have noticed the accent."

"Well, it wasn't my fault was it?"

"No. Sorry. You're right. I guess I lived in Belfast for too long. It gets to you after a while. Come on let's go see who we can find in ER."

"ER?"

"Yeah, the emergency room - that's A&E to us," Teresa said with a smile.

They walked around a corridor passed the separate obstetric ward, the sound of babies crying and a woman screaming could clearly be heard. Teresa just walked further down the corridor to a door labelled ER. When they entered the room Becky's mouth dropped open. She looked around and saw that the emergency room was just that, consisting of a small cupboard lined room and two stretchers. A few seats in the room opposite served as a waiting room.

A doctor was bending over a Bahamian man listening to his chest with a stethoscope. Becky looked at Teresa, her eyes sparkled, she pulled back her shoulders ever so slightly, jabbed her hair into its pins and smiled broadly.

"Stefano, I've someone for you to meet."

He stood up and turned around to face them. Becky found herself looking into the deepest of brown eyes, the sort that her friends used to call 'come to bed eyes'. She felt her stomach lurch. God he was gorgeous! Tall and slim, aged about twenty seven, with dark hair and a beard. She tried to stop herself blushing as he looked her up and down before a huge smile revealed his perfect white teeth.

"Well hi there. A new nurse, what a treat," he said in an accent that was American with perhaps just a hint of underlying Italian. "I'll be with, you, in a minute, girls, don't go away," he said, and turned back to the patient, a hint of cologne, male and sexy, wafted their way.

"Could you not just take him home and pop him between the sheets?"

"Teresa!"

"Don't tell me you don't fancy him!"

"He's OK - if you like that sort."

"Have you got a boyfriend then, Becky?"

"No. I had a boyfriend back home - Tim," Becky frowned, "but he wanted to control me, he got too serious. It's partly why I came here. I want a new start."

"Oh well, as long as you don't want to start with Stefano."

"No, I don't. I don't really approve of mixing work and pleasure. I'd never go out with a doctor. They all think you're easy."

Teresa sighed and raised her eyebrows. "Really? Anyway Stefano's mine... Well, not just mine to be completely correct. He's got a wife and two kids back in Miami. He's just here earning money and having fun for a year."

"Don't you care?"

"Not really. Don't look so shocked, Becky. There are no rules here, you'll see."

"Sorry. It's none of my business, Teresa."

"Don't be sorry, sure, I want us to be friends."

At this point Stefano came out. They chatted about where Becky was from and where she was staying until the ambulance pulled up outside. Clifford wheeled a groaning patient in on a stretcher.

"I'd better go. Great meeting you, Becky. I'll catch you later. Maybe we can all go for a drink."

Teresa shot Becky a filthy look.

"Yes, err, maybe," she said with a wan smile and Stefano went in to see the patient.

At this point a slim black woman dressed in baggy green theatre trousers and tunic top, carrying some sterile packages came towards them.

"Well if it isn't the Irish one," she said in a mock Irish accent. "Top of the mornin', Tess'," she smiled broadly.

"Top of the mornin' to you to, Sister. Becky, this is Sister Patterson - runs the theatre here like clockwork."

"Hiya, Becky. How ya doing?"

"I'm fine thanks. Pleased to meet you."

"Lord you two's look like you could do with some feeding up. You want to come over to my place some time? I'll do you some real nice chicken and okra with peas and rice."

"Sounds great to me," said Teresa.

"Yes, thanks," said Becky.

"Well I needs to get a move on. Mustn't keep Mr Silver waiting." She carried on up the corridor.

"Gosh she seems nice."

"Yeah, she's been running theatres as long as it's been here. You get her talking on the old days and she'll tell you about Elizabeth Taylor and other stars having their face lifts done here, back when it was a private hospital."

"Really!"

"Yes, really. No shit."

"Who's Mr Silver?"

"He's the chief surgeon. He's American, only works part time these days but he's been here forever too. He and Sister Patterson are rumoured to have had a thing going once. He seems really nice - especially for a surgeon. He's got a huge motor launch and he often invites us nurses to parties on board but so far I've always been working. There's one in a few weeks, maybe we could both put in for a day off."

"Yes, that would be great, Teresa. How many qualified nurses work here?"

"Well, there's us, Sister Carey and let me see... about four Bahamian qualified nurses. You'll soon meet us all. Right, well that's the tour done. We'd better go and get on with some work, we don't want to get on the wrong side of Sister Carey."

"What's she like?"

"Her bark's worse than her bite. She doesn't really like us ex-pats but if you work hard she's OK."

"It's all so different, Teresa."

"Well you wanted a change."

"It certainly looks as if I've got one doesn't it?" They both laughed.

Whilst Becky was getting up that morning Josef was limping along a dusty road. Mari was sleeping, carried on his back her head resting on his neck. His arms and back ached and his body burnt with a fever. He was glad that Mari slept, he had no answers for her questions about her mother Eugenie. His cousin Peter had sent word back to Haiti last year ago that he was safe and living in a place called Eight Mile Rock on Grand Bahama Island. He said he had a house with a garden, a job, a life. Josef only had to find him and all would be well.

Josef came across a settlement. Wooden huts some no more than shacks and so like those in Haiti - his heart sank. They were the same as homes for poor people everywhere, made of driftwood, pieces of plastic, corrugated iron with cardboard stuffing up the holes. Here and there were small houses, this couldn't be Eight Mile Rock - could it? A tired looking and obviously pregnant woman was pushing a battered pram, a toddler holding the side and a small boy aged about five trailing behind her picking flower heads off their stalks. Josef thought he might ask her where he was, he looked at her.

"What you looking at, man? You lookin' at me?"

"No, no I sorry. Just want to know what this place is?"

"Why? Don't you know, man?"

"Sort of lost, ma'am."

"Well this is Eight Mile Rock, OK?"

"Yes. That's...That's... great. That's what I thinking." His face fell and he sighed. *Had they done all this for nothing? Had he lost his wife and unborn child for a life where he knew no-one? A life no better than the one they'd left behind.* The woman shook her head and moved on. More people were coming into the dirt streets now. Conversations drifted around Josef as he wandered on down the road.

"Heh, man, how you doin'?"

"Tryin' to make it."

"How's that woman of yours?"

Dogs ran around barking and the sun was already high in the sky. The smell of tropical flowers mingled with decaying rubbish. Small children ran around completely naked and the occasional old car bumped over the potholed main road. *Maybe it wasn't quite so bad though,* he thought. Many of the houses were clean and painted, everyone seemed well fed and there were no police with guns and batons out looking for trouble like at home.

He risked approaching another woman. This one was good looking, she wore a brightly coloured short dress.

"Excuse, ma'am I looking for Peter?"

"Peter who?"

"Peter Leblanc."

"I ain't never heard of no Lee... Lee what?"

"Leblanc. No problem, ma'am. Thanks."

"Where you from, man? What you doing here?"

"Nothing. I'm just meeting a friend. Thanks."

He turned and walked away quickly aware of her gaze on his back.

After about half an hour he saw a large Bahamian woman going into a church with a mop and bucket.

"Excuse me, ma'am."

"What can I do for you, honey?" The woman put her bucket down, turned around and smiled at him. She had crinkly brown eyes that lit up her tired face, Josef thought that she looked to be around thirty.

"I'm looking for my cousin."

"You ain't from round here is you?"

Mari stirred and started to cry.

"Maman, je veux Maman," she said.

The woman looked at him sharply.

"It's OK. I'm going."

"No, no don't go," she said touching Josef's shoulder as he turned to leave. "The Lord he say, 'Suffer the little ones to come unto me.' You looks all in and the child too. You fancy some grits for breakfast."

Josef hesitated.

"Papa, j'ai faim"- I'm hungry.

He looked at the woman. He couldn't walk much further anyway.

"Thanks. That's very kind. And my daughter she's...It's been a long time..."He trailed off.

"Don't worry we'll find your cousin. But first breakfast."

The same morning, Steve and Jennifer were standing at the jewellery counter of the tiny boutique, in the lobby of the Hotel Marina. Steve fidgeted with the elastic of his blue checked Bermuda shorts. He'd certainly eaten well since bringing Jennifer his much younger girlfriend on holiday to the Bahamas and he guessed the cocktails weren't helping his expanding waistband much either. His floral shirt was rubbing on his sunburnt shoulders and Jennifer was whining on about the diamond necklace which the assistant had quickly got from the display case and was fastening around Jennifer's slim neck.

"Oh, darlin' look how great it looks," she said leaning forward and displaying the ample cleavage of her thirty eight D breasts which were straining to be contained in a low cut red satin top. Steve swallowed hard. He couldn't help but think that her long golden legs which finished somewhere around the level of his paunch, were also looking particularly good today in a pair of skin-tight, high cut, white shorts.

"Gee, honey, it looks nice but you look just as good without it."

"Well you'd have me stark naked if you had your way, Stevie."

He groaned softly to himself and pushed away the picture starting to form in his mind. "That's not true, honey. You know I always think you look great."

"Don't you try and sweet talk me out of it, Steven."

"Well to tell the truth, darlin' I'm a bit short at the moment and anyway I've left my wallet in the safe in our room. Why don't we just go get one of those cocktails by the pool that you like so much?"

"I might be blonde but I'm not dumb, you're just changing the subject. I think you left your wallet there on purpose, Steven C. Clarke."

"Aw, no, honey bunch I wouldn't do that."

"Anyways don't you just love the way it sparkles?" she said thrusting out her breasts at him again. Steven started to feel distinctly uncomfortable in his Bermuda shorts.

"It sure suits you, madam," said the assistant.

"See even she agrees."

Steven had spent a fortune on this holiday in order to get Jennifer away with him. He'd spent almost up to the limit on his American Express card and he decided to put his foot down.

"No. I'm sorry. It looks good, baby, but hell it's five hundred dollars."

"Well aren't I worth five hundred little dollars to you?"

"Well yeah of course you are, but what with the holiday and the alimony for Helen and the kids, I think we're all gonna have to make a few little sacrifices."

"Why did you bring up that bitch's name!"

"Now don't raise your voice, sugar, people are looking."

"Don't you sugar me! She's got everything. I've got nothing. I don't think you really love me like you said you did! You ain't even married me!"

People were turning around now some of them smirking as they walked through the lobby.

"Aw, come on..."

Jennifer tore the necklace off and threw it onto the desk. "No! I've had enough! You're taking me for granted, Steven C. Clarke! I'm going for a walk and I just might not come back!"

She stomped off her breasts swaying magnificently and the shorts showing off her tight, neat bottom to perfection. Steven watched her go. *Christ! She looked hot when she was angry!* He sighed and walked back across the lobby to get the lift back up to their room and retrieve his wallet.

Jennifer walked down the steps of the hotel smiling to herself. Passing the beach bar next to the one hundred foot swimming pool she paused for a moment and watched the other tourists swimming, sunbathing and drinking cocktails. The current pop hit, 'Jive Talking,' by the Eagles, was blasting out of the speakers. She started to hum and wiggle her bottom in time to it. *I bet you're going back for your wallet right now Steven C. Clarke,* she thought to herself.

She reached the edge of the hotel grounds. A scarlet hibiscus fringed path led to the silver beach and sparkling turquoise sea. She took her sandals off, the sand felt warm and sensual between her toes. *Lord she felt hot.* She wandered along the deserted beach and noticed that someone had left a pile of clothes down by the sea.

Strange, she thought and wandered across.

She drew closer. Even the fake tan that Jennifer wore couldn't hide the way that the blood drained from her face. Her mouth dropped open. She stood stock still for a full minute. Unable to take her eyes off what lay in front of her. Watching the flies crawl in and out of the young girl's mouth and her open staring eyes. The fish nibbling at the girl's feet. The dried blood staining her face. Her distorted limbs. Her bloated body. The smell of putrefaction and the heat rose up at her.

Jennifer staggered backwards and vomited in the sand. Then she started running and screaming all the way back to the hotel. Stumbling over sun loungers, knocking over drinks, pushing tourists out of the way, crashing into a waiter. Eventually she reached the lobby still screaming.

Steve wandered out of the lift his wallet in his hand. He stopped dead. Arrested in his tracks by the sight of the screaming, dishevelled Jennifer. "Gee, if I'd known you wanted it that much, honey, I'd have bought it straight away."

Chapter 3

Back in Eight Mile Rock the friendly woman took Josef and Mari into her house near the church. A boy aged about ten was inside repairing a fishing line.

"Eli, I want you to go to Rosa see if she know a Haitian man name of Peter. Peter... What?" she turned to Josef.

"Le Blanc, Madam."

"Don't you madam me," she said laughing. Everyone here calls me Rach, short for Rachel. Rosa's from Haiti too, if he's here she'll soon find him."

"Thank-you, Rach."

"Come on, let's get you two some grits, you look all in."

She sat Josef and Mari on a rickety but clean settee in her tiny room. On one wall was a picture of the Madonna and Child that looked as if it had been carefully cut out of a magazine. On the black and white T.V., the Flintstones cartoons played, interspersed by adverts in which earnest men in white coats and dark rimmed glasses stood in a 'laboratory', extolling the virtues of washing powder to bemused looking housewives in floral aprons.

When they'd eaten Rachel turned to Mari, "Would you like to go and play with Helen, the little girl next door?"

Mari looked at Josef enquiringly.

"She's got a new dolly that she'd like to show you," said Rachel.

"Yes, go on, cherie."

"OK, papa," she said and skipped out of the room.

"Will she be OK?"

"Yes. Don't worry. Ain't no crime here. Everyone knows everyone here and anyways we can watch her from the door."

Josef slumped back on the settee exhausted.

"So, what happened?" Rachel asked softly. Josef looked startled. "It's OK. You can tell me. It ain't gonna go no further than these walls."

Josef told her everything. It seemed unreal, as though it had happened to someone else. Rachel looked at him with pity in her eyes. "You know she may still be alive. If she didn't drown they would have taken her back to Haiti. What's done is done. Those men - they'll get their punishment. What goes around comes around as we say here."

"Thanks, you've been good to us."

"There are lots of you Haitians living here. Don't worry, the Lord will provide. You'll see."

Josef glanced outside at Mari who'd been playing with Helen the little girl next door. A black woman was crouched next to Mari and seemed to be talking intently to her. "Who's she?"

"Oh that's Isabella. She's from Haiti too." Rachel's face darkened, "Let's go and see what nonsense she's talking today."

They went out and Josef heard Mari saying in Creole, "Like I told you the nasty man had a gun, and then me and mummy we all fell in the sea, and it was dark, and I swallowed the horrid water and..." Mari started to cry.

"Isabella! Can I get you something?"

Isabella stood up. She was an impressive woman, about six feet tall. Her face was gaunt with high cheek bones and dark flashing eyes.

"No. I was just passing. The child looked troubled." She spoke with a heavy Haitian accent.

Josef felt uneasy, a shiver went down his spine. For some reason he quietly crossed himself.

"The child's just fine, Isabella. These is Christian people."

Josef looked from Rachel's angry face to the impassive one of the woman's. "Perhaps we should go, we..."

Eli appeared around the corner with a man. A man who started to run towards them shouting. As he got nearer Josef recognised him.

"Josef! Josef!"

Mari ran up to him squealing, "Uncle Peter! Uncle Peter!" He swept her up into his arms laughing and crying at the same time. Peter embraced them both unable to speak.

 In the greetings and introductions, the hugging and crying, the strange Haitian woman Isabella, slipped away. Peter tried to give Rachel a little money for looking after Josef and Mari but she wouldn't take it. "No, you just make sure you drop by with the child now and then to see me. If you want to come to the church Sunday, I goes to the one you saw me cleaning. We'd be real happy to have you."

Peter took Josef and Mari home with him. Home was a tiny but clean two roomed hut. Later that evening when Mari was asleep Josef asked Peter, "I met a Haitian woman just before you arrived - Isabella do you know her?"

"Yeah. Well, no, not really. Everyone knows of her. I stay well clear. She's into the old ways."

Josef looked puzzled, "Old ways?"

"Yeah you know." He lowered his voice, "The old religion, all that stuff. They say she's not right in the head."

Josef crossed himself. "Mari was telling her everything."

"Don't worry. She won't hurt us or Mari. She says she only uses it for fighting evil. It's all a nonsense. I think she just a bit crazy."

"Yes, you're right. But we must keep Mari away from her. We've left all that behind us. This is a new start."

"Yes, a new life for you both. Don't worry you'll be fine here, you can make it. But tell me, where's Eugenie? When I asked you earlier, in front of Mari, you said something about her joining you later."

Josef looked at Peter. His eyes filled with tears. "I said that, 'cause that's what I tell Mari. The truth is..." He started to sob, he covered his face with his hands. "I think... I think she drowned. And my baby. Our precious unborn baby..." He slid to the floor and howled, rocking backwards and forwards.

"Oh my God!" Peter slid to the floor next to Josef, put his arm around him and cried with him.

The seventeenth of July, three p.m.
Corporal Woods and Harris along with Constables Lightburn and Johnson were on duty in the office of the small police station in Freeport. It was hot and noisy, the rackety air conditioning system having no effect, other than to compete with the radio station playing, Bob Marley, at top volume. Constable Johnson was humming under his breath to it, as he arduously typed with one finger. At twenty two years old with his boyish looks and ready smile you could be forgiven for thinking he was far too young to be in the police, but in fact he was married with two children.

He started to cough. "You think you could blow that smoke in another direction, you two?" he asked.

Corporal Woods a heavy set man in his forties, who looked older than his years due to a fondness for Becks beer and cigarettes glanced across, "Cool it, man," he said sending more smoke in Johnson's direction and continuing talking to Constable Lightburn. They often drank together when off duty. "Then they made a run for it and scored. I'm telling you it was somethin' to see."

"Next season I'm goin' across to see the Miami Dolphins, I went last year and man you should have seen..."

Constable Harris was as usual on the phone to a woman. Aged thirty, light skinned and attractive, he had a ready smile and a smooth and charming manner. The women tourists often hired Mopeds and he was particularly fond of pulling them over for supposed driving offences.

"Are you aware of what speed you were doing, madam?" Of course they never were. Usually they were horrified at being stopped by a policeman in a foreign country, especially when he explained to them how low the limit and how high the fine was.

He looked good in uniform so they would often smile at him tremulously and ask if he was going to charge them. "Well I oughta, I could get in a whole lotta trouble if I don't." He would raise his eyebrows slightly, "But I kinda got a weakness for a pretty woman..." If they gave him an encouraging smile or giggle he knew he was in luck. "I know a real nice restaurant on Taino Beach. You want to discuss this over a steak and a beer?" Very few refused and his charge sheet was never as full as everyone else's.

His side of the phone conversation could be clearly heard.

"You know that ain't true, honey. You's the only one... Where! No I swear on my Mother's grave I wasn't in the Lucayan last night...Aw come on... You sure gonna look great in the little present I've got for you..."

Luther the sergeant erupted into the room slamming the door behind him. He seemed to fill the room. Standing with his hands on his hips he surveyed them with a furious face.

"Shit, honey. I gotta go." Harris put the phone down.

"You pieces of shit! What the hell you all think you're doing!"

"Heh, man, I'm typing," said Johnson.

"Don't you, 'Heh man' me, Johnson! I want some respect"

"Sorry, sir," muttered Johnson.

"You will be. You'll all be damn sorry. While you're sat on your arse typing we've got bodies washing up on the beach."

"Oh Jesus," said Lightburn.

"Well Jesus didn't help them. Two Haitian women, one of them pregnant and a man. The customs say they just missed the fishing boat the other night."

"What happened?"

"Damn skipper heard customs coming and ordered the lot overboard. They fished about a dozen out."

"My God!" said Johnson.

"They don't know how many drowned or how many made the shore."

"So now we got another boat load to add to the rest here," said Harris.

"Inspector Mills is ranting fit to bust a gut! Some idiot Yankee tourist found one of them washed up on the beach. She's going round squawking like a parrot, moaning on about her mental health and how she's gonna sue us and Lord knows what. Our esteemed M.P.'s on the chief's back ranting about tourism and image and Mills is on my case.

"We're doin' our best, Sergeant." Woods said.

"Well it ain't good enough. That isn't all of it. Miami customs have picked up another boat crammed with cocaine. The idiot carrying it hoping for a little less time in the slammer in Miami, told them all about how it comes by boat from South America and then some of our local lads looking to make a little dough take it to Miami on their fishing vessels."

"We're out on patrol, we're doing searches," said Harris.

"Well it ain't working is it? This island's flooded with the crap. Tourists going to the casino are getting offered any drugs cocktail they fancy. It's not doing our reputation any good."

"Yeah but it's the Mafia running it, everyone knows that," said Lightburn.

"Yeah, everyone knows but no-one knows the main man do they!" bellowed Luther. "Someone is running their operations here, and someone must know who it is."

"We've been looking for him for twenty years," said Woods.

"That's what I'm saying! You ain't looking hard enough. I want you all to get out and work over your contacts. Bring them in and see what they've got to say. This week-end you'll be patrolling the beaches all night."

"All night! You joking?" said Harris.

Luther was a big man. He bulged out of his uniform. He towered over Harris and jabbed a fat finger in Harris's face, his brown eyes menacing, his lips narrowed. "Do I look as though I'm joking, Harris?"

"N...no, no, sir," stuttered Harris.

"You'll be keeping your dick in your pants this week-end I'm telling you. You're on patrol with, Lightburn."

Lightburn groaned quietly.

Luther slammed the table with his fist, "Any more from you and you'll find yourself on a charge!" he yelled looking at Lightburn.

"I never said nuffin', sir."

"You'd better not. Meantime, Johnson and Woods come with me. We need to get down to Lucaya beach and clear up some of this mess!" Johnson and Woods got up and started putting on their jackets.

Luther blew the smoke from his cigar into Lightburn's face before throwing it to the floor and stubbing it out with his foot. "Have I made myself clear?" he said looking around the room.

"Yes, sir," they all said in unison.

"I want results - understood?"

"Yes, sir," came the reply again

"Come on, you two." They went out the door slamming behind them.

"Ah shit," said Harris.

This is Radio Grand Bahama - your sunshine station. It's the eight of August and that sun is shining. There will be a high of ninety degrees Fahrenheit, humidity eighty percent. You all relax and have a real cool day. Here's Barry Manilow, singing, 'Mandy', for you...

After the first day Becky decided to walk to work. It wasn't far and it avoided the attentions of Clifford. She was on a late shift starting at three p.m. and the sun beat down on her. As she walked down the drive from her apartment block, flame coloured petals from a gently swaying royal poinciana tree fell around her like confetti.

She wandered down the quiet road and couldn't resist picking a scarlet hibiscus flower from the plants that bordered the road. She delighted in the variety and intensity of the flowers that grew so profusely - the massive bird of paradise plants, with their fluorescent orange pointed petals resembling an exotic bird, demanded that you notice them, purple morning glory rampaged over gardens and scrub alike.

She breathed in the warm air carrying a tang of the sea and the perfume of the flowers, and felt herself relax. She stopped for several minutes to gaze in fascination at the exquisite tiny humming birds. Their wings were a whirring iridescent blur in shades of turquoise and emerald as they darted from flower to flower, hovering at each one as they gathered its nectar.

When the hospital came into sight Becky's face clouded over. She sighed at the thought of another hot and confusing day. She was struggling with the many differences between working here and in England. She was embarrassed to find that she often couldn't work out what people were saying to her, the heavy Caribbean accent rendering English into a different language.

There were never more than two qualified nurses on duty and it was always hectic. On her second day a patient needed an injection of morphine. Becky had approached Sister Carey.

"Mr Evans needs some post-op morphine, Sister."

"Yeah OK, Lewis."

"Can you check it with me?"

"Can't you see I'm busy?"

"Yes, but we need to check it, count the amount remaining and sign the controlled drug register don't we?" In England the administration of all potentially addictive drugs was strictly controlled by law. They were never even taken out of the cupboard except in the presence of two qualified nurses.

"Yeah and I need to get three patients ready for theatre or Mr Silver's gonna have my arse. This ain't England, Lewis. Just give him the morphine. We signs the book for everyone at the end of the day. OK?"

With that Sister Carey swept out of the office carrying forms and theatre gowns leaving Becky perplexed. She stood still for several minutes, unsure what to do.

"Heh, Lewis." A Nurses' Aide came into the office. "Mr Evans he's a moaning and groaning fit ta bust. He say he's gonna make a complaint if he don't get something real quick for his pain."

Becky sighed, "OK, Nurse Rolle, tell him I'm just coming." She carefully checked the drug out on her own, counted the number left, signed the controlled drugs register and re-locked the cupboard within another locked cupboard that it was held in.

The Nurses Aide returned, "Lewis, Miss Hilary's drip's run out and Mr Peters says his dressing's leaking all over the bed."

"OK. I'll be there in a minute," Becky snapped and picked up the morphine to give to Mr Evans. The Aide went off muttering, "These English, comes over here..."

"Sorry..." Becky said but the Aide had left.

Becky found that strict protocols in Britain were routinely disregarded on the ward and that everyone accepted that the drug register was often wrong at the end of the day. She thought it hardly surprising, they were so busy that sometimes she couldn't remember what she had or hadn't done. She found that being 'The New Girl,' she was pressured into falling in with Sister Carey's suggestions, that so and so was on morphine or pethidine, and they must have had an injection at some time in the shift. Teresa was laid back about it, "It's just how things are here, Becky. Don't try and change the system or lack of it. We're only here for two years, you've got to adapt."

At about seven p.m. Becky was working on the ward when the bell rang signalling that a patient had arrived in the ER. A Bahamian girl aged about nineteen was slumped in a chair moaning, there was no sign of anyone else around.

"What's the matter? What's wrong?" Becky asked feeling the girl's cold and sweating forehead.

"Bleedin' Nurse. I's bleedin.'"

Clifford was passing the door.

"Clifford! Can you help me please? I need to get this girl on the couch."

"Sure thing, Becky." He effortlessly lifted the girl on to the couch. As he put her down he said, "Oh shit! Jus' look at my jacket! My wife's gonna be furious." His jacket was smeared with blood.

"Sorry, Clifford, do you know which Doctor's on call?"

"No can't say I do." He wandered off shaking his head and muttering, "These girls they coming in like flies these days. God, Ellen's gonna be real mad"

Becky quickly took the girl's dress off. She found that the girl's underwear was soaked with blood. She lay moaning and shivering as Becky covered her with a blanket. She took the girl's pulse. It was weak and rapid, and worryingly, her blood pressure was too faint to hear with a stethoscope. Becky had to detect it by feeling for the girl's pulse as the blood pressure cuff deflated. The systolic reading was only ninety. It should have been between one hundred and ten and one hundred and thirty approximately. Becky was horrified. The girl's lips were tinged blue. She suddenly opened her huge brown eyes. Her pupils were massive, dilated by circulating adrenaline.

"Help me, Nurse. I feels real bad."

"Yes, I know, I can see you feel awful. What's your name?"

"I'm May Lee. They calls me May."

"What happened, May? Are you pregnant or what?

May started to cry, "Don't tell anyone will you?"

"May, I just need to know so we can help you."

"I committed a sin and now I'm gonna pay."

"Don't be silly May, you'll be fine, just tell me what happened."

"I got rid of the baby." May grabbed Becky's hand. "I'm gonna die. I know I am."

"No. No. Of course you're not. Lie back, I'll get the doctor."

Becky got the on call doctors rota. She found it was a Doctor Rooks, a medical consultant that she hadn't met. She quickly dialled his number.

"Hello, Doctor Rooks' residence. How may I be of assistance?" a cool Bahamian woman's voice answered.

"This is the hospital. I need to speak to the doctor immediately." She waited. The girl moaned on the couch. Sweat trickled down Becky's body. The girl's colour worsened, her breathing was fast and shallow. Her eyes closed.

Stretching the phone cord she held the phone under her chin and struggled to tip the end of the couch up to send blood to the girl's vital organs. "Come on. Come on," she muttered. She managed to get the oxygen switched on and put a mask on the girl's face with one hand whilst holding the phone in the other. "It's OK. It's OK," she said to the girl who didn't respond.

Eventually an English man's voice came on the phone, "Doctor Rooks here. What is it you want?"

Becky quickly explained the situation.

"What do you expect me to do about it?"

"Do! Come in of course. You're the on-call doctor."

"I'm a medical consultant. I don't know anything about 'Gynae' problems."

"But you're on call!"

"Sorry. No can do."

"But you must come in!"

"I'm not accustomed to being told what I must and mustn't do, Nurse. You're interrupting my evening," with that he put the phone down.

Becky stood in a state of shock for a few seconds then muttering, "Damn, damn, damn," she looked up Stefano's phone number and rang it.

"Stefano, it's me, Becky."

"Becky! What a lovely surprise! To what do I owe the pleasure?

"Stefano, could you come in please? I wouldn't ask but it's an emergency and Doctor Rooks won't come."

"God damn it!"

"Stefano this girl's very young, she's going to die if someone doesn't help me."

"OK, honey, don't worry. I'll be there as soon as I can."

Ten minutes later Stefano arrived. Becky had got a drip ready and attached May to a cardiac monitor. Stefano quickly looked at May. "What's the problem?"

"She told me she's had an abortion. She's bleeding profusely."

"OK. Vital signs?" He rapidly washed his hands.

"She's in sinus rhythm at about one hundred and thirty and her pulse is really faint. Systolic B.P. is eighty five. Respirations are shallow, about twenty five a minute."

"Damn," he frowned. He took a plastic cannula out, applied a tourniquet to May's arm and tapped the back of her hand trying to find a vein. "Can't find a vein," he muttered. He needed to give her an intra-venous infusion to replace the blood she'd lost. "She's shut down. Get me a cut down set."Becky was opening the sterile pack when the girl gave a sigh and stopped breathing. Her pallor deepened. Becky felt for a pulse at May's neck. There was none. The alarm sounded on the heart monitor. May's tracing was in a straight line.

"Damn it! She's arrested!"

Becky gave May a single hard blow to the centre of her chest and started doing chest compressions, counting aloud, "One and two and three and..." Stefano reached across to the emergency trolley and took out a laryngoscope - the instrument that he could use to illuminate May's airway so that he could put a tube down it.

"Yep, that's it," he successfully got the Endo-Tracheal tube in place and attached a re-breathing bag connected to the oxygen. He started to use it to inflate May's lungs.

"Becky carry on with this as well, I need to get a vein."

"OK." Becky interspersed chest compression with inflations. She had to move rapidly backwards and forwards from the side of the trolley where she gave May ten compressions, to the head of it to inflate May's lungs with the bag. Sweat was pouring down her body.

Stefano got a cannula into May's vein.

"Stop a minute, Becky." He looked at the cardiac monitor it was still in a straight line. "She's still in asystole. Adrenaline! Where's the adrenaline?" he said rifling through the disorganised drug cupboard.

"It should be there somewhere."

After a couple of minutes he found some, drew it up and gave it directly into May's vein. He looked up at the heart monitor and asked Becky to stop for a few seconds. The tracing from May's heart was completely erratic.

"She's in ventricular fibrillation."

Clifford wandered past the open door.

"Clifford, is the defib' on the ward?" asked Becky.

"I don't rightly know, Becky."

"Well could you go and ask and get it please?"

He shrugged, "OK," and sloped off.

Becky continued resuscitating May. Stefano tried to stop the bleeding by inserting a pack into May's vagina. Ten long minutes later Clifford returned with the de- fibrillator machine.

Stefano plugged it in set it to two hundred mega joules and pressed charge - nothing happened. "What the hell is wrong with this?"

Clifford was just leaving. He turned around, "I think it got wet in the last storm, man. She dead now anyway."

"Just sod off!" said Becky.

Clifford gave her a filthy look and disappeared, Stefano looked startled. Becky looked at him, "Sorry."

"No, don't be," he said and gave her a quick grin.

They tried for another half an hour to resuscitate May but it was no good.

Stefano wiped his sweating brow. "We'd better stop hadn't we?"

Becky swallowed, "Yes. We'd better."

"If we carry on, even if we're successful she'll have brain damage and I don't think we can do anything more."

"No, you're right, Stefano." Their eyes met. A silent confrontation of their failure. Stefano swallowed and Becky bit her lip. They sighed and stood in silence looking at May for a moment.

"Damn shame," said Stefano.

"What do you think happened?"

"Botched abortion. Not the first."

"Is it illegal here then?"

"No, but it costs. It costs plenty, plus everyone knows everyone here. Maybe you don't want your husband to know, or your boyfriend wants lots of babies and you don't, or you just can't feed another one."

Becky looked shocked.

"Don't worry, Becky. We did our best. It was her time. She's out of it now."

Becky just shook her head and pushed her hair off her sweating forehead with the back of her hand. At that point a patient arrived.

"I only had a couple of drinks and I tripped over a damn rock!"

"Look, I'm off," said Stefano.

"Yes, of course, thanks, Stefano. Thanks a lot." She turned to the patient.

When Becky came off shift an hour later at ten p.m. Stefano was waiting outside in his white MGBGT. He shouted across, "Becky!"

Becky walked over, smiling as she pushed her hair up from her sweating forehead.

"Get in."

"Why?"

"You need a drink."

"No thanks, Stefano. Anyway I'm in uniform."

"This is Freeport not England. You owe me. I was off duty."

Becky laughed, "Yes, yes you're right, and I could do with one."

Stefano drove off with a squeal of tyres. After a couple of miles they left the main road and went down a long pot holed dirt track, at the bottom it opened out to the sea. On a tiny wharf stood a small thatched bar with a mooring for boats next to it. A dilapidated notice half fallen down announced that it was 'Harry's Bar.' Outside on the wooden wharf two old fishermen sat playing cards and drinking beer with Harry. A young couple gazed into each other's eyes, whispering and giggling whilst drinking cocktails out of massive glasses.

Stefano and Becky gratefully sank into some old squashy fabric seats enjoying the balmy night air, whilst looking at the light of the moon reflected in the still waters. A calypso played quietly on the radio in the background, the perfume of the flowers and the salty sharp tang of the sea drifted around them and they both relaxed.

Stefano drank 'Jack Daniels' and Becky had martini and lemonade. Harry was generous with his measures and Becky and Stefano were soon laughing and chatting. Stefano told Becky about his old-fashioned parents who'd settled in Miami from Sicily, he was good company and he made her laugh as they forgot the trauma of the evening for a while.

Eventually Becky said, "I must go. I've got an early shift in the morning."

As he drove she glanced at him. His driving was confident and assured and she felt attracted to him. On the way back Stefano stopped at a deserted beach. The moonlight glinted on the gentle waves rippling the sand. The only other noise was the rustle of the palm trees and that of the little lizards darting in and out of the bushes.

"It's so beautiful here," said Becky.

"But?"

She laughed, "How did you know there's a 'but'?"

"It's written all over your face."

"It's not what I expected. Why didn't Doctor Rooks come in?"

"Becky, it's different here. Life is cheap. He's been here for years and forgotten everything but medicine. Plus he knows the girl wouldn't have had any health insurance."

"But that's dreadful!"

"Yeah. But that's the way it is." He reached into the glove compartment and took out some cigarettes. "Here do you want one?"

"No thanks, I don't."

Stefano lit one and a distinctive herbal smell drifted across.

"Stefano! Is that pot?"

"Yeah, sure it is."

"But you're a doctor!"

"Becky, loosen up! Everyone does it out here."

"I don't. Look, Stefano it's getting late. I want to go home please."

He stubbed out the joint carefully between his thumb and forefinger and put it back in the glove compartment. His hand rested on her thigh. It lay there - burning. He turned towards her and she felt attracted to him. He put his arm around her shoulders and started to pull her to him. Then she remembered his wife and Teresa.

"How about a kiss then, if not a smoke, with a lonely Doctor?"

She was suddenly angry - more with herself for being tempted than with him. She pulled away and shoved his hand off her leg. "If you're lonely go and see Teresa!"

"There's more to you than meets the eye isn't there? I like my women fiery."

Becky started to open the car door, "Well I don't like my men two timing."

He grabbed her wrist, "You know it's nothing serious with Teresa."

"Not for you maybe."

"Heh, cool it. I can take a hint. There are plenty that will say yes. Get in, I'll drive you home."

Becky sighed. She didn't know exactly where she was so she reluctantly got back in the car.

Stefano grinned at her, started the car up and whistled, "Brown girl in the ring," all the way back to Becky's apartment.

As they drew up Becky looked at his profile and found herself wondering what it would have been like. That made her even more annoyed.

"Good-night, Stefano, I'll see you at work," she said and got out and slammed the car door.

"Bye, Miss Hoity Toity. See you at... what do you Brit's call it? ... Ah yes, the coal face."

Becky ran upstairs slamming the door after her. *Little shit,* she thought as she kicked off her shoes and slumped into a chair. She'd thought that coming here would be an exciting adventure. Everyone at home was so envious, but it wasn't turning out as she'd expected. Everything was so different. She felt more alone than she ever had in her life.

She thought about Tim her ex-fiancé. When she'd left he'd said, "You've got no idea what you're getting into. You'll never manage in a foreign country on your own"

"You'll see! I'll see you in two years when my contract expires," she'd said and stormed off. Tim had looked astonished. Up until Becky broke off their engagement, which he still didn't understand, she'd never disagreed with him. She'd wanted to see more of life before settling down. *Oh well, she was certainly achieving that ambition,* she thought ruefully.

Thinking of this Becky got up to go to bed. *She'd show them! Sod the lot of them!* Becky smiled to herself then, as she thought that her language was one of the things that was changing and maybe not for the better. She got undressed and fell asleep only to be disturbed by dreams of blood and the feel of Stefano's hand on her thigh.

This is Radio Grand Bahama your sunshine station. It's the ninth of August, we expect a high of ninety two degrees and eighty percent humidity, watch out for the possibility of a heavy rain shower later today. Now just get on down to a hit from five years ago, it's the Rolling Stones with 'Honky tonk woman'...

The more Becky thought about how May had bled to death in the ER the more annoyed she became. Just before going on duty she went to the Matron's office and knocked on the door.

"Come in," said a woman's voice. Sitting behind a large mahogany desk Matron looked elegant as usual. She was a black woman always immaculately dressed in a navy suit and white blouse, a white starched hat perched on top of her curly black hair. She was rarely seen on the wards, seeming to spend all her time on paperwork. Becky had heard rumours that she was related to the local M.P., but no one ever wanted to say much about this.

"Good morning Matron. I wanted to talk to you about something that happened last night."

Matron continued reading the papers in front of her. Becky hesitated. Matron sighed and looked up with a frown. "Yes?"

Becky told her about Doctor Rooks not coming in and May dying.

She looked Becky up and down over pince-nez glasses. "Well it's true, Dr Rooks is not a gynaecologist is he?"

"But he was on call!"

"Don't you raise your voice to me, Nurse!"

"Err...Well... Sorry."

"The stupid girl shouldn't have had an illegal abortion should she?"

"I'm sorry, Matron but I think that's beside the point."

"Oh you do, do you? Look this isn't Surrey or Sussex or wherever it is you're from. We do things differently here. Dr. Rooks has been here for twenty five years, you've been here for five minutes."

"But...."

"Don't interrupt me, I'll speak to him. I happen to be revising the ER rota with Mr Silver just now and we may well be changing things. How are you settling in?"

"OK. It's all very different."

"What did you expect? A cushy job in the sunshine?"

"No I didn't. I don't mind hard work but I thought you might care about patients dying needlessly!"

"I do care. And I can see you do too. Look I'll see what I can do, Lewis. You'd better get on duty now. Leave it with me."

Becky left with a mixture of feelings. Nothing she did seemed to work out here.

The next day Becky had a day off and went shopping. Outside the only supermarket were lots of stalls where local Bahamian women sold the fruit and vegetables that they'd grown. Wooden tables were laden with tomatoes, avocadoes, red and green peppers, sweet potatoes, bananas, mangoes and other tropical fruits.

A large woman, dressed in an even larger pink and yellow floral dress was talking to Teresa. "Honey these is the hottest," she gestured to some red chillies. "You cook these for your man and you both be smilin' tonight." She laughed heartily and layers of fat wobbled concertina-style from her overflowing bosom to her well padded bottom.

Teresa laughed, "OK I'll take two." She turned and saw Becky and gave her a huge smile, "Hi, Becky! How great to see you. How are you doing?"

Becky smiled back, "Fine thanks, yes I'm fine." Teresa noticed that Becky's smile didn't reach her eyes.

"You sure?"

"Yes, of course."

"If you're off today why don't we go snorkelling at Taino beach this afternoon? Then we could go out for a drink and a bite to eat at the Anchor Inn."

The Anchor Inn was a pub where the English hung out.

"Oh, I don't know..."

"Come on, Becky! Have you been snorkelling?"

"Well no."

"Do you swim?"

"Yes, of course. I swam before I could walk!"

"You're in for a real treat then. I'll pick you up around three p.m."

Becky loved the sea and was a strong swimmer. She'd been tired or busy since coming to Freeport so she hadn't gone to the beach, but had just swum in the pool every day. Teresa arrived in an ancient blue Hillman Minx and they rattled and wheezed their way along the main highway that crossed the island, before turning down a sandy track.

"Teresa, this car smells awful, what is it?"

Teresa laughed, "It's petrol. For God's sake don't be lighting a cigarette or we'll all be blown to Kingdom Come! It's the only car I could afford and it gets me from A to B."

When they reached the end of the track Becky gasped, "My God it's beautiful Teresa!"

"Yes, it's grand isn't it?"

In front of them lay a beach of virgin white sand, fringed by gently swaying palm trees. At the edge of the water the completely calm sea broke into tiny wavelets of sparkling white surf. Beyond lay shimmering shades of turquoise advancing to ultramarine, deepest emerald and indigo. The sun reflecting on the water looked like a hundred thousand sparkling diamonds. It was a paradise that Becky had only dreamt about before and the reality was breath taking.

For the first time since she'd stepped off the plane Becky felt herself completely relax. She took a deep breath of the balmy salt air. "Incredible," she muttered. They wandered onto the beach and found a spot in the shade underneath some palm trees where they got changed into bikinis. Teresa produced a set of snorkels and masks each.

"I've never used one before," said Becky.

"Sure, it's easy," said Teresa.

When she'd shown Becky, they wandered down to the edge, "Watch out for these," said Teresa pointing out a sea urchin. "If you tread on one you'll end up at the hospital having the spikes taken out."

"God forbid!" said Becky and they both laughed. But she took care where she walked.

When the water lapped around Becky's feet she squealed with delight. "It's warm! It's warm like a bath!"

"Better than Dorset then?"

"It's better than anything I've ever felt in my life."

"Really?" said Teresa with a dirty laugh and Becky blushed and smiled. Even as they walked in Becky could see the fish. Tiny multi-coloured angel fish darted around her toes, schools of grouper meandered past.

"Look! Look!" shrieked Becky.

"Put your mask on and float looking down through the water, then you'll really see something," said Teresa.

Becky put her mask on and when she put her face in the water the world changed irrevocably, as she entered an enchanted place for the first time. The only noise was the sound of her breathing. The reality of the world and everyday life vanished.

A moving carnival of jewelled brightly flashing colours was displayed beneath and all around her in the crystal warm waters. There were angel fish of all types. She noticed some orange and blue queen angel fish were swimming around nearby rocks. A few yards away she saw black striped sergeant major angel fish, black and gold French angel fish nibbled on the coral then swiftly darted on and vanished. No sooner were they gone then, just underneath her a whole shoal of grunt with dark yellow stripes swam in formation like soldiers on a parade ground, closely followed by silver grouper and snapper. Her mind reeled with the ever-changing fantasy of colour and shapes displayed all around her.

The fish were feeding on the coral. Gently waving purple and yellow sea fans looking more like exotic flowers than a primitive animal, faced the water currents to trap their food. Elkhorn coral stretched out its long fingers, fish darted around the white brain coral its surface mirroring the surface of the human brain with its intricate patterns.

A huge conch shell lay on the bottom, in shades of pink like the Bahamian sunrise. Becky gently moved her feet and floated over an exotic new world. She could never have believed that so much beauty lay just beneath the surface. She was completely entranced, hypnotised by the constantly changing kaleidoscope of colours. When she finally looked up more than an hour had passed.

Teresa was already sitting on the beach, she waved at Becky to come in. Becky reluctantly wandered out of the water, dry before she even reached the sands under the sun's blazing rays.

"That was just incredible, Teresa! I've never seen anything so beautiful. I had no idea it would be so lovely and so... so amazing."

Teresa laughed, "Yeah I thought you'd like it. How could you not like it? But it's just as well you've come in now, there's a shark out there."

"Oh yes, very funny."

"No really. Look. You can see his fin. Just over there at two o'clock."

"Oh my God! Why didn't you warn me?"

"Sure it's no big deal, Becky. A diving friend of mine says that there are more than forty different types of sharks here."

"How many!"

"Forty. But really, it's not a problem. There's loads of fish for them to eat. They don't need to eat us! Don't look so worried. He says there's never been a shark attack here."

"Oh great! I don't want to be the first!"

"You won't be."

"You know, Teresa, that seems like everything here. You think it's paradise and then something happens and you're not so sure..."

"Not sure? About what?"

"Oh I don't know... It's not what it seems...There's something... something lurking...lurking under the surface."

"No you're wrong, Becky. It *is* paradise, you just need to keep your eyes open. After all we've got sharks in Britain as well haven't we? It's just that they're the male kind."

Becky laughed.

"Come on. Let's eat," said Teresa. She'd brought a cold bag with beers, fresh bread, cheese, a pineapple and bananas. It was the best picnic that Becky had ever eaten. Teresa was great company, full of laughter and jokes.

"I love it here," she said after a while. "So different to Belfast and all that shit! I worked in A&E, fits you for anything that does... You cope at the time but it comes back to you...It was when they brought them in... You can't imagine what one human being is capable of doing to another, not until you've seen it..." Teresa's face clouded over.

"Yes, I guess we haven't got a clue in England," said Becky and reached over and gave Teresa's hand a squeeze.

Teresa gave her a smile, "You know what?"

"What?"

"Me, I'm never going back."

The words seemed to hang in the air for a moment and Becky felt uneasy.

"What about your family, Teresa?"

"Well I miss them I guess. I'm one of nine..."

"Really!"

"Yes, really. Dear God, Becky my parents were that strict! My Mum wasn't so bad, but Dad ...We lived in a village outside of Belfast near the border - cowboy country, you could say." She laughed, "My Mum's typically Irish, she's still having the holy water blessed for me. They'd die if they knew the half of what I get up to out here. I miss my sister Deidra and her two wee ones Dermot and Rosaline, but that's all. What about you?"

"Me? I'm really boring, Teresa. I've got two brothers, Phillip and my little brother Harry, except he's not that little now of course. Dad's a solicitor, Mum's a teacher... I miss them, I really do."

"You won't leave will you?"

"No, I've too much to see and do here. In fact come on, Teresa, I can't see that damn shark now, let's go back in!"

They ran down and back into the warm sea. At the end of the afternoon they went back to Teresa's flat.

"Sorry about the mess," said Teresa going into the kitchen to make coffee and a tuna sandwich for them both.

Becky moved some clothes off a seat and surveyed the glass coffee table which was overflowing with half drunk cups of coffee, two laden ash trays, several empty glasses, paperbacks and magazines. A plant sat wilting on the window sill.

On the wall was a photo of a woman aged about thirty with auburn hair like Teresa's and two small children.

"Is that your sister and her kids?"

"Yes. Aren't they the best?"

"Yes, they look lovely. Would you like kids, Teresa?"

"Yeah. I'm fixing to have a whole bunch - not just now of course!"

They laughed and ate the sandwiches and later on Teresa opened a bottle of white wine and poured them both a generous glass.

"I should go really, I need to shower and change," Becky said.

"No problem. We're only just down the road from the pub, why don't you shower here? We're the same size I'm sure you can find something that suits you from what I've got."

Becky felt warm and relaxed, "OK, it doesn't make sense to go home and then come back, that'll be great."

Becky showered and washed her hair in Teresa's bathroom. When she came out, Teresa had put a black linen halter neck dress on top of her double bed which was covered in sheets of bright orange and lime green swirling flowers. Becky put the dress on and looked in the mirror. She was surprised by what she saw - a more confident and sexier Becky. She wasn't sure about the change and went into the lounge.

"Wow! You look a million dollars!"

"It's a bit low and short isn't it?"

"Don't be silly, Becky, it's the fashion. Just look in the mirror."

Becky looked in the mirror. "Yes. You're right. It's not what I'd usually wear but I think I need to be more adventurous. OK thanks, I'll wear it."

Teresa went to shower next and emerged from her bedroom wearing tight white jeans with a red boob tube that left little to the imagination. She wore her long auburn hair loose and when she moved Becky could smell the 'Chanel Number Five' which Teresa said an ex-boyfriend had given her.

They set off in Teresa's Hillman Minx chugging and rattling down the road. They pulled up outside a low white modern building with well kept gardens of hibiscus and bougainvillea. A swinging pub sign reminiscent of England was emblazoned with, 'The Anchor Inn,' and had a painting of a sloop and an anchor on it.

Becky laughed, "You could think we were back in Britain," she said.

"Wait 'til you get inside," said Teresa.

They pushed open the door and were instantly engulfed by a wave of smoke, laughing, and English and American voices. Becky was astounded. Almost everyone was white. The only black person was serving behind the bar. It made her feel slightly uncomfortable.

Several couples sat at low tables, many of the women dressed in either ankle length or mini skirts, the two extremes were in fashion. Becky could tell the ones on holiday or honeymoon - they dreamily held hands and gazed into each other's eyes, but most people seemed to live here. The pub was packed and they had to push their way to the bar, where a group of young English and American men wearing shorts and T-shirts were drinking pints of beer and sounded as if they'd been doing so for some time.

"Teresa! Who's your friend?" shouted an attractive blond guy.

"This is Becky. Becky, meet Chris and this is Harry, Steve, John and Troy. Most were members of the island's rugby club and all worked on the island. They were soon buying the girls drinks and Troy who was American bought Becky a PIna Colada. Becky didn't realise that the innocuous sweet tasting drink contained two or three generous measures of white rum.

The conversation swirled around them and Becky felt herself bobbing about on a tide of moaning about the Bahamas.

"You can't get decent bacon here."

"They don't want to work."

"It's so damn hot."

"I can't wait to get back home."

"Roast beef and Yorkshire pudding, decent food..."

"The telly's crap."

She began to wonder why anyone stayed, especially when she found that the people complaining the most had lived there for about five years or more.

Teresa was standing with Chris's arm draped around her. She didn't look as if she minded. He was a tall guy, a good six foot with dark hair and he was making Teresa laugh a lot. Becky saw him bend down and whisper something in Teresa's ear that made her giggle, and then his hand dropped onto Teresa's bottom. She was drinking Bushmills Irish whisky and the measures were huge. Becky was pleased that Teresa was enjoying herself. She thought that maybe if Teresa went off with Chris, she'd be less besotted with Stefano, who she was sure was just having fun with her, especially as he was married.

She was thinking of leaving when an American voice said, "What brought you here then?"

She turned round and found herself looking into Troy's green twinkling eyes.

"Oh... Err... Change of scene, bit of an adventure I suppose, what about you?"

They chatted for half an hour or so. Troy was easy to talk to. Charming. He was tall and blond with a muscular body. Becky couldn't help but notice his tanned firm legs in his white shorts. He bought her another cocktail. This one was called a Hurricane. It was pink and sparkling and tasted of fruit juice. Troy was from San Francisco and Becky enjoyed hearing about the places she'd only seen on T.V. in England.

After a while Becky half realised that she was giggling a lot and she felt slightly giddy when she went to the loo. When she got back she looked for Teresa but she'd vanished.

"Something wrong?" Troy asked.

"No, it's just that I think I'd better get home and Teresa seems to have disappeared."

"Ah. Yes. Teresa..."

"What do you mean?"

"Well if I know Teresa she's probably pretty busy just now - if you know what I mean?"

"Damn. Oh sorry," Becky blushed. She didn't often swear.

Troy smiled and shrugged, "What's the problem?"

"I need to go home. I've got an early shift in the morning."

"That's no problem, I'll take you."

"Are you sure?"

"Yes, of course come on."

On the way to the car Becky stumbled on the path and Troy put his arm round her. He was about six foot two and strong, easy to lean on.

"Carefully does it," he said and smiled at her. Becky got into his yellow Ford Cortina and they roared off. She must have closed her eyes because when she opened them she found that they were parked at a beach.

Troy got out of the car and opened the passenger door.

"Come on, let's go for a swim."

"No, sorry, I need to get home I'm working in the morning."

"Oh come on. We won't be long."

"I think I'd drown the state I'm in."

"Oh, don't be a spoil-sport," he said with a big smile. "Let's just try the water. It's really warm at this time of night."

He ran down to the edge and took off his shoes. Becky sighed. She really was tired but he'd gone straight ahead so she got out of the car and wandered down to the beach. It was beautiful, still and calm, the moon reflecting on the water. She took off her shoes and paddled. It was true it felt very warm and inviting.

Troy turned and looks at her, "It's great isn't it?"

"Yes, it feels wonderful."

"Let's go then!"

Before she knew it he'd pulled off his t-shirt and got out of his shorts. He stood in just his white 'boxers' and Becky thought what a good body he had, tanned and kept trim and muscular by playing rugby.

He smiled at her boyishly. "You have to join me or I'll feel a right prick," and he laughed.

"But I haven't got a costume."

"Well you may not have noticed but neither have I. Just wear your underwear. I won't look I promise," he gave that engaging laugh again and held out his hand. The moon illuminated his grin and his blond hair flopped into his eyes.

Becky thought, *Blow it! Why don't I just loosen up like everyone else?*

"OK then hang on, I'll just take this dress off it belongs to Teresa. Promise not to look?"

"Sure thing."

The moon illuminated Becky as she pulled the dress over her head. Troy got a glimpse of her full breasts clad in a white plunging lacy bra and matching panties showing off her brown slim legs.

When Becky looked up Troy had swum a little distance away and wasn't looking at her. *How sweet,* she thought to herself.

She got in quickly and started to swim, loving the sensation of the warm water caressing her body.

"This is fantastic," said Becky, "It's even warmer than in the day."

"Yeah it's great. You look pretty good too."

Troy swam to her and put his arms around her. They were about waist high in the sea. He leant towards her and they kissed, Becky relaxed. Troy's hands went to her breasts and she moved them off. He kissed her again more urgently and moved his mouth down her neck to her breasts.

"No, Troy."

He pulled her to him more firmly, holding her bottom, his mouth still on her breast.

"No, Troy. Sorry. I mean it"

"Aw, come on." He put both hands under the elastic of her panties and holding her buttocks pulled her close.

"No. Really, Troy. It's too soon." She said trying to wriggle away.

"It's never too soon out here, honey." He pulled down her panties and biting her breast put his hand between her legs.

"Troy! No! Stop it!" she shouted, struggling in the water to take his hand away.

"You know you love it really. You've been teasing me all night. You're just a little prick teaser." He turned her around forcefully so that her back was to him. Holding her arms across her breasts with one hand he forced his fingers into her with the other hand.

"No! No!" Becky was screaming, "You're drunk!" She pushed him with all her strength and they struggled and slipped in the water. She managed to get away and stumbled out of the sea crying and trying to pull her panties back up.

She reached the shore but he was too quick for her and with one experienced rugby tackle he had her down and pinned underneath him

"No! NO!" He roughly turned her over face down and spread her legs apart.

"You know you want it!" His breath was on her neck, he was strong and she was completely helpless.

Chapter 4

About the same time that night a few miles down the road in Eight Mile Rock most people had gone to bed. The occasional TV and radio could be heard, somewhere an old woman was humming a black spiritual, a stray dog was turning over some bins and a drunk mumbled and cursed as he stumbled down the road. The lateness of the hour and the heat meant that most people slept or tried to sleep, tossing and turning, hoping to get some sort of a breeze from their open windows.

If anyone had listened carefully they would have heard the hint of chanting from one of the tiny dwellings. This particular house, wooden and small, no different from the others, like many had a small strip of land at the back of it. Three chickens and a cockerel were kept here. They were quiet now in their tiny hutch. Earlier the cock had crowed and the chickens squawked vociferously, as one of their members was dispatched with a sharp knife. Sweet potatoes and peppers grew here, and in amongst them marijuana and other plants with distinctive and foul smelling odours.

The door of the house was closed tight and bolted in three places. Inside, Isabella, the Haitian woman who'd met Mari outside Rachel's, was lighting candles. Her eyes glinted fiercely and her expression was grim. She placed three of the candles under small burners, the saucers set above them contained a mixture of oils and substances that gave off a heady scent.

Isabella moved slowly and methodically, all the time quietly chanting in a sing song voice. As she drifted around the room she took several sips from a pungent smelling drink, held in an ancient looking, dark red, pottery chalice. She grimaced and put it on a table decisively, lips and teeth stained red from the potion. Her chanting was a little louder now. If anyone listened they would have found it impossible to decipher the words which were a mixture of Creole and French, interspersed with others that originated in Africa.

Isabella moved towards the wooden table, her long black dress brushing the floor. She put her hand carefully underneath the table and released a hidden catch. A drawer sprang open. Taking out a small bag covered in strange symbols, she placed it reverently on the black oil-cloth that covered the table. The candles flickered and the smell of the burning oils became stronger, as her chanting assumed a louder and more rhythmic quality.

She sat at the table and pushed her long dark hair that smelt of exotic unguents away from her face. Her hand shook slightly as she pulled the bag towards her and for a second she hesitated. Reaching for the chalice, in one decisive move, she drank the remaining contents. Then she seemed to stiffen a little, giving a chilling smile, before with a set face she resumed her chanting and opened the bag. From it she took, some black fabric, a needle and thread, and some cloth stuffing. Reached to the bottom of the bag, she removed a tiny parcel of brown paper and unrolled it carefully. Glinting in the candle light lay six long and very sharp, silver tipped pins. Placing everything carefully on the table, she picked up the fabric and started to sew. Her hands completely steady now, the needle darted in and out. Swift and sure. In time with her chanting.

The pictures grew in her mind and she saw them reflected in the shadows on the walls. Hazy figures of people obscured as if in a dark night, rocking on a cruel sea. A little girl and her mother appeared clinging to each other. She smelt the people's fear. Heard the children crying. At last He came into view. The man she sought. His eyes cruel and glinting. Screaming rose up around her. In his hands she saw he held a gun. Isabella rocked backwards and forwards. Chanting. No longer conscious of what she was doing, as she sewed and fashioned the image.

A few huts away a couple lying in bed woke and heard her. They glanced at each other and looked away. Their child stirred in his sleep and murmured. They pulled their sheet around them a little tighter, and the man tilted the woman's chin and kissed her.

"Ain't nothin' to do with us. Don't worry. She just crazy."

They moved together. Started to make love, needing the closeness and to shut out the sound.

Josef also stirred in his sleep, dreaming again of their nightmare voyage, seeing Eugenie's face, the dark seas, hearing Marie call to him. Seeing the skipper and his gun.

In the hut the figure was made. A miniature man. Resembling a strange doll for a child. Sweat poured down Isabella's face and body. The candles guttered and the smoke made shadows and forms in the room. Isabella picked up one of the long sharp pins, gave a cry and pushed it into the stomach of the figure she'd made. She fell back in the chair, her eyes closed and her chest just moving, her breathing shallow.

The couple in the nearby hut cried out in their pleasure.

Josef woke to find Marie trying to shake him awake. "Papa! Papa! You making a strange noise."

"Sorry, ma petite. Just a bad dream. Go back to sleep."

Across the island another man woke from his sleep. He groaned, yelled out and doubled up in sudden pain. He swore and clutched his stomach.

"Troy! No! Please!" Becky was sobbing.

"I think you'll find the lady's not interested," said a cool American man's voice.

"For Christ's sake," said Troy, turning his head to see a tall blonde man aged about thirty standing a short distance away. "Who the hell are you?"

"I don't think that's important."

"Well, sod off, whoever you are!"

"No. I don't think so."

The stranger had drawn closer. He bent down and in one forceful movement pulled Troy off Becky.

"What the hell do you think you're doing?" Troy swung a punch at the stranger who ducked and missed it.

"Look, I don't want a fight just leave the young lady alone."

"Mind your own business and clear off!" Troy squared up to the man. Becky took the opportunity to roll away and she pulled on her dress with shaking hands, too shocked to say anything.

The man glanced at her movement. Troy took advantage and punched the man full in the face. He staggered backwards. Put his hand to his mouth and found that it was bleeding.

"You son of a bitch," he said quietly and moved towards Troy. He hit him squarely under the chin. Troy crumpled and he hit him again, this time in the solar plexus.

Troy collapsed on the sand muttering, "Shit, shit, shit," and clutching his abdomen. The man went to kick him. Becky yelled, "NO! No! Leave him! That's enough!"

Troy was doubled up and groaning. "OK, honey," the man said, and turned away from Troy. As he walked away there was a click. Becky saw Troy spring up, the moonlight glinting on a knife in his hand.

"Look out!" she screamed.

The man turned around and grabbed Troy's wrist forcing him to drop the knife. He delivered a mighty punch to Troy's jaw. "You don't learn, do you?"

Troy swayed and fell silently to the sand.

"Oh my God. Are you OK?"

"Yeah. Idiots like him are just plain stupid."

Troy lay unmoving.

"And Troy... he's not..."

"Dead?- No - 'course not."

The man went across to Troy and pushed him over onto his side with his foot. Troy groaned softly. "He's fine. He's just going to have one hell of a hangover in the morning."

Becky stood up and pain shot through her ankle. She hobbled across to Troy. She could see that he was still breathing.

"Oh, dear God," she said quietly. She felt cold and started to shake.

"You OK?"

"Yes, yes I'm fine."

"If you don't mind me saying so, you don't look it."

Becky managed a smile. "No, I'm alright, really. Sorry, I should thank, you."

"You're welcome. Lucky I came along. I jog along the beach at night when I can't sleep."

Becky saw then that he was wearing trainers with white shorts and a t-shirt. He pushed his blond hair off his sweating forehead. He had an angular strong face and looked a little older than Becky.

"I don't know what would have happened if you... If you hadn't come along." She bit her lip, passed a hand over her face and sighed.

"You're OK though aren't you? He didn't..."

"No, no. Thanks to you."

"Good. No harm done then. Where are you from?"

"England."

"Yeah, I'd worked that one out," he said, with a smile.

"Yes, the accent's a bit of a give away isn't it. I'm working here in Freeport and I live in Lucaya Sun apartments."

"You look all in. My car's just at the end of the beach, come on, I'll drive you home."

She hesitated for a moment, "Well, if you're sure."

"Yeah, it won't take more than five minutes."

"That's kind of you." Becky tried to walk and stumbled, "Ow! I think I've sprained my ankle."

"No problem." In one movement he'd swept her up into his arms. Their eyes met and she saw that his were of the deepest blue, clear and sparkling. He smiled at her and she smiled back unable to breathe for a moment. They were silent. Then they both laughed a little. Becky blushed.

"Maybe I should know your name, if we're going to be this close?" he said with a smile.

"It's Becky."

"Well, how do you do, Becky? I'm Michael and it's sure nice to meet you."

"Thanks, Michael. Are you certain Troy's OK?"

"Yeah. You don't need to worry about that little mother fu... Sorry."

Becky laughed.

"He'll be just fine." He carried Becky effortlessly to his red Alfa Romeo and she found herself relaxing against his chest. He put her down gently next to the car and helped her in. She lay back against the seat and closed her eyes as he drove quickly to her apartment. As Becky got out she winced with the pain in her ankle.

"Which is your apartment?" he asked.

She pointed to the first floor and he picked her up into his arms again. "Are you sure I'm not too heavy for you?" Becky felt flustered by the conflicting emotions of the evening.

He just laughed as he carried her effortlessly up the stairs, putting her down at her front door. "You OK now then, Becky?"

"Yes, I'm fine. Thanks." Their eyes met again. They moved together almost imperceptibly and, as Becky's weight shifted, she felt a sharp pain in her ankle and jerked away.

"Ow! Think I need to put some ice on my ankle."

He ran a hand through his blond hair and Becky struggled to take her eyes off him.

"Yes, of course, you go on in I'll be off. But can I call by tomorrow to see how you're doing?"

"Yes. I'd like that, Michael. I'd like that a lot. Good night."

"Good night, Becky."

She went inside and closed the door. In spite of the pain in her ankle and the night's events, she found to her surprise that she was smiling.

Becky's doorbell rang about eleven a.m. She got out of bed and groaned as her left foot hit the ground. Limping past the mirror she noticed that her hair was a mess, and last night's mascara was streaked and black under her eyes. The door bell rang again.

"OK. I'm coming, I'm coming."

She pulled on a flimsy dressing gown and opened the door. Michael was leaning nonchalantly against the frame, a bunch of exotic flowers in his hands. He wore jeans and a white t-shirt and smelt of expensive cologne. Becky gulped.

"I thought you might like these."

"Oh... Michael, yes, thank-you. They're beautiful. God I look a mess." She pulled her dressing gown together. "Come in. Come in. Well that's if you want to. Sorry. Not very awake yet."

"No, no. I'm sorry I didn't mean to wake you," he gave her a smile. "I can come back later if you like."

"No, really. Coffee. Would you like some coffee?" Becky was cross with herself for being so flustered, but Michael just grinned.

"That would be just great. Do you mind if I smoke?"

"No, of course not."

He lit up a Marlborough cigarette whilst Becky put the kettle on and hastily washed her face, pulled on jeans and a t-shirt and brushed her hair. They sat in chairs opposite each other with their coffee. When Becky looked into his eyes she found he was looking into hers, she glanced away quickly, embarrassed when she realised that she was blushing like a teenager. There was a pause. Neither seemed to know what to say. Finally Becky said, "Where are you from then, Michael?"

"Just forty miles away, in Miami," he said with a warm smile.

"Gosh, I didn't realise it was so close."

"Yeah, just half an hour away in a plane. I'm in Real Estate and I'm over here for a couple of years."

"Why here?"

"Well there's been a boom here in Freeport. Up until 1955 there was virtually nothing on this island, just scrub and a mangrove swamp around Hawksbill Creek. Then an entrepreneur, Wallace Groves, conceived a plan for a free port and an industrial centre."

"Oh, I see – a free port. I'd wondered where the name came from. So then what happened?"

The government was pretty smart and guaranteed freedom from all taxation until 1985 and from customs and excise until 2054. So by 1966 they'd created the area called Lucaya, with roads, hotels, a casino, a shopping centre and a hospital clinic, which is I guess, where you come in."

"Gosh, that's really interesting."

"Yeah, they built a cement plant and an oil bunkering facility as well. The only problem was, as I understand it, that all the work force was crammed into a shanty town called Eight Mile Rock, so eventually they built the centre of what's now Freeport."

"Yes, a lot of the patients seem to come from Eight Mile Rock."

"Anyway that's enough about me. What brings you here?"

Becky found that she was soon telling Michael all about herself and her family in England. She thought it was crazy and she knew it was a cliche, but she felt as if she'd always known him.

A worrying thought crossed her mind. "You don't think Troy will have been admitted to the hospital do you?"

A shadow crossed Michael's face, "No. I don't. I didn't hit him hard enough," he laughed, "but if you don't mind me asking what were you doing with a jerk like him? Is he your boyfriend?"

"Good God no! I only met him last night. He was just supposed to be giving me a lift. No, I never want to see him again." Becky bit her lip as the evening before came flooding back to her.

"Don't you worry. You get any more problems with him just ring me." He gave her his phone number on the back of the Marlborough cigarette carton. "You know, Becky if you're not working this Sunday would you like to come with me for brunch at the Xanadu Hotel?"

Becky looked at him and smiled, "Yes, I'd love to, Michael, thanks."

"OK. See you Sunday at eleven then."

"Sunday at eleven."

When Michael left Becky put his flowers into water. She thought, it was kind of him to bring them. Sunday - it couldn't come soon enough.

A couple of days later Becky was back at work, her ankle now fully healed. She walked into the office carrying a tray of empty medicine pots. Sister Carey was talking to a tall Doctor with silver hair, who stood with his back to Becky.

"Well Mrs Hughes has had all the medication and inhalers that you prescribed and she still breathless."

"I think we'll give her some cortisone, Sister."

Becky met Sister Carey's eyes and she seemed to give her an almost imperceptible nod in the direction of the door.

The doctor turned around and looked Becky up and down over the rim of his half moon glasses. He was aged about sixty and so white that he looked as if he never ventured outside. "You must be, Lewis."

"Yes. I'm Staff Nurse Lewis."

"Well, I'm Doctor Rooks."

"Really."

The bell rang that signalled someone had arrived in the emergency room.

"Yes, really. I've got some advice for you, Lewis. If you want to continue working here, I'd appreciate a little courtesy the next time that you ring me out of hours."

"Well, Doctor Rooks, I'd appreciate you coming in when you're on the on call rota."

Sister Carey made some sort of snorting noise behind. Doctor Rooks turned round and glared at her. The emergency room bell rang again.

"How dare you! I'll have you know I've been a consultant here for more than..."

A Nurse's Aide wandered in. "Sister Carey, sorry to interrupt but there's a man in E.R. and he bleedin'. He bleedin' real bad and his wife she kicking up and yellin' an'..."

"OK, Fletcher. Lewis, get round there quick and sort it."

"Yes, Sister."

As Becky turned to leave Doctor Rooks stepped forward and placed a firm hand on her shoulder, his face menacing. "You need to show a little more respect. I know a lot of people here and you are very much 'The New Girl.'"

"If you'll excuse me I've got work to do, Doctor Rooks." Becky shook his hand from her shoulder and stormed out of the office.

"Bastard!" she muttered to herself as she strode down the corridor.

Later that day, just as Becky was leaving, she bumped into Teresa arriving for a late shift.

"Heh! How you doin', Becky?"

"I'm fine."

"Wow! What did you and Troy get up to the other night?"

"What do you mean?"

"Well you've been off sick with a sprained ankle and he's vanished."

"What do you mean vanished?" Becky said frowning.

"Well, no, not exactly vanished. They say he's gone to the States or something."

"Oh. Oh, I see."

"You OK? You're awfully pale."

"Yes 'course. I'm fine."

"Anyway, how did you get on?"

"Get on?"

"Oh, don't be coy, Becky!"

"No. He wasn't my type, Teresa. I only had a lift with him because I couldn't find you."

"Sorry. I guess I'd a wee bit too much too drink. I did have a great night though. Chris knows what he's doing, if you know what I mean."

Becky gave her a wan smile. "Look you'd better get on. You're going to be late."

Teresa looked slightly puzzled, "Sure, sure OK, I'll see you soon." As she walked away, Becky noticed that you could see straight through Teresa's uniform against the light. She shook her head, watching Teresa jabbing pins into her auburn hair with one hand as she walked, whilst yanking her uniform down with the other.

Becky sighed. *She was relieved that Troy was OK in spite of what had happened. She didn't really know why she hadn't told Teresa everything, except that Teresa already thought she was a prude. She felt that Teresa probably wouldn't have believed her and would have thought that she was exaggerating.*

Anyway at least it meant that she'd met Michael. She walked home enjoying the sunshine and humming to herself.

This is radio Grand Bahama, the sunshine station, and that sun is sure shining today folks! On this sixteenth of August we have a high of ninety three degrees and humidity at eighty four per cent. Now here comes Terry Jacks singing, 'Seasons in the sun,' for you all...

Becky had tried on six different outfits by the time she heard Michael's Alfa Romeo screech to a halt outside. She looked in the mirror. She was wearing an emerald green short strappy dress, with white high heeled sandals which showed off her long legs, which were fast becoming golden brown.

She'd washed and brushed her blonde hair and tried arranging it in several different styles. First she'd put it up - *too stuffy*. Then she'd tried it in a pony tail - *too teenage*. Then loose - *too hot*. Finally she'd caught the sides up with gold clips. She'd shrugged and decided, *it would have to do*.

She could hear Michael whistling as he took the steps two at a time before reaching the door and giving a long confident ring on the bell. When she opened the door he gave a low whistle of appreciation.

"Gee! You look good enough to eat."

Becky looked at Michael in his tight blue jeans and a white open necked shirt and thought that he looked pretty good too. There was a pause and then they both spoke at once.

"Ankle better?"

"Is your hand OK?"

They laughed and then both said "Yes" at the same time and laughed again.

"Come on," said Michael, "Let's go eat."

She shut the door behind her and they went downstairs chatting, passing Margaret coming back from the shops, a bag in her hand making a chinking noise. Becky introduced them.

"Any time, you both fancy a drink, you know where to find us," said Margaret.

"She seems nice," said Michael.

"Yes, she's very friendly."

They drove to the Tropical Hotel, an imposing almost totally glass structure, ten floors high. It overlooked a beach of pure white sand and was set in manicured grounds with a massive swimming pool and thatched bar. The strains of Harry Belafonte's record, 'Island in the sun,' drifted from the bar as they walked down a long hibiscus-lined path to the immense glass revolving doors of the hotel.

Inside the lobby Becky's heels sunk into a deep pile, cobalt blue carpet. Comfortable velvet chairs and settees were in the same shade and small mahogany tables with elegant lamps were dotted around. Tourists sat reading papers and magazines or just chatting and drinking coffee, the aroma of which filled the air. The tinkle of a piano in the bar playing 'You make me feel so young,' could just be heard.

Two women wandered out of a jewellery boutique wearing long flowing beach dresses and large hats.

"Well gee, Suzy, I think Daren will be just crazy about those pearls."

"You can't go wrong with pearls can you, Mercedes."

They smiled in Michael's direction and every tooth was brilliantly white and impossibly perfect. Their arms were sagging and their necks wrinkled, but their faces showed no hint of the passage of time. Only Becky noticed the tell-tale little scars, just tucked underneath the hair that draped the sides of the women's faces.

Becky was struck by the differences between the hotel and the hospital with its peeling paint and rickety chairs, scuttling cockroaches and noisy back ground radio. She shivered as the icy air conditioning encased her and wished that she'd worn something more sophisticated and a little warmer.

Michael however only had eyes for Becky. "You cold, Becky?"

"Not really. I think I've just got used to working in the heat that's all."

"What, no air-con?"

"No. No anything, more's the pity," Becky said and laughed.

"You want to tell me about it?"

A shadow crossed Becky's face. "No, not now, thanks. Let's enjoy lunch."

They rode up in the elevator to the tenth floor restaurant. Becky gasped as she saw the views from the huge picture windows that lined three sides of it.

"Pretty cool huh?" said Michael.

"Yeah, pretty cool," echoed Becky. "It certainly beats Sunday in my local pub in the rain, hands down," she laughed. Then she saw the brunch spread out over several long tables, covered by immaculate white cloths. There was a dazzling array of hot and cold dishes. Dressed local lobsters and fish - snapper, grouper or conch, prawns and fresh tuna from further afield. Pork, chicken and beef dishes in different sauces, salads and vegetables. Another table held an impressive number of tempting hot and cold sweets and fresh fruit.

"Wow Michael! Roast beef and Yorkshire pudding at home will never be the same again."

"Yorkshire pudding?"

Becky laughed and soon they were deep in conversation about the differences between England and America. Becky recognised one of the waiters as an ex-patient at the hospital and after that the champagne kept flowing at their table.

Chatting to Michael was easy. He seemed fascinated by her conventional and to her mind boring upbringing in Dorset, with her two brothers Henry and Phillip. Becky's eyes sparkled and Michael listened attentively, she told him how much she loved walking around Corfe Castle and swimming at Studland and Shell Bay near Bournemouth.

"Do you like swimming?" he said.

"I love to swim and sail more than anything else."

"You sail! That's fantastic!" I've got a dinghy on Lucaya Beach. When's your next day off?"

"Let's see." She looked in her diary, "It's Friday the twenty first."

"Great. I can pretty well work what days I please in the real estate business. We could go for a sail and have a picnic if you like.

Becky looked at Michael's eager face, his blue eyes sparkling.

"Yes. I'd like that. I'd like that very much."
They clinked champagne glasses, the sunlight glinting on Michael's gold signet ring. "To sailing in the Bahamas," he said.

Lunch lasted until about six o'clock and, when they finally got back to Becky's flat, she swayed slightly. Michael put his arm around her waist. He seemed to be on the point of kissing her when he drew back.

"Do you want to come in for coffee, Michael?"

He smiled and then looked serious. "Err...No. Thanks all the same. Better not. Work tomorrow, maybe another time."

"OK - another time, Michael. It's been great. The meal was fantastic."

"Yeah."

"I'll see you Friday then?"

"Yeah...of course. See you Friday." He turned and was gone.

Becky was puzzled. *Maybe Americans were different,* she thought. She was slightly drunk and she'd had a great time. She wasn't sure what would have happened if he'd come in. She'd made Tim wait six months before she slept with him. *She* smiled. *Perhaps the tourist board slogan was true after all,* it boasted that, 'Everything's better in the Bahamas.'

When Becky had closed her apartment door Michael banged the steering wheel with his fist. "Damn!" he muttered and roared off. He sure as hell had wanted to kiss Becky and in truth a whole lot more. He'd wanted her from the instant he'd held her in his arms on the beach.

He'd had plenty of women in his time, even been in love a couple of times when he was young, but any sort of commitment could be a problem just now. Recent girlfriends had been the sexy, hard-nosed type who'd seen him and his car and hadn't looked too much further. A quick tumble with no strings, that was the way he liked it.

The problem was that Becky was sweet. Sweet and sexy, and he really liked her. He thought back over their conversation, how much she loved her family at home, her obvious dedication to her job, her innocence and naivety.

He mused, *maybe, just maybe, she was so naive that he could go out with her without her causing problems. She always saw the best in people and God damn it, she was gorgeous.*

He arrived at a new apartment block next to the marina and parked the car outside. An elderly, smartly dressed doorman opened the door. His face was lined, he looked as though he'd waited on a lot of people in his time, but his smile was warm and sincere.

"Hi, George how are you?"

"I'm doin' jus' fine, sir."

"For Christ sake, will you please just call me Michael."

"OK , if you insist. Sure thing, Michael."

"That's better. I'll see you in the morning, George."

Michael grinned at him and took the lift to the sixth floor. Closing the door his feet sank into a cream shag carpet and he went across and put a music cassette on to play in his state of the art stereo system. He threw his keys on the glass stainless steel edged coffee table and poured himself a Jack Daniels.

Going through to the bedroom he looked at the massive king sized water bed with its silk sheets and muttered, "It sure would be good to bring Becky back here."

Lighting a Marlborough cigarette he went across to a scaled down copy of Picasso's 'Guernica' painting hanging on the wall. "Genius, sheer genius," he muttered. Taking it off the wall revealed a safe which he opened with a small gold key. He reached inside and took out an envelope of papers, three passports and a wad of one hundred dollar bills. He placed them all on the desk under the window that overlooked the sweep of Lucaya Beach. He started reading the papers but Becky intruded into his thoughts. *She really was the last thing he needed now.* The problem was he couldn't get her out of his head. *There was something about that snub nose and cute English accent.*

He sighed. Even with the air conditioning on it was warm and he decided to change out of his shirt into a t-shirt. He took off his tie and undid his cuff links. Opening the bedside cabinet drawer he tossed them inside, next to a Browning 9mm pistol.

Chapter 5

It's the twentieth of August and you're listening to the sunshine station - Radio Grand Bahama. It's hotting up so get your air con' switched to high as the temperature is soaring! Today the forecast is for ninety five degrees and eighty three percent humidity. Just relax with our next record, here's, John Denver with, 'Sunshine on my shoulders' ...

Becky worked a lot with Stefano as the weeks passed. She had to admit he was a great doctor, cool under pressure and kind, but it was his way with women that astounded her.

"Are you here long?" he would ask of the leggy American tourists in their skimpy shorts and tight t-shirts.

"No, just the week," they would reply with an inviting smile.

"What can I do for you?" His huge brown eyes would gaze into theirs, and you could almost see the women melting, sweat breaking out and gently trickling down their cleavage.

Sometimes they'd explain that they'd just fallen off their moped that they'd hired locally, or got an upset stomach, or forgotten to bring their contraceptive with them.

The more 'up front' ones would just say, "What couldn't you do for me Doctor!" or something similar. At this point Becky would usually start to leave the room, calling back, "There's a lot waiting, Doctor."

"Yeah, yeah, I'll be there in a minute." Then he'd mutter, "Do you fancy a little lobster and white wine with me tonight? I know a secluded place that overlooks the ocean." He would give them a beautiful smile and look into their eyes.

How could they refuse? Becky never stopped to hear the answer. She couldn't understand why Teresa put up with his behaviour, although she was no saint either.

After Sunday brunch with Michael, Becky found that the week dragged past. Michael intruded into her thoughts in every spare minute. She lost her appetite and struggled to sleep. Suddenly none of the problems of living and working in Freeport seemed so bad. She felt as if she was behaving like a teenager and told herself sternly to pull herself together.

But at night she lay awake going over and over their time out together. It all felt so different from going out with Tim at home. He only ever wanted to go to the pub or watch TV whereas Michael was sophisticated and sexy, confident and attentive. He seemed to love the same things that she did. She wished he could meet her brothers as she was sure they would get on.

She was bright and bubbly at work. Stefano looked at her closely after a patient had left, "You've really settled in here now haven't you?"

"Yes, thanks. I love it."

"It's more than that though isn't it? More... Yes, you're different, more alive."

Becky blushed, "I don't know what you mean. I'll get the next patient in."

"Yeah, you know," he muttered and smirked at her.

Becky had bought a new bikini in the London Boutique in the International Bazaar, a collection of shops next to the casino. She'd been looking at a pink one when the sexy young owner Caroline had said, "What about this?" She held up a red one- a strapless bandeau at the top secured by a little silver clip, the bottoms cut high on the thighs and tied with little bows at the sides.

Becky hesitated, "I'm not sure if it's really me."

"Go on, try it."

She looked in the mirror with it on. She didn't look like the old Becky from Dorset any more.

Caroline looked at her, "Wow! Some lucky mans going to love that!" she said, with a laugh.

"OK. I'll take it," Becky surprised herself. Her confidence was growing along with her deepening sun tan, *and yes,* she thought, *Michael probably would love it.*

That night In Eight Mile Rock it was hard to sleep in the heat. Josef lay awake tossing and turning for hours, thinking about Eugenie before drifting into a restless sleep. Mari didn't ask often about her mother now, she played with the other kids and next year she'd be going to school. They all went to church on Sunday and Rachel had taken to inviting them back afterwards for some peas and rice or Jerk Chicken.

Tonight he was dreaming again. They were back on the boat and suddenly the skipper with the gun loomed over them twenty foot high. He was chanting, "You're going to die, you're all going to drown." He started to laugh and his laughter filled Josef's head. He saw Eugenie and Mari fall in the water and disappear without a trace. He was trying to shout but no words would come out. He was terrified.

Suddenly he was back in the room and there she stood - Eugenie dressed in white and holding a baby. "Look, Josef, look what we have, a beautiful boy." She was smiling and he was filled with joy. She vanished as suddenly as she'd appeared and he woke suddenly, his pillow wet with tears. His disappointment was so great that it was only a dream, that he had to put his hand in his mouth to stop from crying out.

Mari lay next to him a smile on her lips, sleeping peacefully. He gently kissed her head and crept outside. He could hear something strange now. *What was it?* The noise came to him on the hint of a breeze. Isabella was chanting in her hut. He looked at the night sky and guessed it must be around one a.m. "Crazy woman," he muttered to himself, shook his head and went back into the house.

Isabella lay back in her chair, her eyes closed, her breathing laboured, sweat pouring down her face in the oppressively hot and darkened room. The candles were guttering, their smell mingled with that of the herbs. She was totally spent. On the table in front of her was the effigy of the man. Three of the silver pins were now embedded in it.

The twenty first of August, eleven a.m.
At last Friday arrived. Becky looked outside when she woke and the sun was already high in the sky. There was however an unusually refreshing breeze which would make it a perfect day for sailing.

Becky had been up early showering and washing her hair. She put her bikini on under her shorts and t-shirt. She looked at the time again and twirled a strand of hair in her fingers whilst vaguely listening to the radio. Every two minutes she got up and looked out of the window to see if Michael had arrived.

Maybe she'd got the time wrong she thought. Quarter past and then half past eleven came and went. She picked up the phone and put it down again. She was starting to feel sick when she heard his car.

Michael roared up with the top down and his blond hair blowing in the wind. *God he looked fantastic*! she thought. She could hear his car stereo blasting out The Beach Boys, 'Barbara Anne.' Becky's face broke out into a huge smile and she felt her heart racing. She picked up her things and rushed out, to find Michael taking the stairs two at a time.

"Sorry, Becky. Really sorry. I got delayed."

She was running down the steps and they collided half-way. Laughing and talking at once they tangled up with each other.

"That's OK. As long as you're here."

"God! You look great!"

He put his arms around her and drew her to him. Suddenly they were kissing. Long, deep and sweet. Warmth flooded their bodies. Eventually they pulled apart and realised they were still on the stairs. They looked into each other's eyes and smiled.

"Perhaps we'd better go before Margaret comes out," laughed Michael.

"Yes. Perhaps we had. It's a perfect day isn't it?"

"Sure is," said Michael and taking her hand they walked to his car.

Michael drove to the marina where he had a large dinghy tied up, 'The Sea Breeze'. They quickly rigged it and Michael threw a bag of things in the hold. With Becky's skilled help they were soon sailing out into the bay, red sails gently rustling and flapping in the light wind. Becky felt so exhilarated. She was never happier than when sailing, there was a cooling breeze on her skin and the sun sparkled on the turquoise waters.

Michael let Becky take the helm. "You're pretty damn good aren't you?" He said, as she expertly tacked her way across the bay.

"I'm used to sailing in freezing weather and English gales," she laughed. "This is almost too easy."

Michael grinned back at her, his eyes shining and looking deep into hers for a moment before lingering on her long brown legs.

With Michael's directions she sailed effortlessly to a beach at the quiet East End of the island. They dragged the boat out and put it under some palm trees at the edge of the beach.

Becky looked at the deserted white sands, "Wow! This is beautiful Michael." They were the only people there.

"Glad you like it. It's one of my favourite places."

They wandered along the beach and Becky found an exquisite small tulip shell in shades of chocolate and cream. She picked it up to take home. The sun was beating down on her back.

"Do you fancy a beer?" Michael asked.

"Yes, I'd love one, but where?"

"Just down this track."

They walked down a dusty track, lizards darted around in front of them and lining the edges were massive century trees, with huge yellow flowers on the end of great stalks. There was nothing to hear but the gentle sound of the waves lapping and birds singing. Michael pulled her close and they kissed again. Becky felt herself melting into him and after several minutes they pulled reluctantly apart.

"Hungry?" asked Michael.

"A little."

"Come on then let's get this beer."

The track opened out to a tiny settlement of a dozen wooden houses and a small bar. They sat outside at a table in the shade of a huge deep pink flowering oleander bush and some trees. A smiling old man with white curling hair and a big smile came out. In the background a calypso was quietly playing on the radio.

"What can I get you, folks?"

Michael ordered Budweisers and Conch fritters. The fritters came hot and steaming, crunchy and delicious.

"These are great, Michael, What are they made from?"

"Look," he pointed to a pile of enormous shells, their inner surfaces gleaming in shades of pink, the lustrous skeletons of the conch. "The fishermen catch them and when they get them back, they make a hole at the top and then pull out the 'meat.'"

Becky went and picked one up, "They're beautiful." Shades of pink from salmon to rose shimmered in the sunshine.

The old man came out, "You want one - take one. We got plenty," he said with a smile. "You know my grandma told me that way back in the eighteen hundreds, they sent them to Italy and France to make those fancy cameo brooches."

"Really, that's fascinating. I think my Mum's got one. I'd love to have a shell. Thanks, thanks so much." She chose one and went back to Michael.

"I'll take you diving for them sometime if you'd like," he said.

"That would be fantastic." Becky smiled at him and they sneaked a kiss before the old man returned. When they'd eaten they wandered back down to the beach hand in hand.

"It's so hot, Michael."

"Yeah it must be over ninety degrees. Shall we sit in the shade here?"

On a secluded part of the beach a semi-circle of sand was almost enclosed by palm trees, it looked deliciously cool.

"Yes, that would be great."

Michael went to the boat and pulled out a bag containing towels, a rug and some water. He spread the rug under the trees and they sat looking out at the sweep of the sands and the turquoise sea gently lapping the shore, framed by the palm trees. Overhead a buzzard soared on the thermals.

"I don't think I've ever been anywhere more perfect," said Becky.

"Me neither."

They both turned to each other at the same moment and suddenly they were kissing, touching and caressing each other, warm hands on warm skin. Michael hesitantly put his hand under Becky's t-shirt, and caressed her breasts through her bikini.

"Oh, Michael," she said and moving apart slightly, she let him pull her t-shirt off. Then his hands went under the elastic of her shorts and he looked at her. Saying nothing she lifted her bottom up so that he could ease her shorts down her legs.

"My God, Becky," was all he said, when he saw her in the red bikini. Then he took off his own t-shirt. His chest was broad and muscular and she breathed in the smell of his fresh sweat. Kissing his neck she tasted the salt on his skin. He undid the little clasp at the front of her bikini, and laid her back, as he kissed her firm breasts and large brown nipples. He groaned softly.

Becky moaned and gripped his shoulders whilst he touched and caressed her tanned and firm body. He took off his shorts and they kissed urgently now. He undid a bow on her bikini bottom, "Becky, Becky," he said, as he saw her golden pubic hair. Touching and kissing her there, he found her warm dampness, and teased her gently with his tongue. Becky dug her nails deep into his back as pleasure filled her body.

"God, Becky! You're perfect, really perfect."

"Michael... Michael."

She felt his hardness against her and was consumed with longing as he touched her. Arching her back she moved against him and gasped as he entered her. Michael was an expert lover and she let herself go surrendering to the intimate pleasure. They moaned and cried out together, until at last the waves of pleasure exploded, and Becky lost all sense of time and place. They lay satiated in each other's arms.

Becky opened her eyes to find Michael quietly watching her. They smiled and kissed.

"That was incredible," he murmured. "You're special you know, Becky.'"

"You too."

They kissed again, warm and tender and lay together for some time. Michael stroked Becky's hair which had come loose from its pony tail.

"Shall we go for a swim?" asked Becky.

"Yeah, great idea."

Becky moved to put her bikini back on.

"You look better without it."

Becky laughed.

"Ever gone 'skinny dipping?'"

"No."

"You'll love it, I guarantee. Come on"

He took her hand and they ran laughing down the beach and into the warm water. Swimming and diving. The feeling of freedom was incredible as the sea caressed their skin.

They swam back in a little. "Wow! This is fantastic!" said Becky standing up and running her hands through her wet hair. Water streamed over her gleaming taut tanned breasts, her nipples standing huge and erect.

Michael swam to her smiling. "Christ, Becky," he said. He pulled her to him and they kissed again. Becky giggled as she found he was erect against her. She touched his hardness, and he took her breast in his mouth and kissed it whilst fondling her. He stood up, gently moved Becky so her back was against him, and felt round to the softness between her legs. She leant back against him and gave out a small groan.

They had sex. Desire pulsating equally between them. Becky cried out as she climaxed and then Michael came. Together they stumbled in the water, laughing and giggling. Michael picked her up in one easy movement and carried her to the shallows. There they lay arms entwined around each other in the gently lapping turquoise water.

"I didn't mean that to happen," said Michael.

Becky laughed, "Liar."

"Oh well. Maybe just a bit, honey."

A dozen or so brightly coloured angel fish swam by in the clear waters, right next to them.

"God, this is heaven, Michael."

"Yeah, it is, especially with you." They kissed again. "Maybe we'd better think about getting back though."

They wandered up the beach, stopping to kiss as they walked.

"The sand's pink, Michael!"

"Yeah, it looks that colour here in certain lights."

"This is an amazing place." They reached the palm trees and got dressed. "Could I just look for some more shells, before we go, Michael?"

"'Course you can, honey."

Hand in hand they walked along the beach and Becky suddenly stopped dead. "What on earth is this, Michael?" In front of her in the sand, was a completely round hole, about two metres in diameter. Becky looked closely, "My God, Michael! The sides of it just look! " The sides vanished steeply and within the hole dark water swirled.

"It's a Blue Hole, Becky. They connect with the ocean. No-one knows how deep they are. They say that divers have gone down them and never come back." A cloud suddenly went across the sun, Becky shivered. She couldn't take her eyes off the rippling water.

Michael gave her a strange look, "People get out of their depth here, Becky. They don't realise what lies beneath the surface."

Becky was silent. The words hung between them and she shivered.

Michael laughed nervously. "Come on. Let's get back before it gets dark."

Becky felt uneasy, but once they got the boat out and started sailing she forgot all about it. They sailed back chatting and laughing again. That night Michael stayed at Becky's apartment.

This is Radio Grand Bahama. It's the twenty eighth of August and there's gonna be a high of ninety one degrees with that humidity at seventy eight percent. If you're visiting our beautiful island you can't do better than to get on down to one of our hundreds of beaches, get yourself a sun lounger and a cocktail and have yourselves a real nice day.

Becky was working on the ward when Nurse Wright came round from the E.R. "Stefano, he want to know if you got a cut down set."

"Yes, why what's the problem?"

"Some girl she bleedin' all over the place."

"OK, Nurse Wright, you go back, I'll bring one."

Becky found Nurse Wright on one side of the room admitting a man with a severe asthma attack. Stefano was a couple of feet away with a young Bahamian girl aged about seventeen, who was lying on a stretcher. Becky noticed that the girl's dark skin had a grey shade to it and her breathing was shallow. Nurse Wright had already undressed the girl and put her in a white gown. Her discarded blood stained clothes lay on the floor in a corner.

"Thank God," said Stefano glancing up at Becky and seeing her holding the sterile cut down pack. He'd got a small tourniquet on the girl's forearm, and sweat was dripping off his forehead. Several cannulas of various sizes lay discarded around the stretcher.

"OK, Stefano. I'll get it open," she said whilst quickly opening the pack which would allow Stefano to literally cut down to where the girl's collapsed vein lay, so he could put in a drip to replace the blood that she'd lost. Stefano took a scalpel and cut down to a vein, whilst Becky ran and got the oxygen cylinder and started giving the girl some oxygen.

"Stefano, it's the same as May Lee isn't it?

"Yeah, Becky, we get one every month or two."

"But that's awful! We need to find out what's going on!"

"Becky, I'm a doctor not the frigging FBI! Now help me get this drip up and then ring theatre and tell them they need to get her in straight away. Her name's Millie Smith."

Stefano managed to get the cannula in and quickly ran through five hundred millilitres of dextrose five percent solution to rehydrate Millie. He sent a blood sample to the laboratory, so they could issue blood that matched Millie's group. Becky ran and got a pack from theatres which Stefano inserted into Millie to temporarily stop her blood loss.

"Go and get her Mum to sign the consent form, would you, Becky?"

"Yes, OK." Just outside in the corridor a middle aged Bahamian woman was standing against the wall, rocking slightly, her arms tightly crossed against her chest.

She turned quickly to Becky, "What's happening, Nurse? How's my baby?"

"Don't worry she's going to be OK. You need to sign this form though so we can get her to theatre for a D&C."

"D&C!"

"Yes, it's to scrape out the womb to stop the bleeding."

"I know what it for. I'm not stupid, Nurse."

"Sorry."

"No, I'm sorry. I must be the stupid one anyway. I didn't even know..." She bit her lip as tears filled her eyes.

Becky put her hand gently on the woman's wrist. "These things happen."

"Yeah. Ain't that the truth. She'll be OK?"

"Yes, she'll be fine."

"Give me the form then."

Becky gave her the form and read it through to her.

"You know, I don't write too good. The only schooling we got on the Out Islands, when the British were here, was from the church. We lived a bit away and Mom always was wanting me to help with the little ones an' that. But we starting to train our own teachers now we's independent," she added proudly.

Becky felt surprised and slightly embarrassed to find that the British had done so little to help the Bahamian people, but she just said, "It doesn't matter at all. Just put your name as best you can."

The woman signed, 'Sarah Barnes,' in a mixture of capitals and joined up writing. "Is that OK, Nurse?"

"Yes, of course, it's fine."

"Becky, can you give me a hand?" shouted Stefano.

"I've got to go."

"Thanks, Nurse. You're very kind."

Becky just smiled, "Coming," she called and went back in to prepare Millie for theatre. The remainder of her shift passed uneventfully.

The next day Becky found Millie, sitting up in bed reading a magazine, in the Women's Ward waiting for her Mum to pick her up. Millie looked a little pale but otherwise she was completely recovered.

"Hi, how are you feeling today, Millie?"

"I's OK, Miss, thank you"

"That's alright, Millie. My name's, Becky, I was on duty when you came in yesterday."

"Sorry I don't remember nothin' 'bout that."

"No, I know you don't, that's because you were really sick when you came in."

"Oh, I know, Miss and I's real grateful."

"There's no need to thank me, but, Millie whoever did that to you was wrong. They shouldn't be doing it."

"She just tryin' to help."

"She? A woman. It's a woman?"

"Well, I don't want to get no-one into no trouble."

"But whoever, SHE is, she nearly killed you. Girls like you are dying here. We need to stop her from doing this. Something should be done about it."

"Lewis! Ain't you got anything better to do than speak to this silly child!" Sister Carey had approached from behind Becky.

"But I just think something should be done."

"Lewis, you ain't paid to think and you're gonna get yourself into a whole heap of trouble if you don't keep out of Island Matters. Now go and see to Mrs Peeks, she look like she gonna fall outa that bed in a minute."

"But..."

"No buts, Lewis. You jus' get on with what we're supposed to do here and you won't get no bother."

Becky just looked at Sister Carey and frowned. She turned and left, but walking down the ward, Becky decided that she wasn't going to be put off that easily. Going off duty she bumped into Teresa.

"Hi, Becky, how are you doing?"

"I'm great thanks. Look, do you know we just had another one of those girls in after a botched abortion?"

"Is she OK?"

"Well, yes, she is now."

"So what's the problem? You look really worried."

"Well don't you think we should try and do something about it?"

"No, not ...."

"Hi, you two girls."

Sister Patterson from theatres had come up quickly from behind them.

"How are you doin'?"

"OK thanks. I'm fine, but were you on yesterday when that girl Millie came in?"

"Yes, why?"

"Well don't you think we ought to go to the police or something?"

"Lord no, Becky! I can tell you're new to the island or you'd know that's not how things work here," she said with a warm smile.

"Don't you think we should inform someone?"

"Dear girl, I got enough to do. Teresa, can't you talk no sense into this girl?"

Teresa shrugged and smiled, holding up her hands.

"But what I really want to know is, if you're both off duty a week next Saturday?" said Sister Patterson.

"I'm not sure," said Teresa. Teresa and Becky pulled their diaries out of their uniform pockets. "It's my week-end off," said Teresa.

"I'll have just finished nights, so that's fine," said Becky.

"Great. Mr Silver is having a party on his launch and all you girls are invited. Bring a friend if you like."

"Wow! Fantastic!" said Teresa.

"Thanks," said Becky.

"Great, see you then." Sister Patterson carried on to theatres.

"I'd better go," said Teresa.

"OK. See you a week Saturday if not before."

Becky was tired. It was four a.m. and she'd been busy all night. She'd admitted a patient with a ruptured appendix at eleven p.m., a severely dehydrated baby with diarrhoea and vomiting at twelve, and at two a.m., a young man who'd been hit over the head with a heavy pan by his girlfriend when he came home late and smelling of perfume. The ward contained another thirty or so patients in addition to these.

"That girl in room fourteen, she say she hurting real bad, Lewis," Nurse Rolle wandered into the office chewing gum.

"OK .Thanks. We'd best get her some 'post op.'" Becky unpinned the keys to the Controlled Drugs Cupboard from her pocket. She opened the locked cupboards and took out three boxes of pethidine, checking the number of ampoules in each box against the drugs register.

"Ok that's great," Becky held the ampoule up to the light to check the contents and dosage as Nurse Rolle wandered off.

"Nurse Rolle, don't go! Look there's something wrong here. This isn't pethidine - it's water!"

Nurse Rolle wandered back in, took the ampoule and squinted holding it up to the light, "Yeah, it is."

"But this is serious, Nurse Rolle, someone must have swopped this!"

"Could be a mistake, man."

"No. This can't be a mistake!"

"Yeah OK. Ain't nothing to do with me. I don't hold no keys."

"Yes I know but..." Words failed Becky. This would have been a serious problem in England where the controlled drugs such as pethidine, morphine and their derivatives were strictly controlled by law. In all the five years that she'd been nursing in Britain she'd had never known the numbers to be wrong, let alone substituted for something else. There was a noise from further along the ward.

"That girl, she starting to yell now. Anyways most anyone could have changed it, 'cause when we's busy that cupboard often got them keys a hanging outa it."

Becky nodded. It was true that she frequently came on duty to find the keys in the lock when legally they should have always been held by the person in charge

Becky heard a wail. "OK Let's check out another one. Then you'll have to sign a statement."

"Jesus! They gonna make a load of fuss about that, Lewis," Nurse Rolle raised her eyes heavenwards.

"Yes I know, but I'm not risking losing my S.R.N. qualification because things aren't done correctly here."

Nurse Rolle shrugged and the girl wailed loudly again.

"Come on. Let's get her sorted then," Becky said, and they checked out and gave the girl some pethidine. Later that night

Becky checked the rest of the pethidine ampoules but found they were all OK. She wrote a report about it and gave it to Sister Carey in the morning.

"Yeah OK, I'll give it to Matron," she said leaving it lying on the desk and turning to start the medicine round.

Becky could see that as usual Sister Carey thought she was making a fuss. Becky sighed quietly. "I'll be off then."

"Yeah, you get on home."

This is radio Grand Bahama your sunshine station. It's the sixth of September and we've got a high of ninety degrees and seventy six percent humidity. Whatever you're doing today you can get on down with us. Just move your body to our next record, it's Barry White, with, 'My Everything'...

The Saturday of Mr Silver's launch party dawned dry and sunny as usual. Teresa picked Becky up at ten a.m. in her car to go to the West End of the island where Mr Silver had his launch moored up.

"Teresa, you look fantastic!"

"Thanks, I bought it the other day," Teresa wore a very short halter neck shocking pink dress that showed off her lovely legs and ample curves. Becky was wearing skimpy navy shorts and a blue t-shirt.

They went down to the car. "Teresa, this car still stinks of petrol!"

"Don't I know it, Becky! Don't light up whatever you do!"

"You're quite safe, Teresa, you know I hate smoking."

"Talking of the car I know it stinks, Becky but I'm kind of broke at the moment. You wouldn't like to share it with me and just pay for the petrol would you?"

"Yeah, OK... that would be great. I'd love to be able to explore a bit more of the island on my own on my days off."

They drove down flat roads fringed by bougainvillea, and palm trees, deep and pale pink oleander bushes grew down the central reservations. Passing a restaurant that had been built in the last few months Becky asked, "Why hasn't this restaurant opened yet? It's been finished for ages."

"They say they haven't paid their dues to the Mafia."

"The Mafia!"

"Sure, did you not know? They've got a finger in every pie here. The casino of course is the big attraction, but you must have realised that the island's awash with drugs."

"Well, yes, I've been offered all sorts just walking round the shops. The other day a man came up to me and offered me snow, sugar, grass and a load of other things too. At first I thought he was deranged and talking about the weather!"

Teresa snorted with laughter. "God, Becky I don't think I've ever met anyone quite as innocent as you!"

"Thanks!"

"Sorry, it's nice. I like the way you are. There's a history of smuggling here, just as there was in Devon and Cornwall in previous centuries. In fact Clifford told me that, if it hadn't been for prohibition in America, after the first war they would have all starved to death here, even though men had gone from here to fight for Britain!"

"Really! How did prohibition help?"

" Motor boats from here and the island of Bimini went to Florida laden with booze and schooners were chartered to go to what they called 'Rum Row' off New York, Boston and Philadelphia. Planes went from Bimini to deserted lakes in the Everglades. In fact when they repealed prohibition the Bahamas went into a depression."

"That's amazing."

"So now the same things happening but with drugs. They smuggle marijuana from Jamaica and cocaine from South America."

"How do they get away with it?"

"Just look around. It's easy. It comes to any of the little coves and deserted beaches here and then is moved on to the States. They say they bring the Haitians in that way too. Mind you everyone smokes pot here."

"Not everyone."

"Sure, you should try it sometime. Loosen you up a bit!" Becky just laughed.

"Look, here we are. Wow! Who's this smiling at us?"

"It's Michael. The chap I told you about at work the other day."

"More to you than meets the eye, Becks! Great taste."

Becky laughed again and blushed. Michael stood on the marina wearing white shorts and a t-shirt that showed off his tanned and muscular body.

Becky had a flashback to the beach and smiled to herself. Teresa shot her a knowing look. They pulled up next to an enormous, white cabin cruiser, which was berthed in the dock. The sun sparkled on its immaculate paintwork and gleaming stainless steel. A group of about twenty people stood around carrying small bags, or holding towels and beachwear under their arms. Many were already drinking Budweiser from cans in their own insulated containers, and a buzz of talking and laughter greeted Becky as she got out of the car.

Michael rushed up and kissed her. Pulling apart, Becky blushed as she realised that several members of staff from the hospital were watching and smiling, whilst looking slightly surprised. Only Teresa had known about Michael before today.

Becky introduced Michael to Teresa, Sister Patterson, a couple of other nurses from the hospital and Stefano. Teresa took Stefano apart from the rest, supposedly to look at the boat, and she started to talk animatedly with him.

"She's pretty interested in him isn't she?" Michael said.

"Yes, Teresa's completely besotted with him, though not exactly exclusively if you know what I mean."

"Yeah, she looks real hot."

Becky shot him a glance. He noticed and said, "Well, nice dress she's not wearing!" Becky laughed and he said, "You look a lot cuter, honey."

They were interrupted by a line of workers from a local hotel going past. They were heaving crates of beer, bottles of champagne and boxes of food on board. A chef and several immaculate white clad waiters were also going up the gang plank.

"Gosh, this is some boat trip!" whispered Becky in Michael's ear.

Mr Silver's black Porsche was being driven away by a chauffeur as he approached Becky and Michael, with his wife Suzy hanging on his arm. Like most people he wore shorts and a t-shirt. Becky had met him doing his ward rounds and she was surprised by how much younger he looked than when he was dressed informally. She thought that he must worked out or jog because although he was middle-aged he looked slim and fit.

Becky noticed as Suzy came closer, that, although she was wearing a lot of make-up, her skin was clear and unlined. She was probably younger than herself. With one hand Suzy pushed back her long blonde hair, which was falling over a strappy, gold sequinned T-shirt, low cut and revealing a not inconsiderable amount of cleavage. Her legs were shown off by white shorts, which looked as though they would take more time to get into than out of. She tottered towards them on gold high heeled sandals, still leaning on Mr Silver's arm.

"Hi y'all. My, you're cute," she slurred at Michael, with an underlying Southern drawl.

"Suzy this is...It's, Becky isn't it?" said Mr Silver.

"Yes, that's right, pleased to meet you, Suzy."

"Oh! What a cute accent. Is she one of your little nurses? And who are, YOU?" She gave Michael a two hundred watt smile.

"This is Michael. My boyfriend," said Becky firmly.

Mr Silver's smile seemed to freeze a little. "Nice to meet you," he said shaking Michael's hand.

"Yeah, real nice," said Suzy, offering her hand and leaning forward to reveal more of her golden tanned breasts.

"Well, I hope you have a really good time. Let me know if you need anything. If you'll excuse me I'd better get everyone organised," said Mr Silver ignoring her.

"Thanks, thanks a lot."

"Come on, Suzy."

"See y'all later."

"OK! Let's get this show on the road!" Mr Silver shouted and led the way up the gang plank, everyone else following behind, all talking and laughing at once.

Becky and Michael wandered around the deck looking at all the luxurious fittings, before going through an open doorway into a large lounge.

"Wow! Just feel the pile on this carpet," said Becky as her feet sank into a thick ruby coloured carpet.

Michael sat down into one of the matching chairs, whilst looking about him at the massive bar that took up one side of the room and the walls which were adorned with studies of nude women.

Michael whistled, "Nice taste." Becky smiled and laughed. "Not as nice as you though, darling," he said, and pulled her on to his lap. They kissed. There was a barely perceptible shudder and a light vibration carried through the boat. They were moving.

"We'd better go and socialise," Becky said, pulling away from him reluctantly. They hurried back to the deck and after chatting to some of the other hospital staff, went and sat on two of the many comfortable sun loungers that were spread around. Soon they'd left the turquoise waters behind them, and were sailing through a completely flat and calm indigo sea. They left their things on their seats and got up to stand by the rail where there was a gentle cooling breeze.

"Look! Look!" Becky suddenly yelled. A shoal of flying fish were skimming the water beside the boat putting on a display for them. Sparkling silver in the sunlight, they leapt from the water in perfect synchronisation, before disappearing as fast as they had arrived.

A waiter wandered around with glasses of champagne and Michael got them one each. They changed out of their clothes. Becky had bought another bikini from the same shop. This one was black with gold fastenings and she looked stunning. She thought that Michael looked great in his navy swim trunks. They went back to their seats which they positioned close together and lay back lazily chatting.

Suzy teetered across to them. "How y'all doin'?" she slurred.

"We're great, thanks," said Becky.

"Well that's jus' fine." She looked Michael up and down and looking into his eyes said, "You sure look great, honey. Us Americans should stick together. I'll see you later." She tottered away.

Michael just laughed and then noticed Becky's frown. "Don't worry, sweetheart, she's sloshed already. She's gonna pass out real soon."

"I wasn't worried."

At this point the boat stopped. The water here was the deepest of blues.

"We must be over the reef," said Michael.

Ropes attached to the boat were flung over the side by the crew.

"Come on let's snorkel," said Michael.

Many people produced their own snorkels and flippers from their bags and others were distributed by the crew. Becky and Michael jumped in together each holding one of the long ropes which were attached to the boat. As Becky snorkelled, she enjoyed the feeling of security the rope gave her, especially when the ocean floor suddenly seemed to drop away beneath her to a depth of sixty feet or more.

The real world was blotted out now as they entered the enchanted landscape of a Caribbean reef. Beneath them, shoals of fish, in fantastic colours and patterns, swam in and around gently waving coral, in shades of rose, lilac, tangerine and lemon. They saw a star fish which had settled on a rock, and then, to Becky's delight, a turtle lazily swam underneath them. She nudged Michael excitedly and he nodded back at her. They slowly propelled themselves with their flippers over the kaleidoscopic, magical display beneath them.

After about an hour they went back on board. Michael went to get them a drink whilst Becky dried herself off and put on a blue silk sarong. Dr Rooks walked past Becky, with his wife.

"Who's that, darling?" Becky heard his wife say.

He gave her Becky a cursory glance, "That's no-one. Just a new nurse from the hospital."

Becky shrugged, she wasn't going to let his rudeness spoil her day and then Teresa appeared.

"Isn't this great?"

Teresa and Becky were still chatting when Mr Silver came up to them. "Everything OK?" He smiled as he looked at Becky in her sarong and Teresa in her emerald green bikini, which complemented her red hair.

"Yes, it's fantastic, Mr Silver," said Becky.

"Come on, there's no need for formality here, please, call me, Tony."

"OK. Err, Tony," they both said.

"You girls sure look different out of uniform," he said with a laugh.

"Thanks, and thanks for inviting us," said Teresa.

"That's OK, I know how hard you girls work at the Royal and this is just my little thank-you. I'd best go and get this lunch served now. I don't know about, you girls, but I'm starving." He left to go inside.

"What a really lovely guy," Becky said.

"Yes, not like the usual surgeons with their orders and temper tantrums," agreed Teresa.

Michael returned and they went into the salon where a buffet was set out on two huge mahogany tables. There was something for everyone. One table was laden with crawfish, prawns, conch, steak, chicken, exotic salads, sweet potatoes, and rice. On the other lay freshly prepared, pineapple, mango, bananas, and fruit salad.

It was an uproarious lunch, everyone laughed and talked at once and the champagne flowed. Afterwards most people drowsed or slept in shady spots on the yacht, or sunbathed. Becky fell asleep and when she woke up Michael had disappeared.

She needed to go to the toilet and found she was a little unsteady when she got up. *Too much champagne*, she thought ruefully to herself and went to look in the now deserted salon. There didn't seem to be a toilet there, so she took the stairs down to the deck below. Her eyes struggled to adjust to the dim light after the bright sunshine on deck and she pushed open a door. She couldn't find the light switch and blinked screwing up her eyes trying to see in what little light there was that filtered in from the corridor.

Still drowsy from the champagne, she suddenly realised that she was in a cabin where she could half make out a bed just in front of her. As her eyes adjusted to the light, she realised to her horror that a woman was on the bed facing the door, kneeling, legs straddled over a man. A man whose penis she was vigorously sucking. The man's face and blond hair were buried in the woman's crutch, both were groaning intermittently. The light from a porthole glinted on the woman's gold sequinned T-shirt which was rucked up under her arms, her breasts swinging free.

Becky backed out hastily, stumbling over a pair of gold sandals on her way. At the noise the woman looked up. It was Suzy. She smiled benignly at Becky for a second, put her fingers to her lips and then carried on.

Becky got outside the door her head reeling. "Good grief," she muttered to herself, she didn't know whether to laugh or not. She'd never seen a couple having sex before, not on the TV or at the cinema, let alone oral sex. She was astounded.

Carrying on down the corridor, her need for a pee was getting desperate. She opened another door very carefully. *Thank God*, all was quiet inside and just on the left was a door labelled the Heads. Gratefully she went in, sat down and started to pee. To her horror she heard the door from the corridor open. A man's laugh and Teresa's voice were just discernible, as they went into the cabin a little further inside.

Becky froze. She didn't know what to do. She tried to finish peeing as quietly as possible and cautiously came out. The sounds of sex could clearly be heard, a bed was squeaking and both people were breathing heavily. Glancing back at the cabin on her way out she saw that Teresa seemed to be already half laid over the very end of the bed her knickers around one ankle. Becky could see a man's bottom vigorously going up and down as they had sex hard and fast.

She could hear him muttering something like, "Yeah, you know you like it. That's the way. God you're tight."

Teresa was moaning and grunting.

Becky rushed out. *My God, I must be so naive*, she thought. *Was this what other people did? Suzy enthusiastically having oral sex with someone who obviously wasn't her husband; Stefano and Teresa also having sex, and, in the middle of the day, on someone else's yacht.* She felt really shocked.

Becky went back on deck but Michael wasn't at their sun lounger. She wandered about the deck trying to find him and bumped into Sister Patterson from theatres.

"Are you Ok, Becky? You look a bit..."

"Yes...Yes I'm fine."

"How are you getting on? It must be very different here for you."

"Err... yes. You can say that again!" Sister Patterson gave her a quizzical look. Becky suddenly realised she meant at work. "I'm getting used to it, thanks." They chatted of the differences between England and the Bahamas and after about twenty minutes, Michael came up to them.

"Now then, you make sure you and Teresa come for supper real soon."

"Thanks, Sister."

"Call me Ellie."

Michael and Becky left Ellie Patterson and wandered along the deck. "Alright, honey?"

"Yes...yes. Where've you been?"

"I didn't want to disturb you, as you were sound asleep, so I just went to get us some iced water, hon'. You, Ok? You seem a bit distracted."

"Well, you're not going to believe what I've just seen."

"I think I will," he said with a grin.

She walked with Michael to a quiet spot and told him everything. "Well what do you expect? They're all either high or pissed or both."

"I guess so. I think I must have led a sheltered life in England. I'm certainly seeing life here! Bit more than I wanted to really!" They both laughed.

"Well, sex seems to be Teresa's weakness doesn't it?" said Michael.

"She's pretty infatuated with Stefano and I've seen him at work. He can be quite charming when he wants to be."

"You're pretty cute too, honey," he pulled Becky close to him and they kissed. "That was some beach party we had."

"Yes, it was." said Becky and she blushed. They kissed again.

"Come on, let's see if we can see any more flying fish," Michael said and they walked back to their vantage point.

Becky didn't see Teresa again until they were back at the marina around seven in the evening. She was leaning on Stefano who shouted across, "Can you take her car, Becky and I'll get her home?"

"OK"

He threw the keys across to Becky.

"As for you," said Michael to Becky, "I've been looking forward to showing you my water bed for some time now, follow me in that car of hers and let's see if we can finish the day in style."

Becky giggled and they kissed again before she followed him home.

Chapter 6

This is radio Grand Bahama your sunshine station. It's a sunny day and you'll feel a little cooler now that humidity's coming down. A high of eighty eight degrees and seventy four percent humidity. So relax yourselves and sing along with us to the Beach Boys...

Johnson strode back into the police station from the streets frowning and looking pre-occupied. He was thinking about what a foul mood Luther was still in. Luther had been on everyone's backs ever since the bodies got washed up on the beach. It was getting Johnson down, he loved his job normally. He'd always wanted to be a cop, hell he'd watched every cop series going as a boy and, even now, he hated missing an episode of Starsky and Hutch - the American detective series on the telly. He knew if he could just get a break, he could get promotion, really go places, maybe he'd even be able to transfer to the Miami police force. He just needed to do a real good drug bust or find out who was running the illegals.

He'd spent the morning going round his informers but they knew diddly shit. Christ he wished he had Huggy Bear from Starsky and Hutch on his patch. He could just see himself and his wife Hyacinth ridin' around in style, in a red Cadillac, like she deserved. Hell, he was pissed at spending his time patrolling empty beaches at night. Hyacinth was none too happy about that too, and if this carried on, not only would he never get promotion, maybe she would start looking at other guys.

As for the rest, Harris treated it all as a joke. He only patrolled the beaches at night to see if he could catch any good looking women having sex. Woods was too old - he had to be at least forty-five, he was just seeing his time out. Lightburn was a good guy, but he just kept his head down, did his job and collected his pay packet

Johnson admired Luther. Luther was passionate about policin'. He got real angry if anyone tried to bribe him. He'd charge them straight off and sling them in the cells. He never let anything go and he really seemed to care about making Grand Bahama a better place to live in. Johnson just knew that somehow he was going to make detective one day, make Luther proud of him, and put the others in their place.

Woods and Harris were deep in conversation when he went into the office, "Hi you two, how's it going?" Johnson said. They barely glanced at him.

Woods had a cigarette in one hand and another burning in the ash tray. He stood by an open window laughing with Harris. "So did you give her a slap, tell her to shut the fuck up or what?"

"Hell no, man. That ain't my style. I told her I'd never cheat on a woman like her. Then I runs her a bath, real deep with all that smelly bubbly shit she likes, an I tells her that we's goin' to the Bahamian Sunset for a classy meal. She softens up a bit and when she done gets in that bath I goes in there, naked as a jay bird, carrying two glasses of fizzy."

"Man!" said Woods shaking his head.

"I tell her I got sometin' special for you, honey."

"She looks at what I got an' I don't mean no crap sparklin' drink an' she starts a giggling. I know I'm past first base then. I don't get no more of that GBH of the ears and guess what?"

"What?"

"We gets too busy to get to that restaurant, so I'm in pocket and by the end of the evening she's 'pologisin for doubtin' me."

"You cocky bastard! I sure remember those days with my Rose. I like my women a good size you know." They both chuckled. "In the old days why I just used to slap her on the rump and ride in on the ripples."

Harris and Woods started laughing and slapping their thighs.

"Ain't you two got nothing better to do than talk about women!"

"Can't think of anything better to talk about," said Harris.

"You two! You don't get it do you?" said Johnson. "We're suppose to be out there catching these drug pushers an that, an you's just in here treatin' it all like a joke! Like it don't matter."

"Look here boy. When you've been in the service as long as I have you'll know it don't matter, 'cause whatever you do, you ain't gonna stop it," said Woods, an amused smile playing on his lips.

"Cool it Johnson! A bit of pot never hurt anyone anyways. What's wrong with you? Ain't you getting any from your precious Cynth?" asked Harris.

"God! That's all you can think about! An you leave my Hyacinth outa it. These kids they start on pot, next thing you know they're taking snow, then they're shoving needles in their arms. I love these islands, man, you got kids too, what's gonna happen if all the kids start doing this shit?"

They looked at him, sighed and shrugged. Woods lit another cigarette.

"I'm finished now anyway. I'm outa here," said Johnson and stormed out slamming the door behind him.

"Wanker!" Harris muttered as the door slammed.

The same afternoon Becky was working in the ER when a man dressed in jeans and a scruffy t-shirt carrying a little girl in his arms rushed in.

"Help me! Help us!" he shouted. Becky stopped bandaging a man's leg to see what the problem was. The little girl was making a rasping noise as she breathed and her lips were tinged with blue.

"Quickly come with me! Stefano! Stefano!" Becky shouted.

"Put her on here. What's happened?" she asked, indicating a stretcher. The man put the little girl on the stretcher and Becky raised the head end of it.

"Sweetie. She eating sweetie."

The little girl's brown eyes were wide with fear and she clung to the man.

"What's her name?"

"It's Mari."

"Mari, it's OK, poppet, let me put this mask on you." Becky turned on the oxygen and tried to put the mask on Mari, but she fought it and pushed it away with her hand.

"She no understand Nurse."

"Tell her she needs to have this mask on, it'll make her feel better. What's your name?"

"Josef. I am Josef."

"OK. Josef, everything's going to be OK. I know you're frightened but be calm with her, it will help her breathing. Tell her she's going to be fine."

Josef spoke to her rapidly in French.

Stefano came in. "What's wrong?"

"This is Mari, she can't breathe, her father's talking about sweets."

At this point Josef produced a small round empty tube of the type that held 'Smarties' in England.

"It's this," he said pointing to where the tiny round lid should have been. "She has it here," he touched Mari's throat.

"Get her down flat and I'll look with a laryngoscope," said Stefano.

Becky tipped the trolley so the girl lay head down and then got the emergency resuscitation trolley.

"Josef, tell her we're going to make her better, and that the doctor's going to look at her throat."

Josef spoke in French again to Mari.

"Becky where are the 'scopes?" asked Stefano.

"Here on the trolley."

"Is this all we have?"

"Yes, I think so."

Stefano tried to look down Mari's throat but the laryngoscope was too big.

"Damn! This is no good, I need a paediatric one."

"I'll try Theatres."

Becky ran out of the cubicle, into the ER waiting room, where she was greeted by a chorus of shouting.

"Heh, Nurse! We been waiting hours."

"What you all doing?"

"They don't care nuthin' 'bout us"

"Sorry, an emergency!" Becky shouted over her shoulder, as she rushed passed them all and round to the Operating Theatre.

She hurried through a side door and found Sister Carey there rootling around the sterile packed instruments.

"What do you want, Lewis?"

"I need a child's laryngoscope."

"Oh. OK." Sister Carey carried on looking for what she wanted.

"Sister! Please! Where can I find one! I need it now!"

"Why didn't you say? It right there above your head."

"Thanks." Becky grabbed it and ran out.

When she got back to the little girl, Stefano looked worried. He'd got Mari sat up again and had put a cannula in the vein of her arm. He was giving her Aminophylline a drug to open up her airways. Josef was stroking Mari's hair and muttering softly, he crossed himself. Becky realised he was praying. She looked at Mari who was making no effort to fight or look around her, but lay impassive with her eyes closed. Her rasping breathing filled the air. *We need all the help we can get*, Becky thought.

"Here, Stefano try this," she gave him the laryngoscope.

They tilted the bed so Mari was head down again and Stefano tried again to get the laryngoscope in. He succeeded but looking down her illuminated airway said, "The trouble is it's all so swollen now." He frowned and sweat started to stand out in beads on his brow. He began to fish around with a long pair of forceps down Mari's throat.

"Give her fifty milligrams of hydrocortisone, Becky, to see if it will help the swelling. It's OK, sweetheart, I'm going to make it better," he said to Mari, shooting Becky a desperate look as he did so.

Becky drew up and gave her the hydrocortisone. After a few minutes the girls breathing was getting worse, her eyes were rolling and her skin had an ashen sheen to it. Her lips were blue. Becky attached her to a heart monitor which showed that Mari's heart was beating too fast and irregularly. She took her blood pressure it was almost undetectable and dangerously low. Becky hunted around in the trolley and found some nasal oxygen cannula which she managed to get in Mari's nose, as Stefano continued to try to get the cap out of her throat.

"I see it!" cried Stefano. "I can see it, it's yellow!"

Josef crossed himself and continued to mutter.

"I have it!"Stefano withdrew the forceps and sure enough attached to the end was the sweet cap.

Josef fell to his knees. "Merci, Merci," he said, crossing himself.

"Well done, Stefano," said Becky as she sat Mari upright. The colour was already starting to return to Mari's cheeks, and her breathing had quietened.

Josef rushed to Stefano, "Merci, merci beaucoup, thank you, thank you, thank you so much. I couldn't live without her, she's all I've got." Then he rushed to Becky and embraced her, "Thank you, thank you," and he started to cry.

"That's OK, it's Dr Rossi that you have to thank."

"No, Becky, he's right, it was a joint effort. Thanks."

Becky said nothing. She hadn't wanted to be friendly with him since he'd taken her to the beach that night, and after seeing him on the boat with Teresa she felt even more uncomfortable in his company.

He turned to Josef, "We'll just keep her in overnight to make sure there are no after-effects, but I'm sure she'll be fine now."

Becky rang the ward to let them know that Mari would be admitted. Teresa answered the phone, when she'd taken down the details she said, "Becky, I need to talk to you about the trip on Mr Silver's launch."

"Oh do you? Go on then."

"No, not on the phone. Can you come round when you've finished."

"Yes, OK," said Becky feeling uneasy. She hoped it was nothing to do with seeing Teresa downstairs on the boat. She'd didn't think that Teresa had seen her and she certainly didn't want to talk about it. Although she'd laughed about it with Michael she wished she'd just asked where the loos were instead of wandering about witnessing far more than she'd wanted to.

At the end of Becky's shift she went round to the ward. On the way she bumped into Mr Silver. "Hi, Becky, how are you doing?"

"I'm fine thanks. A bit tired, I've just finished my shift. Thank you so much for inviting us to the yacht last Saturday, it was fantastic."

"You're welcome, glad you and your boyfriend enjoyed it. I understand you've had a few problems with the on call rota and Doctor Rooks?"

"Well...yes, but it seems to be all sorted now."

"If you get any more problems, just come and see me about them."

"Thanks, that's kind of you."

"OK. See you around."

"Yes, OK, 'bye."

Becky went in to the office and found Teresa writing up a patients report. "Hi, Teresa, how are things?"

"Not bad." She finished off what she was writing.

"I just bumped into Mr Silver. What a nice guy. That was an amazing trip out Saturday wasn't it? Gosh I'm shattered. What a shift I've just had with that little girl Mari coming in."

"Becky, have you got time for a quick coffee in the staff room?"

"Yes, OK that'll be great," Becky said frowning a little. It wasn't like Teresa to look so serious.

Becky and Teresa went into the staff room and Becky started making coffee Teresa suddenly said, "Becky, how did I get back from the yacht?"

"Stefano took you in his car, don't you remember?"

"No, no I don't, Becky, that's it. I don't remember anything after we got back on board, when we'd been swimming over the reef."

"Well I guess we'd all had a lot of champagne."

"But, Becky, did you see me with anyone?"

"Damn! I've spilt the water! What do you mean exactly?" said Becky not looking up, intent now on pouring hot water into the mugs. "You chatted to lots of people."

"No. I mean did you see me snogging or kissing with anyone?"

"Well sort of," said Becky reddening a little, and picking up the coffee cups and taking them across to her. "Would you like a biscuit?"

"Becky! What do you mean 'sort of'?"

"Well it was quite a lot more than snogging, Teresa, if you really want to know."

"What!"

"I'm sorry, I didn't mean to see you. I was looking for the loo."

"What are you talking about?"

"I saw you, Teresa."

"Saw me what?"

"You know..."

"No I don't know. I don't know anything. All I know is, Becky, that I woke up lying on the settee at home on Sunday morning, and I didn't have any panties on and..."

"Well, come on, Teresa. You and Stefano are pretty close. You'd had a lot to drink..."

"NO! No, he swears he never touched me."

"Then he's lying, Teresa."

"How do you know?"

"Because if you must know, I saw him having sex with you on the yacht."

"What!"

Becky sighed and put her coffee mug down firmly. "Yes. I was desperate for a wee and I went into a loo in a cabin. While I was in there you and Stefano came in and by the time I came out you were both... both...you know..."

"Stefano! You saw him having sex with me?"

"Well. No. Not exactly. It was dark. But I heard you speak as you both came in. I didn't see Stefano's face because... because he had his back to me. But I heard him...you know...talking to you."

"You heard him talking!"

"Well, it was more muttering, urging you on so to speak." Becky blushed and fiddled with her hair not looking at Teresa.

"Becky, you're wrong. It wasn't him. I'm sure."

"Look, Teresa it's really none of my business. You're the one who told me there are no rules here."

"Becky, I think I was drugged!"

"What!"

"I can't remember anything! Anything at all."

"Are you sure you weren't just drunk?"

"Yes, I'm sure. You've got to believe me."

"OK. Yes, I do."

Teresa's eyes filled with tears. All I know is that I woke up feeling like shit. I've got bruises on my shoulders and... thighs and I was sore, really really sore," she started to cry.

"Oh my God, come here," Becky put her arms around Teresa.

"Who would do that to me, Becky?"

"I don't know. God! There were a lot of people on board."

Teresa dried her eyes, "Becky I'd better start work."

"Well are you OK to work?"

"Yeah, I'll be fine."

"Let's meet up when you finish and go for a drink. We can talk some more."

"Thanks, Becky, that would be great. I know you think I'm a slut but..."

"Don't be ridiculous, of course I don't."

"OK Let's go to the bar at the casino, the crowd don't hang out there and I don't want to go anywhere where someone I know might see me. Where... he, whoever *he* is, might see me."

"Oh, Teresa," Becky stroked Teresa's shoulder.

"I'd better go. See you at eleven o'clock tonight then." She dried her eyes and stood up.

"Yes, OK, come and pick me up from the flat."

Teresa had changed out of her uniform when she picked Becky up that night and was wearing jeans and a high necked blue blouse. She looked pale and had a slight tremor as she re-started the car.

"How are you, Teresa?"

"Oh. You know."

"Do you think you should get checked out, or go to the police?"

"No! I don't want anyone to know and the police would do sod all. Probably laugh at a stupid ex-pat getting what she deserves!"

"They can't all be that bad surely. I could come with you."

"Becky, I don't think I've got a reputation for being Snow Bleeding White. They won't believe me."

"But we should..."

"NO, Becky, I said no!"

"OK, OK, I'm sorry."

"No, I'm sorry, I know you're trying to help. Come on, let's get a drink."

They drew up at the gleaming white casino, its gold dome lit up from underneath. It reminded Becky of a lesser version of the Taj Mahal. In front of it fountains of water played over the manicured lawns and immaculate flower beds. A Bahamian doorman, dressed in a tuxedo and a red bow tie, opened Teresa's door as she drew to a halt.

"Park your car, ma'am?" His nose wrinkled. "You gotta' petrol leak, ma'am."

"Yes I know!" said Teresa.

"Well, it don't smell too good..."

"Would you just park the damn thing please!"

"You're the boss." He drove off looking annoyed and muttering, "Time was we had film stars come here, *A* class people..."

Both Becky and Teresa walked into the casino laughing, "*A* Class people," parodied Teresa and they both laughed again.

Their feet sank into the royal blue carpet of the vestibule. Immaculate waiters and waitresses walked past carrying trays laden with drinks. Cocktails were crammed to the brim with ice and swizzle sticks and little umbrellas.

American tourists wandered by Becky and Teresa. Some of the women wore beautiful evening dresses, their diamonds sparkling under the light of the chandeliers, the fragrances of Chanel, or Yves St Laurent trailing in their wake. Their partners often several years older and smoking cigars wore DJs and bow ties. Others wore their normal tourist uniform - the men in slacks with bright floral shirts, the women bulging out of skin-tight trousers and low satin tops or boob tubes.

A quartet could be heard playing Frank Sinatra standards – the female vocalist crooned 'Fly me to the moon,' in the bar, and the nightly show in the theatre had already started. They walked towards the bar and to Becky's horror a familiar figure walked towards them.

"Well, if it isn't little Miss Prim and Proper." Troy stood in front of them, wearing a rugby club sweat shirt and holding what looked like a large scotch.

"Hi, Troy," said Teresa with a smile.

"Hi," muttered Becky.

"Where's Sir Galahad tonight then?" he slurred.

"Who are you talking about?" asked Teresa.

"Look, Troy, we've just come for a quiet drink," said Becky.

"You want to go swimming later?" he put an arm round Becky who shook it off.

"Please, Troy, just leave me alone!"

People were starting to look at them.

"Jesus, Troy, you've had too much. Why don't you go home? Can't you see she's not interested?" said Teresa.

"I've had too much have I? Who's this speaking? Saint bloody Teresa?"

A burly door man with a shaven head, wearing a jacket that was straining over his chest, approached them, "Is there a problem here, ladies?"

"No. No, sorry we're fine."

"I think we're just leaving, Sir, aren't we?" An equally burly doorman had joined the first one.

"Yeah, yeah. Not worth bothering with. One's a slut, and, you," he turned to Becky with a menacing stare, "You, I'm going to sort you out properly one of these days."

"Right, Sir. Out!"

They seized him under both elbows and frog marched him to the door.

Troy shouted back over his shoulder, "You'll see Miss Hoity Toity!"

"You OK, Becky?" said Teresa.

"Yes, of course, he's just drunk." They went into the bar, and sat on the plush seats in a quiet spot. Becky found her hands were shaking. Teresa ordered a gin and tonic and Becky a large glass of white wine.

"Becky, why's he acting like that? Didn't he take you home the other week from the pub?"

"No, not really."

"You haven't told me everything have you?"

"No, no, I haven't..." Becky explained what had happened that night.

"Bloody hell, Becky, you should have told me."

"There was no harm done. And besides it meant that I met Michael. Anyway we're supposed to be talking about you, not me."

"Christ! We make a right pair!" said Teresa, and they laughed a little, before it died away and they looked at each other silently for a moment.

"Tell me, Teresa. Tell me, what happened."

Teresa went over again what she could and couldn't remember and then said, "We'd better go, I've got an early shift in the morning."

"OK," I'm pretty tired myself."

"You know what really puzzles me about the whole thing is why someone would drug me. I knew quite a few of the guys there..." she smiled deprecatingly, "really well - if you know what I mean. I'd had a few drinks, I'd have probably... Oh, you know what I'm like, Becky. And they know too. Who would have drugged me? And why?"

"I don't know, Teresa, but I tell you, I'm watching my drinks from now on."

They passed through one of the rooms where a large group of people were gathered around a table.

"Gee, that's some bet!" an American voice said.

"He's been losing all night," said another.

"Twenty thousand on the black," said a young American man's voice.

Becky stopped.

"What is it, Becky?"

"That voice," she said frowning. "Hang on a sec." She pushed through the crowd. He stood sideways on to her, immaculate in cream jacket, white shirt and black trousers. His blond hair shone in the light. Becky caught her breath. Her eyes widened.

The roulette table spun and everyone fell silent as the dice clattered.

"Red sixty-two," said the croupier.

"Motherfucker! God damn it!" said the man.

Becky moved backwards, bumping into Teresa. "Let's go."

"What's wrong?"

"It's Michael!" she said with a puzzled frown. "Michael just lost twenty thousand dollars!"

"What!"

"Shh! Come on, I don't want him to see us." She pulled Teresa away.

"Why not?"

"I don't know. Look I didn't even know he gambled, let alone that much. I just don't think now's a good time for him to know I've found out. I want to go home. I've had enough surprises for one night."

Becky got in about three a.m., she went into the bathroom and picked up the beautiful tulip shell that she'd found on the beach with Michael. As she held it in her hand something black and slimy slid out of it. She dropped it in horror, feeling sick.

It took her a long time to go to sleep, and, when she finally did, she dreamt of sharks circling.

Chapter 7

Twelfth of September.

By the time Johnson had driven back to the tiny house he rented in Hawksbill Creek he was feeling better. *He'd show the others at the station, they'd see. One day it would be him telling them what to do.* He looked at the small house and sighed. *Damn landlord did sweet F.A.* He'd painted the wood himself, blue, 'cause that was Hyacinth's favourite colour but it couldn't conceal where pieces were missing. Several tiles had come off the roof in a storm last winter and he was worried that it was going to leak if it rained hard. He tried to keep the tiny scrap of garden at the front clean, but the fence was broken and rubbish just blew in whenever it was windy.

His neighbour Josie was often drunk. She had eight kids and as usual they were playing in the street when he drew up. As usual too they were screaming and arguing, this time over a chair leg that they were using as a bat in a ball game.

He shouted at them, "Cool it, you kids! Or I'll be takin' you all in!"

"Yes Sir, Mr Policeman!" Max was ten and cocky. Johnson had had enough today, so he let it go. Just shook his head, smiled through gritted teeth and walked up the dirt path to open the door.

The minute he opened the door he smelt the mouth watering aroma of jerk chicken and peas'n'rice. The door entered straight into the living space and there was a small kitchenette off it. Some cartoons were playing on the TV but no-one was watching them.

He could see his Hyacinth standing at the stove cooking. *God,* he thought, *she looks good enough to eat in that kinda close fittin' blue dress, with some sort of yellow and red flowers, looking like they was out of control rampaging all over it.* He stood for a moment, just looking at her and her long black curly hair, which he loved to bury his face in and smell its sweet perfume.

He walked into the kitchen and noticed small rivulets of sweat running down her cleavage, without realising, he licked his lips.

"Hiya, honey! Man that sure smells good!" He glimpsed little Stevie through the open back door, chasing their three chickens around the yard outside.

He went up to Hyacinth and nuzzled the back of her neck. "Don't your man get no kiss, after a hard day, chasin' them criminals?"

"Huh! Can't you see I's busy cookin'," she shrugged him off and carried on stirring the black pot on the stove.

"You ain't never too busy for me, woman," he said with a chuckle.

"Mummy! Mummy! Daddy I got an A in readin' today! Miss Martin, she says I's the best in the class." Daisy aged seven, the oldest of their two children erupted into the house, throwing down her school bag and kicking off her shoes.

Johnson swept her up in his arms, "That's great, honey pie. You's a real clever girl."

"I know, Daddy! Can I go out an' play with Hilly next door, Mummy?"

"No you can't! Go get changed outa that good uniform. Supper almost done ready."

"Argh. OK. But can I play after supper?"

"We'll see. Now go get changed and take your brother with you, get his hands washed. He been running around after them chickens a full hour now."

As Daisy left Hyacinth looked at her and then at Johnson, "She almost growed outa that dress you know."

"Yeah, honey. Where were we?" he started nuzzling her neck again.

"Can't you see I'm tryin' to cook here?"

Johnson frowned, "Sometin' wrong, honey?"

"Why should anything be wrong?" She finished peeling and started chopping up sweet potatoes with a large and very sharp knife.

"Well you looks like you got Mrs MacMeany under that knife!"

Mrs MacAlistar or Mrs MacMeany as all the kids called her behind her back, had been the scourge of the local Sunday school, who didn't hesitate to use a slipper, if she thought anyone was getting what she called uppity.

"I'm fine! I already done told you. Now stop pesterin' me."

"Oh I get it. Time of the month ain't it!"

"No it ain't! An' it ain't gonna be either!"

"What!"

"No good you standin' there with those eyes a poppin outa your head Jo Johnson. I wasn't going to tell you yet but...but...well now you knows."

"But that's great, honey!"

He swung her around and found that she was crying.

"No it ain't great. How we gonna feed another one? We only jus' getting by now."

"Don't, you worry none. I'm gonna get me a promotion. I've got a plan."

She looked at him sharply, "What sorta plan?"

"I can't tell you that, honey, it's police business, but it'll all be Ok you'll see. I ain't havin' my kids growin' up in a place where these drug pushers just bring in any shit they wants to."

"You be careful, Jo. You ain't no Starskey!"

"Yeah. Skin kinda gives it away don't it. Now come here an' give me that kiss."

Hyacinth put the knife down and he pulled her to him, his hands going over her bottom, his mouth moving down her neck tasting salt, and breathing in the perfume of her.

"Mummy! Stevie won't wash his hands for me!"

Stevie came in wailing dragged by Daisy.

"Maybe we could celebrate a little later on, sugar," said Hyacinth.

"Yeah, in the traditional style," he said with a big grin.

"Ain't got nothing to lose now," Hyacinth chuckled and quickly ran her hand over the bulge in his trousers with a smile, before turning back to the children.

The next day, Becky was having a rare quiet moment in the ER. At seven p.m. the great queues of people that they'd treated in the afternoon had gone. It was that in-between time - after the minor accidents and work injuries, and before the drunken incidents and occasional stabbings that came in later.

Becky was still puzzling over Michael's gambling. Maybe it was just a moment of madness when he'd got carried away, perhaps he could afford to lose that much money. She realised that there was a lot she didn't know about him. She wasn't sure how to approach him about it now that time had passed. It might seem as though she'd been spying on him. And then again she'd never been out with anyone quite like him. He was good looking and charming, exciting to be with, and their lovemaking had taken her to peaks of pleasure she didn't know existed. She couldn't wait to see him again.

She found she was daydreaming and remembered she'd still got to fill in some patient details in the admissions book. By chance she opened it at the page for her first shift that fateful Monday, when May Lee came in and died from the botched abortion. She flicked through and noticed another girl had come in three weeks previously on a Monday, also bleeding from the vagina. She frowned, *what day was it when she admitted Millie?* She turned the pages and found her entry - she too had come in on a Monday.

She sat down and started to go through the book noting the dates when other girls had been admitted with the same diagnosis.

"What are you doing, Becky?" Stefano was stood beside her. She stuffed the piece of paper in her pocket.

"Just checking the book's up to date." He gave her a quizzical look. "Stefano, don't you think we should do something about all these girls coming in after botched abortions?"

"You've got a real bee in your bonnet about this haven't you? You know what? I treat them, I put up a drip, I get them to theatre, that's it."

"But don't you think we should go the police or something?"

"God above, Becky! Why can't you just let things lie? It's not our job. I'm a doctor, you're a nurse not a policewoman! It's not our country. I like working here. I don't make waves and if you're sensible you'll do the same."

"You don't care about anything really do you?"

The door suddenly swung open. Clifford appeared pushing a stretcher. "Nurse, I got a patient here. He say his chest hurts real bad." The patient clutched his chest and groaned.

"OK bring him in here," said Stefano indicating the stretcher. "I care about the patients," Stefano hissed. Becky wished she hadn't said anything then, because, whatever else she thought of Stefano, he was, a damn good doctor.

After that the evening passed quickly. Becky got back to her flat and taking off her uniform the piece of paper fell out of her pocket. She made herself a cup of coffee and studied it. Every girl had come in after a week-end. It niggled away at her. *Who had the knowledge to do it and was often off at week-ends? Who had access to drugs and equipment? Who would need the money?* She frowned and twirled her hair, went and made another cup of coffee.

Then it came to her! *Right under her nose! Now - what was she going to do about it?*

Chapter 8

You're listening to radio Grand Bahama, the sunshine station. It's the fifteenth of September and we expect a high of eighty eight degrees and humidity of seventy five percent. Later today cloud is building so watch out for the occasional heavy shower this afternoon. Talking of showers we've got Neil Sedaka for you with 'Laughter in the rain'...

Becky was having coffee with Nurse Carter one of the Aides, in the dingy coffee room where she'd first met Teresa. Nurse Carter was fanning herself with a piece of paper and Becky wished not for the first time, that the coffee room had a window they could open.

"Gosh it's so hot isn't it?" Becky said.

"Man, it sure is. I couldn't sleep last night."

"Have you got air conditioning at home?"

"No we can't afford that, so we has the windows open, but then you can hear everything outside and them walls so thin you can hear them all inside as well. Hell, Sister Carey lives a floor below me and I could hear her laughing last night."

"Where do you live then, Nurse Carter?"

"I lives in town. You know Poinsettia Apartments?"

"I'm not sure."

"It's that small block of apartments just opposite the supermarket, it's real convenient for everything. Why you askin'?"

"Oh nothing. I just wondered. I'd better get back now."

The conversation set Becky off thinking about Sister Carey. She remembered finding her that day at the back of the Operating Rooms, when she went to find a laryngoscope. *What had she been looking for there? She had most week-ends off. Everything fitted together. Surely, It MUST be her that was doing the abortions?*

But, no - if she lived in a block of apartments where everything could be heard then she couldn't be. Maybe Stefano was right and she should just forget all about it.

The next day was a Saturday and Becky had been shopping. It was another swelteringly hot day. She had the car today and as she slammed the boot shut, she pushed her hair off her sweating face and looked around.

Sister Carey was coming out of the flats opposite, a cigarette in her mouth and carrying a large shopping bag. It looked heavy as she heaved it into a yellow rusting and dented Ford Cortina. Becky remembered that it was her day off as well.

Getting into the car Becky started up the engine. Leaning on the steering wheel she twirled her hair and frowned. *It was a stupid idea,* she told herself. She heard Sister Carey's Cortina cough into action and as she pulled out of the car park, Becky found herself pulling out a little way behind. Sister Carey seemed to be going the same way that Becky went to go home, so Becky was driving a couple of cars behind her. When Becky reached the turning to her own apartment, she felt impelled to continue following Sister Carey, even though she told herself, she was being stupid. There were two cars in between them, so she didn't think that Sister Carey would notice. *And after all, she had a perfect right to go where she liked on the island, didn't she?*

The centre of Freeport faded behind them and they went along a fairly empty tarmacked road. Becky had the car window wide open, letting in a refreshing breeze, and the sunshine sparkled on the windscreen. *I must be mad, she* thought to herself, *I could be going to the beach instead of trying to be some sort of detective.*

They entered Eight Mile Rock and one of the two cars turned off. *Well, well,* thought Becky, *if you were going to do an abortion this would be the place to do it.*

Sister Carey turned right and down a narrow dirt road, just as the car in front turned left. *Help! If she looks back now she's going to see me, what the heck am I going to say? Just passing?* Becky hit the brake and dust flew up around her on the rough road, she pulled in between two rusting cars outside some tiny houses, just as Sister Carey stopped a few hundred yards further up.

Becky turned off the engine and noticed the dingy curtains move at the window of the tiny house that she was stopped outside of. Similar to all the others the wood was painted green where it hadn't peeled off. Sister Carey got out of her car and looked around her. She was shading her eyes and seemed to be squinting down the road towards Becky. Becky's heart was pumping hard. She tried to think. *What should she do? Reverse? No too obvious. Drive past? How on earth could she explain what she was doing here? Damn it, in films didn't people have a newspaper or something to hide behind,* she looked around the car, there was nothing. She was sweating in the baking heat now that the car wasn't moving.

Dear God! Sister Carey had started to walk down the road towards her. Perhaps she could say she'd broken down...or got lost...or God - nothing really stood up did it?

"Are you OK, dear?" a woman's voice came through the open window.

Becky jumped. "Oh my goodness!"

An immense Bahamian woman with a friendly smile on her face and a child on her hip was stood next to the open window. "Sorry. I didn't need to startle, you none. Can I be of help to, you?"

Further up the road a woman had appeared and was stood chatting to Sister Carey.

"I err... I err..."

"Yes, honey?" The baby started to wail and Becky looked at it.

"Gosh, she's lovely isn't she?"

"Yeah, she pretty good usually, I got another six."

Becky looked back down the road. The woman speaking to Sister Carey had disappeared. Sister Carey waved at the woman speaking to Becky and she waved back and shouted, "Hi, how you doin?"

Becky could almost see Sister Carey's face now. "Erm... I think I've dropped something." Becky bent over the passenger seat and started pretending to rummage around on the floor. She heard a faint shout from further up the road. Peeking up she saw that Sister Carey had turned and was walking back towards the house. Sister Carey looked back at the woman next to Becky and shook her head.

"Got to go! See you later Sylvia." She opened the boot of her car, heaved out her bag and went into the house.

The woman was looking at Becky puzzled, "Did you find it?"

"What?"

"What you said you dropped."

"Yes. Err...No. Must have left it at home."

"Do you two knows each other from the hospital or something?" the woman pointed at Sister Carey, who was entering the house. She rocked the baby on her hip who was sleeping now.

"No. No. I don't know her."

"Are you sure you're OK, dear? You're awful pale. What are you doing here anyways?"

"Yes, I'm fine. Thanks. Just took a wrong turning. Realise where I am now. Thanks a lot. Got to go, I'm going to be late."

"Well it was nice meeting, you."

Becky started up the car, "Yes, you too, bye."

The woman moved away from the car and stood in the road watching Becky drive off. Becky went slowly down the narrow dirt road and looked at the house that Sister Carey had gone into. It was set apart from the others. The garden was overgrown and rubbish blew around it. There was a rickety fence and the once green painted windows were peeling. Thick net curtains covered them all.

Once Becky got passed the house she drove home fast. She found her hands were shaking. *That had been close - too close. But she knew something else now. Sister Carey had more than one place to live and she went there at week-ends.*

Chapter 9

The seventeenth of September.

Becky was swimming in the pool wearing goggles, as she glanced up she saw a tall figure standing watching her. In her goggles he was indistinct. He stood unmoving. Ominous .When she reached the edge he'd come closer. She tore off her goggles and there stood Michael, looking thoughtful.

"Michael! Heh, what a lovely surprise," she said, effortlessly pulling herself on to the side.

Michael smiled instantly and his face was transformed. "God! You look great, honey!" he said, looking at the way the water droplets stood out on the bronzed skin of her breasts in the black bikini.

Becky laughed, "You look pretty good yourself."

He drew closer and they kissed, "Careful you're going to get your suit wet." Michael was dressed for work in a light beige suit and white shirt.

"Yeah you're right. I guess I can't go back to work soaking wet and I do have to get back. How about you?"

"I'm working tonight starting at eleven o'clock, so at least it will be cool working for once. I'd rather be seeing you though," she said looking sad.

"Well maybe this will cheer you up a little." Michael produced a small package from the inside of his jacket. "It's not much, it's really only the first half of a present."

"Gosh, sounds intriguing. Thanks, Michael."

"Look I'd better go. Unwrap it when I've gone. You're free at the week-end aren't you?"

"Yes, it's my week-end off."

"Great, don't plan anything and I'll give you the other half of the present then."

"The other half? Go on, tell me now, what is it?"

"Nope. That would spoil the surprise."

"Teaser!"

"Don't suppose you need any help getting changed do you?"

She giggled, "No thanks. If you're not going to tell me, you might as well get on back to work, sweetheart."

He smiled at her, his blue eyes sparkling. She thought that she ought to mention she'd seen him at the casino but she didn't know how to approach it. She didn't want to spoil the moment. He leant closer to her again and she melted. They kissed, and Becky felt warmth suffuse her body. She ached for him.

"OK, see you Saturday, darling, about ten a.m.," said Michael.

"Great, I can't wait."

When he'd gone she sighed and frowned. She should have asked him straight away. Why *was* he gambling and such a massive amount? Maybe he'd tell her more about himself this week-end and then she wouldn't have to ask.

The second she got indoors she unwrapped the package. She found it was a small book, 'The old man and the sea,' by Hemingway. She'd read 'For whom the bell tolls,' in the past. She was intrigued and smiled to herself. Michael was so much more thoughtful than anyone else she'd been out with. She wondered what the other half of the present could be. She hugged the book to her. Maybe she would get a chance to read it on duty tonight.

When Becky went on duty at eleven p.m. Sister Carey had been in charge of the day shift.

"Evening, Lewis," she said, looking her up and down without smiling.

Becky felt uncomfortable. "Good evening, Sister. How are things on the ward?"

"Things are like they always are, Lewis. Nothing much ever changes here, as you'll find out when you've been here a whiles."

Another nurse burst in, "Lord, I'm sorry I'm late. Couldn't sleep all day in the heat, an' then fell asleep in front of that stupid 'Mash' programme on the telly. You ever see that, Lewis?"

"Yes. I quite like it. It's the one about the 'medics' in Vietnam isn't it?"

"When you two have finished discussing the TVee, I'd like to hand over and get on home!"

"Yes, Sister. Of course."

Sister Carey handed over and then left without saying anything, much to Becky's relief. Even if she suspected that it was Becky hanging around in Eight Mile Rock, she wouldn't know why. Becky decided she would just deny it if asked. She didn't know what to do next, it all went round and round in her head. She decided she'd maybe try to come up with some better sort of surveillance. Maybe a disguise. She gave a giggle as she thought about moustaches and hats. Nurse Hoskins gave her a curious look.

Becky was kept busy then settling patients down for the night, giving out drugs, and changing infusions etc. It was about three a.m. and she'd just started to read the book Michael had given her, when the bell rang in ER signifying that a patient had come in. Becky walked around and found a man aged about forty wearing jeans. His beige jumper was soaked with blood.

"Oh my goodness! What's happened to you?"

"Been stabbed," the man gasped.

Becky noticed that his lips were slightly blue and there was an unhealthy pallor underneath his black skin.

"OK, let's have a look at you."

Becky helped him to remove his jumper and then to get up on to a trolley, where he lay back semi- upright.

"What's your name?"

"Luther Clarkson, Ma'am."

She carefully undid and eased off his shirt and he groaned. There was what looked like a deep stab wound just below his left shoulder. His breathing was becoming shallow and his lips had become more blue. Blood trickled from the wound.

"What happened, Luther?"

"They jumped me, I couldn't do anything about it, and then..."

"OK, Luther," said Becky interrupting and looking worried, "you just hold this here," she gave him a pad for the wound. She reached behind him and turned the oxygen on to ten litres a minute, through an MC mask. "Now," she said, attaching the mask behind his ears and onto his face, "and just keep this oxygen on and try to relax. I'll go and get the doctor." Becky gave him a reassuring smile, but as soon as she got outside of the room, she ran to the ward. Luckily Stefano was already on duty, putting up an infusion on another patient.

"Stefano, I've got a chap in the ER with a stab wound and I think he's got a pneumothorax."

"OK, I'm just finishing here. You get the chest drain ready and I'll be there."

When Becky got back the man's breathing had become rapid and shallow. He tried to move.

"Nurse, I need to tell someone..."

"No, it's very important now, Luther, that you just lie still please, try not to talk at the moment." She quickly got everything ready for inserting a chest drain so that Luther's collapsed lung would re-inflate.

Stefano arrived and asked Becky to take Luther's blood pressure, it was only ninety systolic over forty five diastolic - figures that were dangerously low.

Luther pulled the mask aside from his face. "Nurse, I need to ring the station."

"Sorry not now, Luther. We need to get you sorted," said Stefano, putting the mask back. He put his stethoscope in his ears, "Breathe in for me, sir." Luther took a breath. "And out." Stefano listened to Luther's chest on both sides, at the back, and at the front.

"But you don't understand..." His voice was muffled behind the mask.

"Yeah, I'm sorry, sir, but it's going to have to wait. Your lung's collapsed and we need to get a chest drain in or you're going to be a really sick man."

Luther pulled the mask off again, "Yeah, but a man's dead."

"What!"

"A man's dead. He's on the beach. Christ, it's just awful!"

"You're sure he's dead?" said Stefano.

"Yeah, I seen enough to know."

"Well there's nothing you can do then. I need you to lie on your side so I can get this chest drain in, before we do anything else."

"OK. Doc. I feels pretty sick."

"Yeah I'm sure you do. I'll get this drain in, your lung will re-inflate and you'll be fine."

They put the mask back on and got him onto his side. Stefano quickly inserted some local anaesthetic. Then he pushed a large needle attached to a cannula through a space in the man's ribs. He placed it expertly between the double lining membranes of the man's lung, which had filled with air, compressing the lung underneath it. Becky attached a tube from the cannula to a bottle a third full of water. Air started bubbling into the water as the man's lung started to inflate.

Luther's colour and breathing began to improve almost immediately. His face relaxed and the relief was echoed on both Stefano and Becky's faces.

"What happened?" said Stefano.

"They jumped me."

"Who?"

"God damn smugglers."

"Do you want me to call the police?" said Becky

"No, I'll do it if I can. You see, I'm a sergeant in the police, here on Freeport."

"Oh, I see. So, how did it happen?" said Becky.

"Well, I 'spect you know we got a load of problems here with drugs and illegals coming in."

"Well, yes, I guess," said Becky.

"Well, Johnson, he's one of my officers, he comes to me on the quiet. He said he'd got a plan..."Luther bit his lip and swallowed.

"And?"

"Well I didn't think he'd have much of a plan, him bein' young an' all, but I likes initiative and he's real keen, not like the rest of them. So I says, 'Ok shoot.' He said, he was going to start patrolling the beaches at night on his own, when he was off duty, so as no-one would know he was going. He thought someone was blabbin' about it in the bars on the island. He was going to keep it real quiet, instead of everyone knowing, and two of them going in a patrol car, and making noise, talking and that."

"So what happened?" said Stefano.

"Well I couldn't let him go on his own, so I said I'd go with him. We went down to a real deserted little cove near the East End. We was sitting there quiet like, smoking when we heard the noise of engines."

"Wow," said Stefano.

"Yeah, I think we both thought - this is it. We're gonna catch them red handed. I don't have my gun or nothin' on me 'cause officially we's off duty. So we crept through the bush and crouched behind a big rock. Sure enough there it was. A rowing boat coming ashore, the other boat just quietly chugging away from it. I wanted to see their faces, so I told Johnson to wait there and I got a little closer - too damn close! Wham! Someone came up from behind and grabbed me."

"Oh my God," said Becky.

"We had one hell of a fight that's how I got this." He gestured to his scratched face. Johnson came down and was tryin' to drag him off, then the bastard smuggler, begging your pardon, Nurse, stabbed me."

"How dreadful!"

I fell to the ground and I think I hit my head on a rock, or maybe one of them hit me, I don't rightly know. But that rowing boat with the other two men in it must have reached the shore. I think I heard a shot and then I guess I must have passed out, because I came round lying on the sand."

"You poor chap," said Stefano.

"Hell no, I was the lucky one. You see I found... I found the boy..."

"The boy?"

"Yeah. The boy - Johnson. God damn it they shot him, Nurse. Bastards shot him in the back!" Luther's eyes welled up and he held his head in his hands.

Becky put her hand on his arm, "I'm so sorry, Luther," she said softly.

"Ain't your fault. I'm gonna get those bastards if it's the last thing I do."

"Would you like us to ring the station and get one of your men in?" asked Stefano.

"Yeah. 'cause we gotta go get his body, then someone's got to go tell his wife...Christ, what a night! I should never have listened to him."

"It's not your fault, Luther. You need to rest now. You'll have to stay in and we maybe need to X-ray your skull to check you haven't got a fracture. I'll just take a look now to see if I can find any obvious damage. Becky, can you arrange a bed on the ward please?"

"Yes, of course."

Becky took Luther round to the ward and got him settled in. She went back to the ER to clear away the trolley and found Stefano writing up the notes.

"Poor chap. What a thing to happen I'm knackered now, I'll be glad to get to my bed," he said.

"Yes, roll on the morning."

"You were great, Becky thanks. You're a really good nurse you know."

"Don't you patronise me!"

"Just trying to be nice, Becky."

"Well after what happened to Teresa on the boat don't bother!"

"What the hell are you talking about?"

"You know very well, Stefano. I saw you with her!"

"Saw me where?"

"On the boat. Downstairs."

Stefano grabbed Becky's arm and pulled her to him. "You know shit! I never touched her!"

"Let go of my arm!"

He let it go with a shrug. "Sorry, Becky, sorry, I didn't mean to grab you. But you're wrong."

"Oh yeah. Mr Pure! Like you're not shagging anything in a skirt - even the patients!"

"Christ, Becky, why are you so down on me?"

"I've got to go. I've got work to do."

"Stuff this. I'm off home for some sleep. You'll find out, Becky. Nothing's ever what it seems here."

Becky snorted and turned her back. As far as she was concerned he wasn't worth the effort of arguing with.

Chapter 10

The year is getting on it's the twenty second of September but radio Grand Bahama is still here for you all. That sun is shining of course and we have a high of eighty six degrees and seventy four percent humidity. Next up is the record that was just made for us. Yes, it's Harry Belafonte and 'Island in the sun'...

Saturday was another beautiful day and Becky wondered what the surprise was that Michael had for her. She was intrigued and was sure it would be something good, because Michael always seemed to know what she enjoyed doing. She put on white shorts and a t-shirt and heard Michael's Alfa Romeo car arrive outside at nine am. She ran down the steps to him.

"Hi, honey. You look great!" he said.

"Thanks." They kissed long and deep and then reluctantly pulled apart.

"Where's this surprise then?"

"Did you read the book?" he asked as they walked back upstairs.

"Yes, it's a quick read isn't it? I liked it. It's a bit different to the other book of his that I've read."

"Yeah. Well, Hemingway loved deep sea fishing, as well as bull fights and war you know."

"So, are we going deep sea fishing?"

"Do you want to?"

"Well, it would be different."

"No. I'm just teasing. We're going to where they say that he was inspired to write the book."

"We are!"

"Yep. Pack an overnight bag, Becky we're off to Bimini."

"Bimini! What's Bimini?"

"Bimini is a little Out Island. You'll love it."

"Fantastic!"

"What do I need to pack, Michael?"

"Just a toothbrush and yourself will be fine."

Becky quickly put a few things together.

"Great! Let's go do it. How are we going to get there?"

"That's all sorted, darlin'. I've hired a plane for a couple of days."

"Cool, Michael."

"You'll be speaking American soon, Becky."

She laughed and they drove to the small airport. Michael drove with his hand casually resting on Becky's thigh. With the top of the car down, a warm wind blew through her hair, the group Meat Loaf played on his car stereo. Becky smiled to herself as she thought of summer in England, sheltering from the rain on a windswept sea front. Life was great here.

When they arrived at the airport Michael left Becky in the lounge for a few minutes, whilst he went to make some arrangements. He came back with some papers in his hand and they walked through to the air field. Sure enough waiting for them on the runway was a four seater plane.

Michael helped Becky up and into the passenger seat in the front, and then to Becky's surprise he got in the pilot's seat.

"I didn't know you could fly, Michael."

"There's lots you don't know about me," he said laughing.

He leant over and kissed her, she felt herself melt. He pulled away. "Come on, let's get this baby airborne, we don't want to miss our slot.

Becky was so excited. She'd never been in such a small plane before. Michael went through his pre-flight checks with the control tower and then they taxied down the runway. The lift off was tremendously exhilarating, so different to being on a large commercial plane. Becky felt dizzyingly high up as the island grew smaller beneath her.

"OK?" Michael smiled at her reassuringly.

"Yes, it's fantastic!" she said raising her voice above the roar of the engines.

Looking down was amazing. The island was spread out beneath them, tiny houses and settlements, inland waterways and marinas, and fringing just a few of the beaches were white hotels. They left the island behind them and flew over the crystal clear sea.

"Look!" Becky shrieked. "There's a manta ray!"

"Where?" said Michael.

She pointed, and the distinctive cape shape of a manta ray swimming beneath the surface could clearly be seen. Michael laughed, decreased their height and they dipped down to take a closer look.

Becky laughed with pleasure. "Wow! This is incredible, Michael." She smiled up at him and reached across to squeeze his thigh.

He smiled back at her. After a short time they reached Bimini a tiny white island floating in the turquoise sea. They landed on a narrow air strip. Customs consisted of a small white washed building with one desk and they were quickly waved through.

"Where to now?"

"Look just over there is the ferry. Alice Town on North Bimini is too small to land on, so you have to land here on South Bimini and catch the ferry."

"Is this it?"

"Yep, it's the only one! Michael helped Becky onto the tiny wooden ferry. She carefully sat on one of the seats, as many had a few struts missing. Only two other people got on with them for the short ride. Becky was enchanted.

When they got off, Michael said, "This is it. What do you think?"

"Oh, it's beautiful, Michael," said Becky, looking around her at the tiny, wooden houses that lined the street. Pink, blue, yellow, each one was painted in a different colour. "Look," she said looking through the gap in between the houses, "you can see the sea on both sides of the road."

"Yeah, this is the main street, and it's also the only street."

"Incredible." They wandered down it hand in hand, a gentle breeze cooling them. An old person on a push bike past them, he seemed to be the only sign of traffic. "Michael, this is lovely. Just look at this fire station!" The passed a tiny, red painted and gleaming fire station.

Bougainvillea trailed its brightly blazing colours over every building, hibiscus grew in wild abandon and the scent of jasmine filled the air.

"Here we are," said Michael. They had arrived outside a small, white painted hotel, with the name, 'Brown's', written on the front. They walked in to a cool shady bar, which doubled as the reception. A smiling middle-aged Bahamian man stood polishing glasses.

"Hi there, my name's Samson. What can I do for, you two."

"Hi. I'm, Michael and this is Becky, we'd like a double room please."

"Sure thing. Where you folks from?"

"Freeport," replied Michael.

"That's real nice. You like the sea?"

"Gosh, yes," said Becky.

"You're gonna love Bimini then. Let's show you the room."

Samson took them through to their room. Becky saw a clean double bed with crisp white sheets, an old wooden wardrobe and a chest with two drawers. Purple bougainvillea climbed around the window. The perfume of flowers and the sharp tang of the sea drifted into the room, along with the sound of birds singing and people quietly chatting in the street.

Becky looked at Michael and smiled, "It's perfect."

"Just as well," Michael smiled back, "It's the only hotel on the island." They laughed.

"You two fancy a cold beer-on the house?"

"Sure thing, Samson. That would be great," said Michael.

They unpacked their few things and, after drinking the beer and chatting to Samson for a while, wandered down to a small and deserted pristine beach. They lay down on their towels on the sand.

"What do you think, honey?"

"It's wonderful, darling. It's like a place that's lost in time. Another world."

"I knew you'd love it."

"It's fantastic to be here, away from work and everything," said Becky.

"Yeah isn't it great? What do you mean by, work and everything?"

"Oh... It's nothing..." Becky looked serious.

"No, Becky something's bothering you. Tell me about it."

"Well..."

"Go on."

"Teresa told me that she thinks she was drugged on the boat."

"What! What makes her think that?"

"Well, she says she had sex, and she doesn't know who she had it with."

Michael snorted. "Nothing new in that is there?"

"Oh, Michael, she's not that bad!"

"Come on, Becky! Wise up! Anyway, I thought you saw her with Stefano."

"Well I thought I did, but she's sure it wasn't him."

"Is she getting flashbacks?"

"What?"

"Is it coming back to her? What happened?" Michael sounded irritated.

"No, no I don't think so."

"Gee, Becky, you're so sweet you can't see what she's like. She was drunk out of her mind we could all tell that. She could have slept with just about anyone. She's just embarrassed because she knows you saw her screwing Stefano."

"Mmm. Maybe."

"Look, Becky there's no maybe about it! She gets drunk and she screws around. That's it!"

"OK ,Michael, you don't need to be so cross. You asked me to tell you."

"Sorry, honey, I just don't like to see you being taken for a ride."

"Let's not talk about problems, darling. Let's go for a swim."

Michael had brought snorkels. They both put them on, the water was warm and as myriad fish swam around them, Becky felt happy and relaxed. She thought it was typical of Michael to bring her somewhere so beautiful.

They were snorkelling together when Michael tugged her arm and pointed at some rocks containing a deep crevice. She couldn't see what he was pointing at, to begin with and then, she saw it. A huge, ugly, black head just visible inside the crevice. A small fish swam by. The huge head opened its massive mouth revealing razor sharp teeth. It swallowed the fish whole.

Becky swam away and surfaced quickly. "Ugh! That was horrible!"

"Yeah, I'm sorry, maybe I shouldn't have pointed him out."

"What was it?"

"It was a Moray eel, Becky. You need to make sure you don't go poking around in any dark holes here. They can be more dangerous than you realise." He gave her a strange look, and for a second, the sun went behind a cloud. Becky felt uneasy.

"Yes...OK..."

Then Michael laughed, "Ugly bugger wasn't he? Come on, let's go and get some lunch."

Saturday passed in a haze of eating crayfish, drinking cocktails, lazing on the beach and dipping in and out of the sea. That evening they went to the bar, where Hemingway was said to have written, 'The old man and the sea.' Becky thought it was really atmospheric. In many ways it resembled old pubs that she'd been into in Dorset or Devon.

Adorning the walls were all the paraphernalia of deep sea fishing; nets, rods, shark's teeth and massive stuffed marlins - the huge fish of the Caribbean. All around were dozens of photographs. Mostly of Hemingway himself, on his own or, with other macho looking men. All the photos seemed to reinforce his reputation. He looked suntanned and confident, always smiling showing off his perfect white teeth. He wore shorts and was shown fishing on boats, displaying the huge marlins and sharks that he'd caught, or drinking in the bar. It felt as though he could walk in at any moment, and find, that here at least, nothing had changed.

Becky was enchanted both with the place and with Michael. She felt as though she'd always known him. They laughed and talked and enjoyed ice cold beers. When they returned to the hotel, they made love for hours, before falling asleep under a sheet, with the sound of the sea in their ears.

They spent the next morning swimming and snorkelling again. They were lying on towels on the sand and Becky found herself thinking about her close shave with Sister Carey.

"You're quiet, darling. Are you thinking about Teresa again?"

"No. No, it's not that."

"What is it then?"

"It's just work, sort of. Nothing really."

"It must be something. Tell me about it."

"OK. It's just that we seem to get a lot of girls in after illegal abortions and I think... I think I know who's doing them."

"What!"

"Yeah I think it's the Ward Sister. I found her just standing once where they keep the instruments for theatre, plus she's got the access to the drugs and she has her days off just before the day they come in."

"You're getting carried away here, honey. It could be anyone. Why are you bothering about this stuff?"

"Michael, one of these girls died when I first arrived here. It's not right."

"Becky, you're not in England now. You don't understand how things work out here. You're getting yourself into something dangerous. Don't you know that everything that's illegal here is run by the Mafia?"

"You sound like all the others, now."

"Well that's because I'm right. You start poking around in these sort of things you'll only be frustrated. Leave it to the cops. It's dangerous to be nosey here."

"Yes. OK, you're probably right." Becky didn't want to argue because it had been such a perfect trip. She thought how horrified Michael would be if he knew she'd followed Sister Carey, so she decided not to say anything more. She began to think that maybe she *was* being stupid. After all no-one else was concerned or thought that she should do anything about it.

At the end of the morning they went back to the bar, to have a lunch of sandwiches and beer. Michael only drank orange juice because he was flying and all too soon they were back at the landing strip. Walking to the plane Becky reflected on what a lovely week-end it had been. Everything had been perfect. She glanced at Michael and thought how lucky she was. She wished the week-end could have lasted forever.

They climbed up into the plane and Becky turned to Michael, "You know that was the most amazing time that I've ever had. Truly beautiful, Thank-you so much."

"That's OK, honey, it was great wasn't it. You were amazing too." He squeezed her thigh affectionately.

"Gosh, I feel really tired now," said Becky, the heat of the day and the beer overwhelming her.

"You just lie back and sleep then, darlin'. I'll be sure to let you know when we get back."

Becky laughed, and then they taxied down the little runway and took off. Her mouth felt dry, she closed her eyes and suddenly she was dreaming of crystal waters and moray eels.

She woke with a start to find that they'd landed. Michael seemed to be stowing something in the back. She looked around her. To her surprise she didn't recognise where they were. They seemed to be on a clearing in the middle of some bush and scrub surrounded by trees. There was no-one to be seen and nothing there except themselves and their plane.

"Where are we Michael? This isn't Freeport."

"Sorry, darlin'. I didn't mean to wake you. I was desperate for a pee and I wanted to rearrange our stuff so it was placed more evenly. I thought I'd just touch down here quickly."

"Oh. OK...Strange place isn't it?"

"Yeah, I guess. They probably just had a bit of a bush fire here. Or maybe kids use it. Anyway, let's go."

"Yes, OK. Have you got some water, Michael? I feel so thirsty and sleepy."

"Yes of course, sweetheart." He handed her over a bottle. "I guess you just had a little too much sun." He kissed her head and ruffled her hair.

"Yes. I expect so." She lay back and when she next woke they were taxiing to a halt at Freeport.

"That was wonderful, darling," she said yawning.

"It sure was," said Michael with an intimate smile." Come on let's go and see if the water bed still works."

This is radio Grand Bahama your sunshine station, the twenty fourth of September. We expect a high of eighty five degrees and seventy six percent humidity. It could cloud up a little later in the day...

Becky woke late the next morning, in Michael's bed, with the worst hangover she'd ever had in her life. Her head was pounding and her mouth dry. Michael had tried to wake her briefly before going to work himself, but had given up in the end when she told him drowsily that she wasn't on duty until that night. A cup of cold coffee sat beside the bed.

She sat up and groaned. Holding her head she went to the bathroom and looked in the cupboard for some paracetamol. All she found was an old bottle of cough mixture and some anti-histamine cream. Going back into the bedroom, she muttered, "I must have some somewhere," and shook the not inconsiderable contents of her handbag onto the bed. She rifled through them and sighed. "Nothing." She pulled open the drawer in the little cabinet next to her side of the bed but it was empty. "Of course not, stupid, he's not going to keep them that side is he?" she said to herself whilst still holding her head with one hand.

She walked round slowly and opened the drawer on his side of the bed. "Oh my God!" She sat down heavily on the bed. She couldn't take her eyes away from the drawer. She put her hand over her mouth. She felt sick. The gun sat there. Black. Ominous. It looked heavy. "Oh my God," she muttered again. She hesitantly reached out with a shaking hand to touch it, but then suddenly withdrew her hand as if the gun was giving off heat. She'd never seen a gun before except in films. She swallowed hard. *He's an American*, she thought to herself. *They're different to us. Probably lots of them have got guns.* She slammed the drawer shut. Her stomach twisted. *Need to get home*, she thought. *Yes, need to get home.* She quickly dressed and left.

She walked home in a daze. *Michael. Her Michael had a gun. A gun! Who could she tell or ask about it? Was it legal to have a gun here?* She didn't think so. *Could she trust Teresa? No, she might blurt it out when she was drunk. Stefano was cool with her since their row. Her parents? God no! They'd want her to come home.*

She thought about asking Michael about it but then it might look as if she'd been looking through his drawers. *What did that make her? God, she adored him so much, she couldn't bear it if he didn't trust her.*

She told herself, that she shouldn't have been poking around in his apartment. As the day went on she decided to forget about it. *It was none of her business and after all he normally lived in Miami. Everyone knew that Miami could be a dangerous place.* The memory of seeing him in the casino came back to her. She went to work that night and no matter how hard she tried, she couldn't get rid of a sense of unease.

Chapter 11

It's the thirtieth of September and you're listening to radio Grand Bahama, the sunshine station. That humidity's going down a little to seventy five degrees, we have a high of eighty four degrees, now you can all chill out listening to an oldie from the Three Degrees, 'When will I see you again...'

Becky walked out late afternoon after an 'early' shift and found that it had just stopped raining. The roads and pavements steamed and the air was fresh and full of birdsong. It was pleasantly warm, a marked contrast from her early days in Freeport when the heat and humidity had seemed more intense. *Maybe she was just getting used to it,* she mused.

A car hooted in the car park and a familiar Irish voice shouted across, "Hi, Becky! How you doing?"

Becky laughed and ran to the car. "What are you doing here?"

"Well I'm off to buy some steaks in Eight Mile Rock. I thought you might like to come along for the ride and maybe get some yourself. You'll never find this place unless I show you."

"O.K. Michael loves steak and I could make us a romantic meal in, so that would be great."

"You two love birds!"

Becky laughed, "I must say it seems like a strange place for a butchers."

"Yeah, I know, but it's a bloody good one!" Becky got in and they drove off laughing.

"How are you, Teresa?"

"I'm great!"

"No, you know what I mean. Are you getting any flash backs or anything?"

Teresa's face clouded over, "Yeah, I've had one or two."

"Do you know who it was?"

"No, no I don't." Then she smiled, "No. Don't worry about me, Becks, I'm the world's original survivor. Believe you me, if you survive a convent education in Ireland you can survive anything!" She laughed and changed the subject, so Becky let it drop.

As they approached Eight Mile Rock it became more difficult to avoid the pot holes and they bounced around in Teresa's car. Advertising hoardings lined the sides of the road and people sat drinking and gossiping outside bars. They passed brightly coloured small houses, shacks that were falling apart and several churches. Rubbish blew across the road and people wandered around, laughing and shouting good-naturedly to each other.

Every now and again Becky would see a man carrying fishing tackle and a plastic bag of fish that he'd just caught for his family's supper. Fish were prolific and easy to catch. Along with peas and rice they were a staple of the Bahamian diet and often served in the hospital.

The only non-Bahamians there were Becky and Teresa. Children were running around playing football and 'tag' in the road, closely followed by mangy looking, excited dogs.

"Teresa, you need to slow down a bit. If we hit one of these dogs or kids we're going to be in real trouble."

"Sure, you worry too much."

"Yes, I know, that's what everyone...God above!"

A blue ball bounced across in front of them, closely followed by a little girl in a bright yellow and pink dress. Teresa slammed on the brakes and Becky's forehead hit the windscreen.

"Shit!" yelled Teresa, as the brakes screeched and she swung the car hard right. The wheels locked up. The girl disappeared from sight, a group of men hove up into view and scattered in all directions, as Teresa narrowly missed them and two dogs. A huge palm tree rose up in front of them. The car came to rest, inches away from it.

Becky groaned, "Oh, bloody hell."

"You OK, Becky?"

"Yes. Just banged my forehead. What about, you?" She turned to look at Teresa, who was lying back in her seat looking pale.

"Yeah, I'm OK, just a bit..."

The driver's door was suddenly opened and a babble of voices surrounded them.

"What the hell you think you two doing?"

"Damn fool girl. You almost hit that kid!"

"Bloody English!"

"I'm Irish!" said Teresa weakly.

"Well, you nearly killed a kid, whatever you is!"

"How is she?" asked Becky. "Is she OK?"

"She ain't movin' none"

"She drivin' too fast!"

"The little girl! Is she OK?" shouted Becky getting out of the car. A knot of people surrounded a pink and yellow bundle on the ground.

"Becky, get back in the car!" shouted Teresa from the car.

"I'm a nurse, let me look at her," said Becky.

Becky pushed her way through the crowd to where the little girl lay on the ground with two men bending over her.

"Who you think you are, girl?" someone said as she tried to reach the little girl.

"Hey, cool it," said a man's voice. "This girl's a real nice nurse, she treated me at the hospital last week."

Becky looked up gratefully and saw a young black man that she'd looked after, when he'd come in with burns the previous week. She smiled at him, "Hi, how are, you?"

"I'm fine, Nurse, real fine."

Then another man spoke in a French accent, "It's OK, she's alright. I think she just fainted with the shock an' that. She ran straight out, it was your fault wasn't it, Mari?"

"Sorry," came a little voice from the girl, who was now sitting up.

Becky found to her astonishment that it was Josef bending over Mari.

"Oh, it's you," she said.

"Oh, yes. You the nurse that helped save her life aren't you?"

"Yes, I was in the ER that day. Small world. Is she OK?"

"Yeah, she fine, Nurse." He looked at the knot of people surrounding them. "You people can all go now, thanks. She good, and this girl, she saved my daughter's life the other week."

Teresa pushed through the crowd, "What's happening, Becky?"

"It's OK."

"These girls they both work at the hospital."

"It true? You both nurses at the Royal?" said a woman.

"Yes."

"Damn fool child."

"They runs round here like it a playground."

The crowd slowly wandered off.

"Are you OK, Mari?" asked Becky.

"Oui, no, yes, yes, I sorry. I was just trying to get the ball back. I never had one before," she started to cry.

"Don't cry, sweetheart. There's no harm done, everything's alright. Did you bang your head.?"

"No."

"Dry your eyes then," Becky gave her a tissue. Mari sniffed and wiped away her tears. "And, you can move your arms and legs OK?"

"Yeah, look." Mari enthusiastically waved and jiggled her legs up and down in the air.

Teresa was deathly pale."I'm so sorry," she said.

"Mari shouldn't have run out, it wasn't your fault. You know, you don't look too good," said Josef. "You want to come back to my place for a drink and rest a few minutes?"

"No, you're wrong, it was my fault... Jesus, I could have killed her," Teresa started to cry.

"Look she's fine. Come on, Mari, let's show the nice nurses where we live. We can all have a drink."

Becky looked at Teresa and gave her a quick hug, "Yes, thanks, Josef, that would be nice," she said. Becky took Mari's hand. "Do you know the song, 'Old McDonald had a farm?'"

"No. I don't think so."

"We'll sing it to you then, won't we, Teresa?"

"You're something else, Becky, you know?" Teresa looked at Becky and smiled gratefully.

"You haven't heard me sing yet!"

They followed Josef down a dirt track off the main road, Teresa and Becky singing and Mari joining in and giggling. They didn't notice a woman watching them from behind her curtains.

Isabella gave a rare smile as they passed. The child seemed happier and she could feel kindness emanating from the two white girls. As the girl with blond hair walked by she felt a prickle of unease. Something was wrong. Danger lurked near this girl. The girl stopped singing for a second and turned suddenly to look straight at where Isabella was standing. Isabella moved away from the window and frowned.

She needed to work more quickly. THE MAN was somehow connected to this girl. She picked up a knife and went out into her backyard.

A few minutes later, Josef and Mari, Teresa and Becky reached a tiny two roomed wooden hut with a tin roof. They stopped singing. The wood was hanging off in places but unlike some there was no rubbish outside. The windows had what looked like clean scraps of coloured fabric suspended at them. It was quiet for a few awkward seconds.

"It ain't much... you two still want a drink?" asked Josef.

"Of course we do," said Teresa.

"I can show you my dolly if you like."

"Yeah. We'd love to see your dolly," said Teresa.

"Come on then." Mari took Becky's hand and pulled her indoors. "My dolly's going to have a lovely drink of lemon and then she's..." Mari carried on babbling half to herself.

When they got inside Josef turned on a fan which moved the hot humid air around. They left the door open and Becky and Teresa sat on a sagging settee. They glanced around them and saw a sink in one corner and a small stove in another. Two clean shirts hung on the side of a shelf, which also held a blouse and jumper for Mari, some packets of black-eyed peas and a Bible.

Nothing was said for a moment. Then Teresa spoke, "This is very kind of you, Josef. You know, where I grew up in Ireland, we lived in a tiny cottage in the country. I have such happy memories of me and my sisters all sharing the same bed. I used to love the craic."

"Crack?" said Josef and Becky in unison.

"It's slang for chatter." They all laughed then and Josef went and fetched them some lemonade.

"This is my cousin Peter's place. He's been great to us. He sleeps on the couch and Mari and I have the mattress in the other room." Josef sat on the floor, "I've got a job here now. I stack shelves at the supermarket. It ain't much but it brings something in."

Mari looked up from playing with her doll, "Papa fishes for us. We get lots of that nice fish, don't we?"

"She means grouper. Yeah, it's a really good fish, cherie."

"My Mama had to go home. She's gonna come see us soon isn't she, Papa?"

Josef looked at them and raised his eyebrows very slightly, "Yeah that's right, sweetheart. Why don't you go and see if Lizzie's in next door?"

"OK, Papa. I'll take dolly with me and we can make her a nice tea." Mari left. There was silence for a moment.

"You both speak English really well now," said Becky.

"Thanks, she's a quick learner. She's been through a lot..."

"What do you mean, Josef? What, what happened to her, mummy?" asked Teresa.

Josef sighed and looked at her sadly, "It's a long story."

"Sorry. I shouldn't have asked."

"No, no. I'd really like to tell you both. I can trust you two can't I?"

They nodded, "Of course."

"I worked hard in Haiti..." As it grew dark Josef told them his story. How they'd struggled to raise the money to leave Haiti for a better life; the dreadful journey on the leaking boat and finally how they were thrown off the boat at gunpoint and forced to swim to the land.

"Jesus, Josef! How awful!" said Teresa.

Becky didn't know what to say, but as Josef's eyes filled with tears she moved closer to him and put her hand on his shoulder.

"The worst thing is I don't know if she's alive or dead, my Eugenie and our unborn child. I hear nothing...I don't know...I just don't know... But I prays to the Good Lord every day, and I just hope that one day they'll be a miracle and she'll walk through that door."

"I'm so sorry," said Becky. "I'd no idea what it was like."

"That's OK, ain't your fault. But those men they're gonna suffer believe me. That Captain, I got a good look at his face. And that mate. I ain't seen him here yet, but I seen his signet ring that night and one of these days I know I'm gonna see it again... When I do..."

Becky and Teresa were silent, not certain what to say.

"Anyways, you girls, what you doin' here in Eight Mile Rock?"

"We came to get steak from Gregory's," said Teresa.

"Yeah? I hear it's good. You know where it is?"

"Yeah, I've been before, thanks. We probably ought to go before he shuts up for the night," said Teresa.

"Well next time you're here, you call in and see us. Perhaps you can teach, Mari some more English songs?"

"Yeah, that would be great, Josef."

"Thanks for the drinks, we'll be sure to drive carefully."

Josef saw them out to the car. "Your car stinks you know?"

They both laughed. "It goes," said Teresa.

"We'll see you again," said Becky and they drove off to buy the steaks. On their return they drove back to Josef's. Mari was playing outside and Teresa called her over.

"Here, Mari, give this to Daddy, tell him it's just to say sorry for this afternoon," said Teresa, and shoved a bag with six steaks in it into Mari's hands.

The fifth of October, midnight.

Lightning illuminated the night sky as Becky walked home after a late shift at the hospital. She wasn't concerned about the lightning. It was beautiful to see the vivid flashes and very often there was lightning without a storm. She'd had a busy shift with several admissions, one just as she was about to finish. Now she was tired.

Becky was worrying about recent events. The gun in Michael's apartment niggled away at her, but it seemed somehow disloyal to Michael to tell Teresa about it and there was no-one else she could tell. She didn't dare speak to Teresa about following Sister Carey either, especially after Michael's negative reaction to her just discussing it. She thought that Teresa probably wouldn't understand and anyway she didn't want to involve her. Sister Carey herself had never been friendly, but ever since Becky had followed her, she hardly spoke and when she did she was curt and dismissive. She must suspect that she'd been in the car that time. Thank God, she hadn't challenged her about it.

Becky didn't seem to see so much of Teresa these days and she seemed a bit cool with her as well. Becky sighed. All in all, if it wasn't for Michael she might have thought of returning to England.

She heard a car approaching slowly from behind her, its headlights showing up the empty road and pavements. There was a stretch here with no houses, just rough scrub, pine trees and the pretty oleanders and hibiscus bushes that attracted the humming birds in the day time.

The car passed at a leisurely pace. It was large, with blacked out windows so you couldn't see the driver. Becky felt uneasy. The lizards rustled in the bushes and in the distance she could hear the sea. She couldn't usually hear it but it had got rougher recently as the weather had cooled a little. There was a faint rumble of thunder. The moon went behind a cloud.

It was still warm although the humidity of the day had gone. Drifting on the breeze came the sound of a radio in the distance and Bob Marley singing, 'No woman no cry.' Normally she would have hummed along to it, but she increased her pace a little, looking forward to getting indoors to her apartment. She wished she'd had the car today to drive back in.

A twig snapped close by. It startled her and she told herself not to be stupid but she walked faster towards the street light that illuminated the entrance to the apartments.

There was a definite rustling in the bushes just behind her. *Was that the sound of a footstep?* Becky glanced back quickly. She couldn't see anyone. She swallowed, her heart was banging in her chest and her hands were clammy. She wasn't far from the entrance now. *Didn't they tell you not to run in these circumstances?* She couldn't remember. It crossed her mind that her scissors were in her uniform pocket.

Suddenly the bushes moved beside her. A loud screeching rent the air. Two cats ran out caterwauling. "God above!" said Becky, literally jumping with shock. She clutched her chest and laughed then, feeling really stupid. She must have been watching too many late films. The thunder was rumbling around now and there was the odd spit of rain. The time between the thunder and the flashes of lightning was shortening. The storm was approaching fast and she needed to get indoors.

There was a massive crash of thunder and as lightning lit up the area, she thought for a second that she saw someone at the entrance to the apartments, but then they vanished. The street light at the entrance went out. "Damn," she swore to herself. She'd been looking forward to a cup of tea. The electric would probably be off for an hour or more now.

On reaching the door of her apartment she fished around in her handbag for the keys. Her elbow knocked the door and to her surprise, it opened. *I must be cracking up,* she thought. Then she remembered she'd been late for work and had left in a hurry that afternoon. She must have forgotten to lock it. Going in she closed the door behind her and pushed in the 'button type' lock.

She tried the light switch in hope, but it was of course dead. Fumbling her way into the lounge, she could see that some light was filtering through the curtains in front of the balcony doors. As the storm grew close to the apartments the rain made a tremendous noise. It hammered its way through the trees and bush, thundering on leaves, bending and breaking branches in its wake. Becky felt uneasy, the skin prickled on the back of her neck and she turned around quickly. No-one was there.

In spite of the noise of the rain, Becky thought she could hear something else. An insistent noise that was close by - a rhythmic sound that seemed to be coming from the bedroom. Biting her lip, she stood completely still for a few seconds. Slowly, she crept towards the bedroom door. Her eyes had adjusted to the dim light. Her right hand was in her pocket and held the scissors. With her left hand she quickly threw open the door. The noise increased. It was coming from the window. Crossing to it quickly she drew back the curtain in one swift movement - a tree branch was tapping against it in the rain which was now a solid grey wall outside.

She felt really stupid and took her hand out of her pocket. "You idiot," she said and laughed. *What on earth did she think she was going to do with the scissors anyway?* She quickly took her uniform off and threw it in a ball into the washing bin. She pulled on jeans and a T-shirt and fished out a small torch that she kept in the bedside cabinet.

In the kitchen she lit two candles and brought them into the lounge. "That's better." She left the torch illuminating the lounge and picking up a candle went into the bathroom. She placed it by the side of the basin and quickly sat on the loo desperate now for a pee.

When she finished she glanced up at the mirror above the basin. She was puzzled for a second. *Something isn't right.* She shook her head and frowned, narrowing her eyes a little to peer at the mirror. She stood, pulled up her underwear and held the candle up to the mirror. The light danced on it as her hand shook. "Go home spook!" was written in large red writing. Then she saw in the mirror something reflected on the wall behind her. She whirled round.

All over the wall were photos. "Oh my God!" She held the candle up to them - they were all of her! Walking to work in her uniform, getting into her car at the supermarket, sitting outside a bar in skimpy shorts and top, swimming in the sea, lying sleeping on an empty beach. They went around a photo in the middle. She held the candle closer to see it clearly. She stumbled backwards one hand over her mouth the other clutched the basin behind her. She felt sick and her legs shook. She wasn't in this photo. It was a photo of her bedroom. On the pillow of her bed lay a large knife.

CHAPTER 12

Becky ran crying from the bathroom through the flat. She stumbled downstairs to her neighbour Margaret. As she hammered on the door all the lights came back on.

Margaret came to the door wearing a pale blue fluffy dressing gown, her hair in rollers and her shocking pink lipstick smudged. She clutched a large glass of what looked like gin and tonic.

"Well, hi. It's real nice to see you, Becky. You look kinda...upset. What's the matter, honey? Something wrong?"

"I...I... Upstairs... Bathroom..."

"Gee, don't you just hate it when the lights all go? But it's OK , look, they just came on."

"No, no. It's not..."

"Sorry, I'm just running on here. You said about the bathroom. Honey, you got a spider? You'd best come in. Don't you worry, my Alex will soon shoo that little ol' spider away. Alex! Alex!" She took Becky's arm and Becky was assailed by the smell of alcohol.

"No! It's not a spider, Margaret!"

"If it's one of them lizards you don't need to worry, they're OK, of course what I really hate are those great big cockroaches you get here. Did you know some of them fly! Gee, I got one on my neck the other day I started hollering...

"Margaret, it's not a bloody cockroach. It's photos!"

"Well I can understand that because I don't take a good pho..."

"Margaret! What's going on here?" Alex her middle aged husband came in tying a dressing gown over his striped pyjamas and looking concerned. "Hi, honey what's wrong?" he said turning to Becky.

"She's got some photos..."

"Margaret, let the girl speak!"

"I'll just go get us a little drink then," said Margaret looking at her half full glass.

"Come in and sit down. It's, Becky, isn't it?"

"Yes."

OK, Becky. Just tell me slowly, what's happened?" He led Becky across to their settee.

Margaret returned from the kitchen with three large brandies, "For the shock, honey."

Becky took a sip, spluttered, swallowed and started to speak. "I just got in from a late shift..." She told them what she'd found upstairs.

Alex looked concerned and then angry. "God damn it, someone trying to frighten a little thing like you! That's dreadful. Don't you worry I'll go and take a look around. You lock the door behind me, Margaret."

Becky looked at Alex and the dressing gown that was struggling to contain his paunch and wondered what he'd do if he met anyone.

"Alex, are you sure that's a good idea?"

"I'm American. We don't scare easy," he said and left.

"Could I phone my boyfriend, Margaret?"

"Course you can, honey."

Alex went up to the flat and Becky called Michael.

"Don't worry, darlin', I'll be straight round," he said. After about ten minutes Becky heard his car draw up and then his footsteps running to the door. She rushed to open it and fell into his arms.

"Thank God, you're here!"

"Are you OK?"

"Yes, I'm fine really. I was just a bit shocked.

Alex came back with the photos and they all went inside. Margaret poured another round of brandies.

"Can I see them?" said Michael.

"Sure thing," Alex passed them across. While Michael was looking at them Alex said, "Do you think it could be some sort of joke, Becky?"

"Well, it's possible."

"Not very amusing," said Michael. Then he reached the last photo showing the knife on the pillow. "Son of a bitch! I'll kill the motherfucker that's done this!"

"Michael!"exclaimed Becky, looking at Margaret.

"Sorry, sorry, Margaret. It just makes me real mad that someone would do this."

"That's OK, honey."

Alex went to put some clothes on and asked Margaret to get them all some coffee. While they were was gone Becky looked around her at the clean and tidy apartment. It didn't have any ornaments or knick knacks and seemed somehow almost too pristine. She'd never taken Margaret up on all the invitations that she'd given her to come down for a chat. The only thing that stood out was a large photo in a gold frame, sat on the empty book shelf. It was a photo of a boy aged about eighteen, freckled and smiling. Alex returned dressed in jeans and a T-shirt.

"Is that your son, Alex?" Becky asked pointing to the photo.

Alex's face clouded over. "Yeah...That's our Chuck. He was a great son. Never any trouble. Loves, loved baseball, same as I do..." He glanced at the kitchen where Margaret was making coffee. "Broke his mom's heart."

"I'm so sorry. What...What do you mean, Alex?"

"Loved his country too. Just like me. Like so many of our fine young men. We were real proud of him... He went to 'Nam... He was in the Tet Offensive. Never came back."

"Oh, Alex," said Becky.

He glanced at the kitchen. "She can't get over it. I guess neither of us can. We moved here to get away...The memories...All the sympathy all the time. I don't know if we did the right thing..."

"How long ago was it?"

"Seven years...Seems like yesterday. Now, now it's all over..."

"I'm so sorry," said Becky.

"Thanks. We weren't the only ones. Everyone's got their problems."

"You must be proud Alex. A sacrifice for our country and freedom," said Michael.

"Yeah. Thanks. Don't say nothing just now."

Margaret came back into the room. "Well it's real nice to meet you two properly at last..."

When they'd finished their coffee, Alex insisted on ringing the police, who said they'd come out to them straight away. After half an hour or so Becky and Michael decided to go up to Becky's flat to wait.

"Thanks, Margaret and Alex, I don't know what I'd have done without you."

"You come down any time and see us, dear," said Margaret.

"Yes, yes I will," said Becky, feeling ashamed of how she'd dismissed Margaret as just a drunk, middle-aged woman, before tonight.

When the police still hadn't turned up after an hour, Becky said, "Come on, let's just go to bed. I'm really tired. I'll be OK if you stay the night with me."

"Are you sure?"

"Yes, I've got an early start in the morning." They went to bed and to Becky's surprise she slept well, snuggled up to Michael.

In the morning he said, "Look, I'll stay with you tonight or you can stay at my place."

"I don't know. It's not as if any harm's done. I think someone just wanted to frighten me. You know some people resent us working here."

"Well, don't you think that's worrying?"

"Yes, of course it is. But why should I give them the satisfaction of changing how I live my life?"

"Becky what about the...the..."

"The knife?"

"Yes, the knife. I mean... Do you want to go back to England? I could get you a ticket."

"What! Don't you want me to stay?"

"Yes, of course, I just wondered that's all."

"No. It's kind of you but I'm not going to let this send me home. I'm not letting whoever did this know that they scared me. I'll get the lock changed and keep the phone by my bed. After all I can always call the cavalry can't I?"

Michael laughed, "Is that me or Alex? But you know seriously, Becky you have to stop snooping around and making waves at work."

"What do you mean?"

"You know. Worrying about drugs and abortions and asking questions."

"Yes, maybe you're right."

"I know I'm right."

Becky didn't want to argue, so just agreed. Michael got someone to come in and change the locks. The more she thought about it, the more she was convinced that this was an attempt by Sister Carey to frighten her. She decided that she'd show her that she wasn't going to be scared that easily, so she went to work as usual that day. On the way in she was distracted and literally bumped into Dr Rooks.

"Watch where you're going, Nurse!"

"Oh sorry, I wasn't thinking."

"Oh well, that doesn't surprise me. Are you still enjoying working here?" he asked, with an impassive face.

"Yes thank you," said Becky coolly.

"Good," he said and nodded. His eyes met hers in a hard stare and Becky looked him full in the face. He seemed disconcerted, "Better things to attend to," he muttered and turned on his heel and walked away.

Stupid man, she thought to herself. Something made her turn round. He was standing in the corridor. Staring after her.

This is radio Grand Bahama on the eleventh of October. It's going to be a chilly seventy four degrees with seventy five percent humidity. Look out for heavy rain storms and remember to keep tuned to your sunshine station.

Teresa woke around seven a.m. and dashed to the loo where she was sick. Leaning back against the basin she muttered, "Jesus, this is all I need." She'd been sick every day for a week now, her period was three weeks late and she had tiny bumps around her nipples. It was only too obvious to her what the problem was. She also knew it was down to whoever had raped her on the launch, as normally she used a diaphragm for contraception.

Jesus, Mary and Joseph! What the hell am I going to do, she thought for the hundredth time since she'd missed her period, which normally, turned up along with her bad temper beforehand, with monotonous regularity.

Her thoughts ran around chaotically; *I can't possibly have a baby. I don't even know who the father is...What can I do? Dear God, how could I ever be explaining to the family? Dad'll kill me if go home pregnant. If he doesn't - all the village will be laughing. I can't bear to see their smug faces when they find out. I can hear them now,* 'Look at Teresa O'Hara. Thought she was too good to stay here - now see. That's what happens if you get above 'yerself'.' *Damn it! What am I going to do?*

She'd had this conversation with herself dozens of times a day, everyday since she'd first missed her period. At first she'd tried the oldest remedy in the book and drunk several large glasses of gin, followed by going for a hard run or having a hot bath. But as she in truth already knew and like countless others before her, she found that it was no remedy. She just became exhausted and it gave her was a terrible hangover.

She loved the Bahamas. She'd been determined to never go back to Northern Ireland. There didn't seem to be anywhere she could go. Nowhere that she could disappear to. She'd have to have an abortion - but how? She'd no money so she couldn't afford to get it done in The States. The hospital was out of the question, everyone knew her, the whole island would know. Jesus! She really wanted children. How was she going to live with herself?

She thought about telling Stefano but he was cool with her lately and she was certain that it wasn't his. *If only Becky had seen clearly who it was having sex with her on the yacht.* She felt embarrassed and stupid that she'd let herself be drugged. And she knew that with her reputation no-one would believe her. She kept coming back to the same solution, but could she go through with it? She vomited again. *Bloody hell, she'd have to do something. And she'd have to do it soon.*

Sister Carey had days off so Becky didn't see her for a few days. When she did see her nothing seemed to have changed. After about a week Becky had convinced herself that the photos were just an attempt to scare her. She had the locks changed, got the phone moved into the bedroom and kept a rape alarm by the bed. Except for the nights that she spent with Michael she went back to sleeping at the apartment on her own. She didn't sleep well but she was damned if she was going to let it alter how she lived.

Things settled down, work carried on as usual. The only difference was that occasionally Becky popped downstairs to chat with Margaret. Margaret told Becky how her son had died in Vietnam and that she was trying to stop drinking. Becky felt ashamed of her previous attitude towards her and arranged for them to go to the beach together on her next set of days off.

October the thirteenth.
Michael picked Becky up for a drink after work late one evening. "Could we just get some bread from the supermarket first, Michael?"

"Sure thing."

They drew up just as it started to spit with rain. The weather had been oppressive lately and the rain was a welcome change, she left Michael putting the roof down on his Alfa Romeo. Inside the store she bumped into Josef who was stacking shelves.

"Hi Becky, how you doing?"

"I'm great thanks. How are you and Mari?"

"We're fine, you down here on your own this time of night?"

"No, I just finished work, I'm buying some bread and then after I get changed my boyfriend's going to take me for a drink."

They chatted and then Josef said, "I'm just coming off shift, I'll walk out with you."

Becky bought the bread and they walked to the door. A short distance away Michael had got the sunroof closed on the car and was leaning against it smoking. A few Bahamians were quickly clearing their stalls of vegetables away, a police officer was getting into his police car nearby, and a group of Bahamians were standing telling jokes loudly and drinking beer out of bottles. Josef suddenly stopped dead in his tracks.

"Something wrong Josef?"

"Think I recognise someone."

"Oh, really?" Becky looked at him curiously. He was frowning and still hadn't moved.

"My boyfriend's just over there. Would you like to meet him?"

"No, no, I gotta' go. I'll see you again." He looked distracted. He turned away and then turned back, "Becky, you watch your back out here."

Becky frowned, puzzled. She opened her mouth to reply but he'd gone. She shrugged. By the time she reached Michael, it was starting to rain hard and people were leaving rapidly.

"Everything OK, honey?"

"Yes...You remember I told you about Josef - the Haitian with the little girl?"

"Yeah."

"Well he works in the supermarket. I was coming out with him and I wanted to introduce you but he just shot off."

Michael took out a Marlborough cigarette and lit it, he took a long drag, "Well, honey if you were an illegal immigrant, you wouldn't want to hang around in a car park with the police in it would you?" he pointed at the police car that was just leaving. Becky thought she glimpsed Luther and another officer driving off.

"No, no, of course not. God I'm stupid at times!"

"No, you're not stupid that's why I... Why I like you so much, you're just naive. You think everyone's like you, with nothing to hide. It's cool." He leant over and kissed the top of her head.

Becky forced a smile onto her face, "Yes, I guess so. Come on let's go for that drink." She suppressed the twin images of Michael gambling and that black gun lying in his drawer.

Back at the far end of the car park Isabella was still standing in the shadows under the trees. Her eyes blazed fiercely and she muttered to herself. *THE MAN had been here and the father of the troubled child.* When Becky had passed by Isabella had smiled for a second. Dressed In her white uniform, Isabella had felt innocence radiating from Becky.

A shiver suddenly ran through Isabella. *It was all coming together. The girl in white, she was part of it. She could feel it. And darkness. Darkness stalked the girl.*

This is radio Grand Bahama on the seventeenth of October. Well it looks like we're in hurricane season folks. Hurricane Bertha is two hundred miles off the Bahamas, so expect grey skies and wind today. Don't worry there's still time for it to change course, if it doesn't...well, keep tuned to Radio Grand Bahama the sunshine station, for all the latest news from the hurricane tracking station and fabulous music.

Becky woke up after a night shift around two p.m. She couldn't get back to sleep and she felt bored and restless. Michael often had free time in the day so she decided to ring his office. "Good afternoon, could you put me through to Michael Vincenzi, please?"

"Sorry, ma'am he's out reviewing some land for a client."

"Oh, where's he gone exactly?" she asked thinking that she might be able to join him.

"He's gone to some Out Island or other I'm not sure which one. He should be back around six p.m."

"OK, thanks," said Becky. She frowned and sighed when she put down the phone, feeling disappointed and a little puzzled. She thought Michael would have told her that he was flying somewhere. She wasn't working tonight and she could have gone with him and caught up with her sleep in the plane or later on in the day.

She made herself some tea and read a book. Glancing outside she saw that it was grey and cloudy, not good flying weather. Going out on to her balcony she looked at the sky. There, in the distance, she could see a dark blot on the horizon. A storm was coming her way.

She stood to watch fascinated. Lightning flashed far away and she could hear the rumble of thunder. Then she heard it. Coming through the trees. Closer and closer, it grew louder and louder, the sound of tropical rain approaching, clearing everything in its wake. The lightning lit up the sky turning it into a bleeding wound surrounded by blackness, thunder crashed around and then the rain reached a few yards from where she stood. The force of the rain blotted everything out. The noise was incredible-throbbing and drumming. A hundred thousand tropical plants and trees swayed and bent, the weak crashed and broke in its path. She breathed in the humid heady smell of the tropics. The force of the storm caught her up in a mixture of exhilaration and excitement. Then the rain started beating into the balcony. She knew from experience that she would be soaked in less than a minute so she quickly went indoors.

She tried to switch on the light but nothing happened and she realised her radio had gone off. As usual the local transformer had tripped out. Remembering the photos she felt uneasy and checked the door's new double locks. Feeling tired now she went back to bed for a while.

When she woke about an hour later the skies were blue, the ground around the swimming pool steamed in the returning heat and the birds were singing. The air was bright with renewal. She decided to go for a run and maybe see if Michael was back.

She changed into shorts, t-shirt and trainers and ran downstairs and along the road to the beach enjoying the sparkling freshness of the air and the birdsong after the storm. As she neared Michael's apartment block she saw him pull up in his car. A flutter of excitement stirred in her.

He got out of the car and she ran up to him and flung her arms around him, "Michael! How great to see you! How are you?"

He dropped the large canvas holdall that he was just lifting out of the car. "Christ, Becky you gave me a shock! What are you doing here?" he said looking annoyed.

Becky was taken aback by his tone. "Well I'm running of course."

"Oh - running. Of course," he said sarcastically.

"Is something wrong, Michael? You don't seem very pleased to see me."

"No, sorry, Becky. I'm just tired."

"Well, yes of course you are. Did you have to fly through the storm? That must have been so ...."

"What do you mean, 'fly through the storm'?"

"Well there's been a storm here."

"I know that! How do you know I've been flying?"

"I rang the office."

"You rang the office! Jesus!" He reached into the car for his briefcase.

"Sorry, Michael, you're obviously tired," Becky went to pick up the canvas bag for him.

"Leave..."

"Good God, Michael!" Becky dropped the bag. "What on earth have you got in here? It weighs a ton!"

"For fucks sake, Becky! Will you just stop interfering!"

"What! What on earth are you talking about?"

"It's like being interrogated! You're always asking questions! Why can't you just forget it!"

"That's not fair!"

"It's true. You ARE always asking questions. You ask questions at the hospital. You ask me questions. You want to change everything. You think you can help everyone. Just leave it out for once!"

"That's unfair. I only asked!"

"Well don't! I'm tired and hot and I need a shower!"

"Sod you, Michael! Just go and have one. I'm going to finish my run!" Becky ran onto the beach absolutely furious.

Miserable bugger! How dare he say she was always asking questions! She was only trying to help. She ran for half a mile, really angry, the row going around in her head until in the end she could hardly remember what had started it.

She sat down under a palm tree and cried. Frustrated, angry and saddened, she lurched from one emotion to the next. Eventually she dried her tears and ran back to her flat. When she got there she slammed the door, tore off her clothes and got under the shower. She started to cry again. She ended up sitting on the floor of the shower, sobbing as the warm water pounded over her.

Eventually she stopped crying, dressed and made herself a cup of tea putting on the TV as she did so. She could hear a State Senator being interviewed.

"It seems to me, Senator that more and more of our young people are becoming addicted to cocaine and then moving on to heroin. What's happening in this great state of ours and more importantly what are you going to do about it?"

"It's not easy. The problem is that Miami and from there the whole of the States, is being flooded with cheap cocaine and heroin."

"Well with all respect, how is that being allowed to happen?"

"Well, Tom, it's like this. A lot of it is coming over the border from Mexico and then a whole lot more is getting here from South America."

"Why isn't the CIA doing something about it then?"

"Tom, the problem is it comes by boat at night from South America. They drop it off at some nice little remote cay in the Bahamas. A local guy picks it up and then it's half an hour on to Miami, by plane or boat or hidden in luggage. It's just flooding in..."

Becky put her tea down on the coffee table with a thump, oblivious that it had spilt.

"Oh my God," she muttered to herself. *It wasn't possible was it? That bag?* In her minds eye she saw him gambling and losing heavily at the casino. She saw The Gun. *No. Not her Michael. It wasn't possible. He hated drugs.* She leant on her elbow and put her hand over her mouth. *The Bag. Why was the bag so heavy? No. She was being ridiculous.* She sat back and closed her eyes.

Then it hit her. *The trip to Bimini. What was he putting in the back when they stopped? No. No. It couldn't be.* She bit her lip and rocked backwards and forwards twirling her hair, unaware of the cartoons that had just started on the TV. *No. There had to be another explanation.*

She turned off the TV and paced the room. *How could she have been so naive? So stupid? Was there an innocent explanation?* She got up and fetched a bottle of Scotch that she kept for Michael. She started to drink it.

In the night she woke sweating, her mouth was dry and her head ached. She could hear a lizard rustling around outside on the balcony. It suddenly occurred to her how quiet it was in the room and she realised that the air conditioning unit wasn't running.

Feeling uneasy she switched on the bedside light and was relieved to find it working normally. She got out of bed and switched the air conditioning on and off, unplugged it and tried again, but nothing happened. "Damn!" she said.

Sighing to herself she opened the window, warm humid air flooded into the room along with the noise of a few cicadas and the waves breaking on the shore just down the road. She got up and put the main light on and went into the lounge, quickly putting the light on in there as well. In the bathroom everything was as usual. Finally she went to the cupboard and got a fan. She took it into the bedroom, plugged it in and went back to bed but by now sleep was impossible.

She kept thinking about Michael and that bag, *there had to be an innocuous explanation.* The fan was noisy. Exasperated she gave up on sleep, put the light back on and got herself a glass of water. Her head ached and she looked at the swimming pool outside longingly. A swim would definitely clear her head and cool her down, but she couldn't risk waking everyone in the apartment block by swimming at this hour.

She remembered that it was one of the days when she'd got Teresa's car and decided she would drive to a quiet beach. Maybe she would even have a swim. She smiled to herself. *Her friends at home would never believe how much she'd changed- quiet, almost timid Becky going for a swim in the middle of the night.*

That decided her. She picked up a towel and left the silent and dark apartment block. Driving to a cove she didn't pass anyone on the road. She parked the car under some palm trees near the beach and getting out felt a cool refreshing breeze coming off the sea. It was very humid and she reflected that the weather was changing, 'I wonder if that hurricane will come this way,' she mused to herself.

The sea was not as calm as usual and she took her shoes off and paddled. *God! It was warm and inviting!* Looking around she listened hard but all that could be heard was the sound of the waves. Suddenly she made up her mind. She was fed up with everyone telling her what she could or couldn't do, fed up with worrying and fed up with her headache. She ran back through the sand and before she could change her mind took all her clothes off, left them behind a rock and ran to plunge into the sea.

It was delicious, it caressed her bare body, sensual and warm. Her headache and worries evaporated. She decided to try to get rid of the alcohol she'd drunk by swimming hard, and struck out strongly. Some distance from the shore she lay floating on her back, bobbing up and down on the waves, looking up at the full moon and feeling relaxed. She felt so much better, *it was heavenly,* she drifted, feeling her headache ebb away.

There was a faint noise. It was somewhere in the distance. *What on earth could it be? The sound of a motor perhaps, a little further out at sea. No, it had gone, probably her imagination playing tricks.* She lay back and closed her eyes. Then she heard it again. *No. It couldn't be. Could it? Yes, there it was. Coming closer. And voices! Shit!* Now she could hear voices. They were coming from the shore. Mens' voices. And a light. *Jesus! There was torchlight on the beach.* She strained her eyes and there they were. Two men pushing a rowing boat into the water. The noise that she'd heard further out was getting louder. It was obviously that of a motor boat's engine.

Oh my God! was all she could think. It went through her head again and again. Then with a start, *I'm naked.* This thought moved her to action and she began to try to swim away very quietly. The men who'd pushed the rowing boat into the water were now heading in her direction. Their voices carried on the night air.

"Jesus, it's bright tonight, man," a Bahamian voice said.

"Yeah, if Custom's or the police are out here we're screwed."

Becky vaguely noticed that the second man had an American accent.

"You worry too much, man, that's well taken care of."

"Yeah I guess. Heh! You see something over there?"

They shone their torches over the sea illuminating the surface. Becky gasped and taking a deep breath dived under the water. She was terrified now. They were obviously drug smugglers. They wouldn't take kindly to being observed. She held her breath and swam under water as gently as she could and came up slowly. *Thank God,* the torch light on the water near her had gone. The men had reached a now clearly visible fishing vessel, as she watched, other men on board, lowered several packages into the rowing boat.

She needed to get away and quickly, while they were distracted. She saw with surprise that she'd surfaced much further from the shore than she'd expected. Puzzled she tried to swim back. *God help me*, she thought, as she realised that she was in the grip of a strong current. "Shit!" she muttered, putting all her strength into swimming for the land without splashing. It was taking forever. It was taking far too long. Glancing back she saw that the men were already rowing towards the beach, they were right behind her. Every now and again one of them would play his torch over the water.

She bit her lip and trembled. *What If they catch me?* Adrenaline surge through her body and she renewed her efforts. The moon started to come out from a cloud just as she reached the water's edge. They were only yards away. Getting out of the sea bent double she realised that she wasn't going to reach her clothes or the scrub at the back, in time to hide. Looking around frantically she saw a small rowing boat a few yards away on the beach. She ran to it still half doubled over, with an enormous effort lifted it up and threw herself underneath it, just as the men dragged their boat out of the water.

"Getting too old for this, man," the Bahamian said, from fifty yards away.

The other chap chuckled. "I need to take a leak before we go any further."

"Don't take too much time about it."

Becky could see them through a small hole in the side of the boat where she hid. She started and suppressed a gasp. She recognised the American! Her mind whirled. It was Troy! He went to pee up against a palm tree. Becky wrapped her arms around her chest and clenched her hands to stop herself from making a sound. Her nails dug deep into her palms. The Bahamian, who had a scarf around his face, came a little closer and turned away to light a cigarette. As he did so Becky noticed the sand between the boat and the man - her wet footprints were clearly visible leading to the boat.

The moon went behind a cloud. It started to spit with rain. The Bahamian walked across to where Troy was standing. Troy did up his pants. "OK, let's go. Get this stuff loaded and stashed, then I think a celebratory drink will be in order. A month's pay for a nights work, not bad eh!" he laughed.

"Hang on a minute. I think I see something just now when the moon was out." The Bahamian took out his torch and flashed it over the sand. "You see that over there, man?"

"See what?"Troy sounded bored.

"You ain't walked over there have you?"

"What are you on about?"

"Look!"

They started to walk towards the boat. Becky's footprints showed up clearly in the torch light.

"No, I sure as hell haven't walked over there! And don't you think they're a bit dainty for my size twelves! Let's go see just what we've got here?" He pulled out a Colt forty five automatic pistol from inside his jacket.

They ran to the boat and upturned it.

"Motherfucker!"

"Shit!"

The only thing to be seen was the imprint of where Becky's wet body had lain. They heard the car start up.

"Come on let's catch the bastard!"

They ran to the road. The car was just in sight. Troy took aim and fired. The car swung wildly to the right. He fired again, aiming for the tyres and missing. There was a crash of gears and it revved away, dust billowing around it.

"Jesus Christ! Who the fuck was that?"

The watched the tail lights vanish.

"Don't worry," said Troy, his face furious, "I think I know exactly who it was."

Becky drove like a demon back to the apartment, naked except for an old towel that she'd grabbed from the back seat. She was shaking and sobbing, wrestling with the wheel and screeching around corners. The rain had come on again. It drummed on the window in time with the mantra going through her head. She was gasping and panting, muttering to herself, "What to do? What to do?" She drew up with a start and clutching the towel around her, leapt out of the car.

She reached Margaret and Alex's door and then remembered that Alex was away for a week in The States. It wasn't fair to involve Margaret, she'd got enough problems. Becky ran up the stairs to her apartment and took out her keys struggling to get them in the lock as she looked around her fearfully. *Had they seen her? Jesus! What to do?*

She got inside, locked the door behind her and ran from room to room, checking the windows and pulling the curtains. She was soaking wet and trembling from head to foot. She got a towel and dried herself, took out the bottle of Scotch and poured herself a large one.

Michael. He'd know what to do. Need to tell Michael, she thought. She picked up the phone and dialled his number. It started to ring. Once, twice, three times. Then the memory of that bag and the gun filled her mind. She slammed the phone down.

Was he in on it? Who could she trust? Not Teresa, who would probably tell anyone the next time she got drunk. The police? Everyone said they were corrupt. She must be wrong about Michael. She picked up the phone and put it down again. A plan of sorts started to take shape in her mind.

The phone started to ring. She jumped - *Shit! Who could it be?* She went to it. Put her hand on the receiver. Bit her lip. Hugged her arms around her body and let it ring. Eventually it stopped. It was four a.m. now, she went and got a blanket and wrapped herself in it.

The old sensible Becky would go home to safety, she thought. *Everything could go back to how it was. She could work in a clean hospital, with lots of equipment, and friendly staff. She could go back to her parents and normality...But what about the girls dying from abortions? The drugs fuelling crime and addiction? What about Michael?*
Michael - had he deceived her from the start?

*No. She wasn't going anywhere. She'd show them all. And if Michael **was** involved, he was going to pay...*

Chapter 13

This is radio Grand Bahama on the eighteenth of October. All you tourists best stay snuggled up in bed today. Hurricane Bertha is still set dead on course for us and you won't be putting up no umbrellas or beach chairs in these winds. A high of seventy five degrees and humidity at seventy percent. Watch out for heavy rain. Us locals can get our hurricane tracking maps from Barclays bank and we'd best start getting our provisions in. Keep listening to radio Grand Bahama your sunshine station...

Teresa got into the car, hardly noticing that it wasn't locked. For a few minutes she didn't move. Looking up at Becky's apartment longingly, she thought of how much she'd love to go and confide in her. To have Becky tell her, "Sit down, I'll make you a cup of tea," - Becky's solution for everything. She'd give anything to have Becky give her a cuddle, tell her that everything would be alright. *But it wouldn't be, would it? Abortion-such a grubby word. Hard and unforgiving like the act itself.*

Gripping her hands together her eyes filled with tears. *It was no good going to Becky. She'd got herself into this mess and she had to get herself out of it.*

She found herself thinking about her mother and the boys in Ireland. Sweet memories from when she was wee. *Of sitting next to the wood fire on winter's evenings, her mother brushing her hair 'til it shone.* She sighed. "Come on Teresa, Bernadette, Bridget, O'Hara," she said. "Get it together. There's no going back. You're going straight to hell anyway the way you've behaved the last few years." How she envied Becky, so sweet, so naive, no idea of the real world. Becky seemed to live in an enchanted place of permanent innocence.

She checked her bag for the fourth time that morning. *A hundred dollars, an old cotton towel and a sanitary towel. Was that really all she needed to end a life?* She looked at the hand drawn map on the tatty piece of paper, beside her on the seat. One night last year she'd been on duty with one of the Nurses Aides. She'd found her crying, and the Aide had confided in Teresa that she'd had an abortion. Last week she'd sought her out at work, taken her into the sluice and asked her to help her. The girl was horrified but, in the end, she did what Teresa wanted; arranged a date and time, drew Teresa a map. She'd said, she'd pray for her.

Teresa blew her nose and got out the car keys. When she started the car up, the smell of petrol made her feel even more nauseated. Clouds scudded across the sky, it was beginning to rain. Shivering she headed out in the direction of Eight Mile Rock.

When Becky woke up it was grey and windswept outside and spitting with rain. She noticed the car had gone. Teresa must have taken it first thing, for work or shopping.

She made herself a strong coffee to clear her head. She needed to act quickly. She wanted Troy brought to justice, but first, she needed to find out if Michael really was involved as well.

After putting on her track suit and jogging shoes she picked up a plastic bag from the boutique in the International Market. Putting a couple of things in it, she reflected on how long ago it seemed from when she'd bought that bikini. When she got outside she felt cold. Margaret was just going in downstairs and looked up as she heard Becky's door slam.

"You OK, Becky?"

"Fine, Margaret. Just fine, thanks," she said, with a smile that didn't reach her eyes.

"You sure know how to party."

"Pardon?"

"You can't fool me. It was pretty late when you got in wasn't it?"

"What! Err... Yes. Sorry, did I disturb you?"

"No, honey. I can never sleep when Alex is away. He'll be home soon. If that hurricane reaches here you come on down to us. We're going to stay in the apartment if we can and hope for the best. Bring that nice young man of your's as well, if you like."

"Yes...OK, Margaret, thanks. I've got to go now."

"See you later then, honey."

Becky pulled up the hood of her tracksuit and jogged to Michael's apartment block. George the doorman was on duty as usual, Becky had met him several times before. He was from Jamaica and his brother lived in London. Like most people with relatives there, he had seemed slightly surprised the last time that they chatted that Becky didn't know his brother. Becky thought that he seemed to have a soft spot for her. Opening the door he gave her a big grin.

"How you doin', princess?"

"I'm great, George. How are you?" She forced herself to give him a tremulous smile.

"Jus' fine ma'am. Jus' fine. What you doing over here? I think I saw Michael go off to work 'bout an hour ago."

"Well, George, you know how it is. He's going to try to get back a little early and I thought I'd surprise him." Becky gave a giggle and opened the bag a little, to reveal a glimpse of a black lace and satin negligee.

"Wow! That's the sort of surprise any man would like!"

"I hope so. Could you let me have his apartment key please? I want to be... sort of ready... when he walks in, if you know what I mean."

"Sure thing, honey. I knows exactly what you mean and I wouldn't want to stand in the way of true love. I can remember myself when I was young, my wife and I we used to..."

"George! The key! Err, please."

"'Course. You get to my age you forgets what a hurry you be in when you's young and keen." He laughed long and hard. "Lord! Lord! You young uns."

"George. The key. Please."

George went into his tiny office and turned to the board where the keys were hanging up. "Let's just have a looky here. Yep. Here you go. Number thirty-five C." He handed the keys to Becky.

"You're a darling," Becky reached up and gave him a quick peck on the cheek.

"Been a long time since a woman did that to me, ma'am,"

Becky laughed, "I find that hard to believe. Thanks, George anyway. Thanks a lot." She went across and pressed the elevator button. She got inside and gave George a conspiratorial look and a big grin. As soon as the doors closed, her expression changed and leaning back against the doors she breathed out a great sigh of relief. She felt bad about deceiving George. Swallowing hard she closed her eyes for a second, holding the keys tightly in her sweating and trembling hands.

She got out of the lift and walked down the corridor to Michael's door, glancing at the other two apartments nearby. The sound of a TV drifted out from one of them, otherwise everywhere seemed deserted.

She put the key in the lock with a hand that was shaking a little. Going inside she called out, "Michael! Anyone at home? It's only me."

Her voice echoed around the empty apartment. Walking through the lounge, she glimpsed the stunning view from the windows, which she'd seen so often with Michael. It felt weird being here on her own. Oppressive. Feeling guilty and slightly sick, she quickly looked into the empty kitchen before going and opening the door to the bedroom. It was completely silent. Looking at the water bed she sighed. On impulse she sat on the end and started to reflect on the great times they'd had.

Michael was at work but he couldn't concentrate. He kept wondering who'd rung him and then rung off again at around four a.m. It made him feel uneasy. Becky was a lot brighter than he'd first thought she was and she asked way too many questions. He was worried that they'd had a row, and even more worried that she'd picked up that bag. *Damn it! What if she was putting two and two together?* He couldn't afford for her to start blundering into everything. *Too much depended on it.*

Running his fingers through his hair, he frowned and lit up a Marlborough cigarette. He couldn't concentrate. Something didn't feel right. He thought that she was probably off duty after working several nights. On impulse he decided he would go around to see her, apologise, and smooth everything over between them. He'd make up some excuse about the bag carrying surveying equipment or some such nonsense. *She'd be easy to convince, she'd want to believe him. After all, she didn't know anything, did she?* He stubbed out the half smoked cigarette in an already overflowing ash tray, told his secretary he was leaving and, as he went through the door, patted the gun in his inside pocket.

Becky realised with a start that she'd been day dreaming. She was so tired. Her limbs felt heavy and her head ached. Everything seemed to be unravelling around her. Hesitantly she went to the bedside drawer and pulled it open. It was empty. She started. The gun had gone. Not wanting to dwell on the possibilities this opened up, she told herself to get on with it.

She began searching for the canvas bag, almost certain that it would hold nothing incriminating and she could tell Michael everything. She looked under the bed.
Yes! There it was. It pulled it out easily. Too easily. It was completely empty. She shoved it back underneath the bed.

Then she opened the wardrobe breathing in the smell of Michael lingering on his designer suits. There was a plastic bag on the floor of the wardrobe, she took it out quickly but it contained only a new pair of shoes. Becky wasn't sure what she was looking for, but yesterday the canvas bag had been heavy. Getting a chair she climbed up and looked on top of the wardrobe but that too revealed nothing. She started going through the drawers in the bedroom, all the time praying that she wouldn't find anything.

Michael drove to Becky's flat, The March of the Valkyries playing on his cassette player. He drummed the fingers of his left hand in time to it whilst holding the wheel in his right. It was raining lightly and the road was slippery. A group of people stood chatting in the road. Suddenly the car went out of control as he aquaplaned on a puddle, "For God's sake!" he yelled as he struggled to control it. The people leapt onto the side walk, cursing him in his wake as regained control. Just missing them, he drenched them with water as the car slew past.

Michael barely glanced at them but he slowed a fraction and lit up a cigarette. *Can't afford to be in an accident, not at this stage of the game*, he thought. Finally he pulled up outside Becky's apartment, jumped out of the car and took the stairs two at a time.

He was feeling uneasy. It was making him nervous. And Michael didn't like to be nervous. In spite of the drop in temperature he was sweating. He scowled. Something felt wrong.

He rang Becky's doorbell long and hard. *Maybe she'd gone out with Teresa last night and was still sleeping. Maybe.* He rang the bell again. The minutes passed. He ground the cigarette out under the heel of his shoe.

"Damn it!" he muttered to himself, "Becky! Becky you in?" he called out.

Margaret came out from downstairs and shouted up at him. "Hi, you looking for Becky?"

"Yeah. Yeah I am. Have you seen her?"

"Sure thing. I saw her go jogging out towards Lucaya Beach half an hour or so ago, she..."

"God damn it!"

Michael clattered down the stairs, pushed past Margaret and roared off in his car.

"Well! Son of a bitch...No thanks or nothing and he seemed so sweet the other week." Margaret went indoors to pour herself a drink by way of consolation.

Becky had gone into the kitchen. She pushed her hair back off her damp forehead and started opening cupboards, pulling things out and shoving them back in. Every now and again she glanced at her watch. The sound of a radio playing Roberta Flack singing 'Killing me softly with his song,' echoed down the corridor to her.

She didn't hear Michael's car roar up outside.

The cupboards contained only crockery, coffee and cigarettes. Going into the lounge she started opening drawers in the bureau.

Michael got out of the car.

Becky stood and looked around and her eyes lit on that picture by Picasso. What was it Michael had said about it? Yes she remembered now. It was the second time she'd gone to the apartment...

"Wow! This is a strange picture, Michael."

"It's called 'Guernica.' Picasso painted it."

"What's it about?"

"It's about the civil war in Spain. The Germans were friendly with Franco and they wanted to try out a little bombing practice, sort of a precursor to bombing a civilian population later on in Britain. It had never been done before."

"So they just bombed a village?"

"Yeah. And they made sure it was market day."

"That's dreadful."

"Yeah. But no-one rushed to help them. That's it you see. People don't notice what's going on. In full view. Right under their noses..."

The words echoed in her head. She walked up to the picture and took it off the wall. There it was. A safe.

Michael ran along the beach but Becky was nowhere in sight. He returned to the car and started the engine. Then he looked down and saw his shoes and socks were soaking wet from the sand. "God damn it!"

He killed the engine and walked through the revolving doors of the apartment block.

"Mornin', Michael. How ya doin'?"

"Oh not bad, George. Just called back to change my shoes."

"Yeah, sure you did."

"What?"

"Awful weather aint it? That hurricane - I hopes it don't continue to head this way. I remembers back in..."

Becky was frantically looking for a key to the safe. Pulling drawers open she rifled through them, her heart pounding and hands trembling. She was almost crying with frustration. The safe. It had to hold the answer to everything.

Think. Think. Stop and think. He wouldn't just keep it in a drawer would he? Looking at the desk it came to her. She'd come in once from the shower dressed only in a towel and surprised him. He'd made a sudden movement. *His hand. His hand had been underneath the desk!* Putting her hand underneath she felt around. "Bingo!" There it was. Taped in place. A gold key.

"My wife an' I an all the little uns we was under a table. That wind it was a howl...

"Look, George, I'm in a bit of a hurry."

"Sorry, goin' on here a bit ain't I?...Oh yeah, 'course, I'd be in a hurry too. I been expectin' you."

"What? What do you mean, you've been expecting me?"

Upstairs, Becky opened the safe.

"Oh don't, you worry, your little secrets are safe with me."

"What the hell are you talking about?"

"Ain't no need to be like that. Your little lady. She got a real nice surprise for you, that's all."

"Becky? You're talking about Becky?"

"Yeah. Becky. She's a real sweet lady. Always polite, always got a smile for..."

"She's here?"

"Sure thing."

"Where?"

"Why, where else would she be? You're, a lucky man, you..."

"What! You let her into my apartment!"

"Yeah, she asked me real nice..."

"For God's sake!" Michael strode to the elevator and started jabbing the buttons.

George shrugged and went back to his office, "He sure in a hurry for that surprise."

Becky took the money, passports and one of the many brown paper wrapped packages out of the safe. With shaking hands she put them all on the desk by the window. There were three passports. All with photos of Michael - all in different names. She glanced through the window. And saw Michael's red car. "Shit!"

The elevator arrived at the ground floor.

Becky prised opened a corner of the packages. She gasped. Then she heard the sound of the elevator starting up to go down to the ground floor. Shoving everything back into the safe, she dropped the package in her hurry, picked it up and quickly pushed it in with the rest.

The bell of the arriving elevator sounded in the hall. Michael's footsteps pounded down the corridor.

Chapter 14

Teresa parked the car as she'd been instructed some half a mile from the house. She took out the hand drawn map and looked at it again. There were hardly any street names to go by and the whole place was a maze. Luckily because of the bad weather the streets were deserted except for the usual motley collection of scruffy dogs. They wandered around in small gangs, looking for food in bins, peeing up the houses and scrapping with each other. Although it seemed quiet she pulled the hood of her black jacket up and kept her head down. She didn't want to bump into anyone from the hospital and have to explain what she was doing there.

It was starting to rain now. Going past Josef's place she noticed that it had been painted white with blue window sills, and where the wood hung off it had been nailed up. It looked as if a proper curtain hung at one window and where the piece of dirt in the front had been tidied, a purple morning glory bush had taken root. Going there with Becky seemed like a lifetime ago. Wondering if Josef had ever found out what had happened to his wife, she reflected that she wasn't the only person with problems.

As she got closer she started to feel sick. Her morning sickness had stopped recently and she knew that this nausea was due to nerves. With her hood pulled well down, she didn't notice a woman come out of a nearby house onto the path, until she collided with her.

"Heh, girl! You needs to watch where you going."

"Sorry. Sorry," Teresa looked up. A woman a little older than herself held a tiny baby in her arms. The baby stirred and snuggled in closer to the woman.

"Don't worry ain't no harm done. Horatio, he still sleepin'"

"Horatio?" Teresa said with a smile.

"Yeah, his daddy really like the sea and he say it some famous sailor. Horatio, you want to meet the nice lady?"

She held the baby out to Teresa. The baby blinked and opened his deep brown eyes. They met her own. For a moment Teresa was transfixed. Then she started backwards, dropping her bag and putting her hands out in a stopping motion in front of her. "No! No!" The towels fell out of the bag.

"OK, OK. No need to take on so."

Teresa hurriedly picked up her bag cramming the towels back into it. "Got to go. Sorry."

The woman's eyes had opened wide when she'd seen what Teresa was carrying. From the expression on the woman's face, Teresa guessed that she knew for certain what she was doing. After all why else would a white girl be there, in her state, with those things?

The woman grasped hold of Teresa's arm. "Would, you like to come in for a drink, an' a chat, or somethin'?" she said, looking concerned.

"No!"Teresa choked back a sob.

"You certain? We could pray together if you like."

"No, no, I've got to go," Teresa shook the woman off and almost ran down the road.

The woman shook her head sadly and looked at Horatio. "Come on sweetie, let's go back indoors, say a little prayer for that foolish girl."

Teresa found the house at last. Not much more than a wooden shed, green paint was peeling from the doors and windows where grubby net curtains were tightly drawn together. A cat was being sick next to a bin of overflowing rubbish in the garden. Weeds brushed Teresa's knees. She walked past a rusting pram and picked her way through a litter of empty beer bottles, discarded cigarette wrappers and empty food cartons.

Forcing herself forward she tapped the door. She waited. Minutes passed. She knocked again, a little louder this time. Still no-one came. Turning away, she started to walk down the path, sighing with relief. She'd give up and go home.

Then she heard it. A sound she was to regret - the noise of bolts being drawn back on the door. Turning around she saw a woman standing there.

"Jesus! It's you!" Teresa said.

Michael slammed the apartment door behind him and strode through the flat. "Becky! Becky! You in here?" he shouted, his eyes hard, his face white.

"I certainly am, darling," Becky's voice came from the bedroom. Michael threw open the door. Becky's track suit and shoes were sprawled about the floor. She lay on top of the bed, facing him. Resting up on her right elbow, her breasts strained to be contained in the skimpy black silk and lace negligee.

"Gosh, you must have driven like the wind to get here so soon."

"What the hell are you talking about?"

"Well I hope you're not going to be cross with me again. I left a message at your office. To let you know I'd got a present for you here."

"Message? No, I didn't get any message."

"Didn't you, darling?" She put her right index finger to her lips and sucked the end of it. At the same time she slid her left hand down to caress her breasts, before sliding it down her body and under the elastic of the tiny black lace panties.

"Well the important thing is that you're here now," she moved her hand suggestively in her panties. "I wanted to make up to you for being such a pain the other day, so as I said, I've brought you a present."

"What sort of present?" said Michael, smiling now, surprise showing on his face. Becky took her finger out of her mouth, slowly licked her lips, and eased herself off the bed. She walked towards him her hips swaying, the negligee just skimming her nipples and the top of her brown thighs.

"Here's the ribbon on your present, Michael." She turned her back to him and holding her blonde hair up above her neck showed him where the top of the negligee was tied in a bow.

Michael kissed the back of her neck. "Wow! This is a bit of a surprise, Becky."

"Well, after I saw what other people did on the boat, I thought perhaps I should be a little more adventurous. I don't want you to get bored with me. You said, I was naive, so I've decided to grow up."

"I could never be bored with you, Becky."

He undid the ribbon and reached around her body to put his hands on her full breasts. She turned around revealing them as the negligee slid to the floor leaving her clad only in the tiny panties.

"Christ, Becky." He went to pull her to him, but before he could she went on to her knees and looking up at him through her tousled blonde hair said, "I might need a bit of instruction with this, Michael," and smiled at him as she undid the zip of his trousers.

"Jesus, Becky!"

The woman looked Teresa up and down. "My, my," was all she said.

"God above! I didn't expect to find you here."

"Likewise, girl. I thought you'd be brighter than to have got yerself caught."

"It's a long story."

The woman laughed, "Ain't it always. Come on in." Chuckling, she led Teresa through a room that doubled as both living room and bedroom, to a dimly lit kitchen. Teresa's nausea increased as she breathed in a mixture of stale blood, sweat and something indefinable; a trace that lingered from the previous girls who'd been here - the smell of fear. A large fly was buzzing over a stainless steel speculum and dilators which sat on the side of the sink like bizarre cooking implements waiting to be washed up. They shone in the light of the bulb swinging from the ceiling.

"Go on get yerself up then." The woman motioned to what looked like an old formica kitchen table, half covered by a torn and stained sheet with a grubby pillow at one end.

Teresa froze.

"Well make yer mind up, girl. I haven't got all day, and now you seen my face you ain't leaving without paying anyways."

Teresa looked at the door, "God forgive me," she muttered, crossed herself and climbed up on to the table.

Half an hour later the woman opened the door of the hut. "You remember what I told you, Teresa. I ain't fooling. You tell anyone about this I'll know exactly who to blame and I've got friends you wouldn't like to meet. You understand me."

"Yeah, yeah, of course I understand. Who do you think I'm going to tell that I just had an abortion? Sure, I couldn't even tell the priest!"

"Well long as you knows. Make sure you don't go telling Little Miss Stuck Up."

"Who?"

"That damn fool white girl friend of yours! She's nosin' around way too much. In fact you care about her, you tell her to keep her nose out of stuff that don't concern her, or she's just gonna disappear into thin air one of these days!"

"What!"

"You heard."

"She's just stupid. She doesn't know anything I promise, you."

"Well she hadn't better. Now get off my door step 'fore everyone start wondering what some white girl's doing at my place." She gave Teresa a shove and slammed the door behind her.

Teresa weaved her way unsteadily down the road trying not to cry. She was cold and shivering, oblivious to the rain soaking her hair where she hadn't pulled up her hood. The pain which had been a low ache suddenly hit her and she bent over double and clutched her stomach. Forced to stop for a few seconds, she moaned, gritted her teeth and then stumbled on.

She couldn't believe how brutal it had all been. The woman had given her an injection of some sort but it had just made her feel groggy, the pain had been excruciating. In a way she didn't mind - it was punishment for her wickedness.

It seemed much further getting back to the car. Waves of pain swept through her. The rain stopped and a watery sun came out. She walked in a daze, passing three boys aged about thirteen. They sniggered as she passed and whispered.

She heard one of them say, "Disgustin.'"

The other one muttered, "That's women's stuff, man, don't you know notin.'"

"My sister she just started all that," said the third one.

Teresa looked down and saw blood trickling down her legs.

"Oh my God! Jesus, Mary and Joseph save me!" she muttered to herself.

She could hear the boys laughing but the world was becoming fuzzy at the edges. Her stomach felt as if it was being crushed between two mighty hands. At last she reached the car, yanked open the door and half fell into the driver's seat.

She didn't know how long she'd lain there when she heard a man's voice.

"Excuse me, ma'am, don't I know you?"

She opened her eyes, the man's face seemed to be coming and going. At last her vision cleared and she realised who it was, "Oh Josef, it's you."

"Ah, yes. It's, Teresa, isn't it? You OK?" Josef asked frowning and looking concerned.

"No. No, I don't feel too good. Can you drive, Josef?"

"No, no sorry I can't. I ain't never learned"

"Damn... Well could you phone Becky and ask her to come out here and get me? Because I feel really, really bad, Josef."

"You sure you don't want me to get an ambulance or somethin'? You looks awful pale."

"No! No! Just Becky. But tell her please hurry."

"OK ,Teresa. What's her phone number?"

"It's...It's, two, four, three...Err...Eight, four, seven."

"Don't you worry. I'll go to the preacher's house and ring her. Two, four, three, eight, four, seven. I'll arrange to meet her there by the church. Else she never find us."

"Thanks, Josef."

As Josef left, Teresa looked down. The blood was starting to soak through her clothes.

Becky looked at Michael sleeping beside her, *so innocent, with his 'tousled hair, all American boy' look. No wonder he'd taken her in!*

She felt sick and angry. Angry with him and angry with herself. *How stupid and naive she'd been. Well, he'd find out that she wasn't as stupid, as he thought she was.*

It had cost her to deceive him. She'd wanted to vomit when she gave him oral sex. Somehow she'd controlled her shaking and played the devoted girlfriend. She'd gritted her teeth when he screwed her afterwards - acted out having an orgasm. She felt physically hurt. Hurt and dirty. Dirty from allowing him to touch her - from what she'd done with him, a drug dealer. And frightened too. She knew now. Knew that she was a long way out, swimming with the sharks.

She whispered, "Got to go now. I'm meeting Teresa," but he didn't stir. She pulled on her track suit and shoes and crept out. As the door closed behind her Michael opened his eyes. He got out of bed and from behind the curtains watched her jog down the drive away from the building. He frowned. *Something didn't add up here.*

When Becky reached her apartment she could hear the phone ringing. She ran up the stairs and opened the door, picked up the phone but whoever was ringing had rung off.

There was no time anyway. A quick shower and change and then she was going to the police. When the phone started ringing again she was showering. As the water washed over her, she realised just how much danger she was in. She could have been killed on the beach, and what if Michael had found her, searching his apartment? Troy, or the other man, had shot at the car last night. Had they seen who she was? Was there any connection between Michael and Troy? "What the hell have I got myself into?" she muttered as she quickly got out, dried and dressed. The phone rang again.

She hesitated before answering it, letting it ring four times. Then on impulse she picked it up.

"Becky? That you? Thank God! I've been ringing you for half an hour now."

"Who is this?"

"It's me, Josef. You need to come! You need to come real quick!"

"What are you talking about? Come where?"

"Here. To Eight Mile Rock."

"What's wrong, Josef?"

"It's your friend - Teresa. She looks real bad. She won't let me get no ambulance or nothin'."

"Where is she?"

"She's in her car. Look, I'm phoning from the preacher's house. You get to the church near my house and I'll take you."

"But, Josef I haven't got a car."

"Becky, she need you. She need you real bad. She won't let me get no-one else. I think she bleeding."

"What!"

"Becky, just get here! Get here now!"

Becky ran downstairs and hammered on Margaret's door.

"What's wrong, Becky? You look kind of..."

"Margaret, I need to borrow your car! It's an emergency."

"OK , honey if it's an emergency." She turned and went indoors to get the keys, Becky could hear her muttering, "Now where did I leave them. I must try and leave them in the same place... I don't know..."

"Margaret! Please! Hurry!"

She came to the door holding them. "You, youngsters, you're all in such a hurry today. You should slow down, enjoy life. When I was..."

Becky snatched the keys from her hands, "Sorry!" She ran to the car, fumbled with the lock, started it and stalled as she found it had been left in gear. "Shit! Shit! Shit!" She got it into gear and screeched off.

"You be careful..." Margaret yelled after her, but she was gone. She shook her head, went indoors muttering, looked at the cupboard where the brandy was kept. Then she looked at Chuck's photo, gritted her teeth and put the kettle on for coffee.

Michael turned back from the window and went to get a drink from the kitchen. Opening the cupboard he was puzzled for a moment, he didn't usually keep his coffee mug on that side. A picture crossed his mind of how Becky had looked when he walked in. He smiled, and made himself some coffee.

Walking back into the lounge he saw it. Just underneath the painting of Guernica. On the carpet. A tiny amount of white powder. He put the coffee down with a start. "Damn!"

Teresa moaned in the front seat of the car. How much longer was Becky going to be? She felt sick with pain and fear and could feel the blood trickling down her legs. As her head lolled back, she came to with a start.

A man was approaching the car. *Thank God*! It was someone she knew.

"Jesus, it's good to see you. Did Becky send you?"

"Becky! Hell no. I was just driving around, hoping to bump into you."

"You were? Well, anyway, God knows I'm pleased you're here. I can't drive and I need a doctor. I need a doctor urgently."

He looked at her more closely then. Saw her white drained face. Saw the blood trickling. "Yeah I can see that, honey. You look in pretty bad shape. You look like you could do with a fag."

"Yeah, you're not kidding! But please, can you drive me to a doctor first?"

He took a packet of Marlborough cigarettes out of his back pocket, tapped one on the packet and casually lit it. Taking a long pull on it he smiled at her.

"Can't beat a fag in a crisis, darlin'....."

"Yeah but I'm really sick, I feel awful."

"This car - it stinks you know."

"Troy! Please! I need a doctor"

Troy smiled at her. "You know, it's a shame, it's a real shame. Seems like a waste really. You, were always good for a quick fuck if there wasn't anything better around."

"Troy, I'm bleeding!"

"Yep. You do look pretty disgusting." He made rings with the smoke, a smile playing on his face.

"What? You don't seem to understand."

"Oh, I understand alright. I understand everything. Not only are you a nosey cow, you've just had a filthy abortion."

"Troy, I don't know what you're on about!"

"I'm on about last night, putting your nose into stuff that doesn't concern you." He took a long drag on his cigarette, his eyes narrowed and he blew the smoke into her face.

Teresa coughed and feebly waved the smoke away. She started to cry.

"Troy, look, OK, it's true, I have had a termination, but what do you mean, 'stuff that doesn't concern me.' Jesus, I've no idea know what you're on about."

"You know. You know exactly what I mean. I saw you."

"Troy, I haven't time for this. Please, please take me. I'm begging you. I need a doctor. I need to go now, Troy! "

"You should never have gone to that beach last night, sweetheart." He turned away from her slightly. Took another long drag on the cigarette. "As for leaving - you're leaving alright, honey." His face hard and angry, he tossed the lit cigarette onto the back seat.

Becky drove with her foot hard on the throttle, changing down through the gears to screech around the corners. "Oh my God. What's happened to her? What's she done? If only I'd been at home." The wipers fought an uneven battle with the driving rain and the car was misting up. She looked at the petrol gauge. It was nearly empty. "Shit! Shit! Shit!"

She peered through the windscreen, *surely it hadn't been this far the last time that she came?* When she reached Eight Mile Rock the streets were deserted, no-one went out here when it rained. Garbage blew around but even the dogs had vanished.

Turning left she found she'd driven into a dead end. "For God's sake!" she yelled and hit the steering wheel. Crashing the gears she reversed back up the road. There was a church ahead, at last, she thought. She looked up and down the street. It was deserted. *Where was Josef? Shit! It must be the wrong church.* There were dozens in Eight Mile Rock. She wiped the inside of the windscreen with her hand. *Maybe she should have turned right before.*

She drove as fast as she dared back down the road, turned left and finally saw another church. As she braked to a halt Josef leapt out into the street, frantically waving at her. He yanked open the car door, "Thank God, Becky. Thank God!" and he almost fell into the car.

"Sorry. I got lost. Couldn't find the right church. I'm nearly out of gas."

"OK . You here now. Let's go! Turn left."

"How did Teresa find, you?"

"She didn't. I was just passing."

"What's wrong with her?"

"I don't know. But she look bad. White. What are you going to do?"

Becky turned to him frowning, "I don't know, Josef. Let's just find her."

"This way, Becky. We're nearly there."

At last they saw Teresa's car. They pulled up a few yards away and Becky glimpsed a man disappear around a corner. There was something vaguely familiar about him, Becky thought, but she was distracted by worry for Teresa.

They got out of the car and started to run towards Teresa's. That's when it happened! The world around them erupted and dissolved in a massive crash! A deafening blast! Screaming, they were blown backwards off their feet. Teresa's car doors flew off. Josef dived on top of Becky as the car windows blew out. Glass and metal rained down on them. A whooshing noise filled the air and the car was engulfed by flames. A blistering heat swept over them.

Josef crawled off Becky. Becky existed in a strange world where everything was happening in slow motion. It was like suddenly being in a nightmare. Nothing made sense. She felt as though she was under the sea, all the noises around her were muffled.

Trying to move she thought for a moment that she'd been punched hard in the stomach. She couldn't catch her breath and her ears were ringing. Looking at Josef she saw that he was bleeding from a cut on his forehead. That, stirred her back to some sort of reality. "Josef! Josef! You OK?" she screamed.

"Yeah, yeah. Just winded I guess. How about you?"

"I'm OK." Becky looked at the car then. Her eyes widened in horror. "Jesus Christ!" She started screaming and running to the car, "Teresa! Teresa!"TERESA!!"

Josef stumbled to his feet and ran after her, blood running down his face. He grabbed her and pulled her back. "No, Becky! No! Ain't notin' we can do. Oh shit!"

There was another massive explosion as the fuel tank went up. Flames lapped the melting metal.

Becky fought Josef with all her might, "No! NO! Have to get her! Have to get her!"

"No! NO! Becky!

"Let me go! Let me go!"

"She's gone, Becky. She gone. You can't do nothin'" He held her tight in his arms as she kicked and struggled. They watched the flames in horror, the heat forcing Josef to drag them back and away from the burning wreck.

Becky collapsed sobbing in his arms. Josef held her. "It's OK, Becky. It's OK." People were running now, coming from all directions shouting and screaming.

"Get the fire engine!"

"Ambulance! Call for an ambulance!"

"Keep back! Keep them kids back!"

Josef started to move then, half carrying Becky. "We needs to get away from here. I can't speak to no police. I need to make sure Mari's OK. Come on!"

Becky just looked at him in a daze.

"Becky! Come on!"

The sound of a siren could be heard in the distance. People were melting away as fast as they'd arrived. Josef physically picked Becky up and carried her to Margaret's car.

"Becky! Pull yourself together! We need to get away from here."

"But Teresa..."

"Becky, for God's sake! There's nothing we can do."

"Your head, Josef. You're bleeding."

"Never mind that. Drive, Becky! For the love of Jesus. Just drive!"

"OK," Becky gave him a strange smile. Started the engine and drove without speaking, no expression on her face. Under Josef's direction they reached his house. Josef stumbled in through the door, Becky sleep-walking behind him.

"Daddy! Daddy!" Mari ran and threw herself into his arms. Peter came out of the back room.

"Where the hell you been? We been worried to death! They say there's been a bomb go off! Oh, sorry I didn't see you there," he said looking at Becky.

"No it wasn't no bomb. It was a car. It caught fire and then it exploded."

"It was my fault. I was late. I was too late."Becky started to cry uncontrollably.

Peter looked at them both then puzzled, "Come in. Come and sit down. What happened to your head, man?" he said, suddenly noticing Josef.

"It was the blast. Christ... wreckage...Everywhere." He looked at Becky who just stood, white faced, saying nothing. "I think we need a drink, Peter."

Mari was looking at Becky curiously. "Are you alright, Becky? Did you fall over?"

"Yes, Mari, I'm fine. There's nothing to worry about," Becky wiped her eyes and gave Mari a tremulous smile.

"Daddy, you're all bleeding. You're not going to die are you?"

"No, sweetheart, it's just a graze."

Becky made a huge effort to pull herself out of a dark place. "Thanks, Josef, you probably saved my life. Let me look at your head."

"I'll go get us some beers," said Peter.

Becky looked at the wound on Josef's head. "It's OK, Josef. I don't think it needs stitching. Scalp wounds always bleed a lot..." her voice trailed off and she stared into space.

Peter went and got a damp cloth. "Here, Becky. You want to wipe it with this?" She looked at him puzzled for a moment.

"Oh... Yes, yes of course. She cleaned the wound as best she could and with trembling hands fumbled around in her handbag. "Got a plaster in here somewhere. Know I've got one. Must be in here. Oh bloody hell." She started to cry.

"You want to lie down or something?"

"No. I'm OK."

"What happened, Josef?"

"Well, it was a friend of Becky's. I found her..."Josef told Peter what had happened.

"If only I'd got here sooner. What was she doing in Eight Mile Rock anyway? You said she was bleeding, where was she bleeding from, Josef?" Becky said.

Josef looked embarrassed, "Becky, I'm not sure." He glanced at Mari who was happily playing with her doll.

"What do you mean?"

"Well...The blood, it was...it was on her skirt. You know like when you ladies have it happen,...Unexpected like."

Becky frowned, puzzled for a minute, then she realised. "Oh my God! And it was heavy? A lot of blood?"

"Yeah, Becky it was a lot."

Becky put her hand over her mouth and gasped. "Oh no," she said and started to cry. She rested her head in her hand. "I didn't know. I didn't know anything. Why didn't she tell me? She's been quiet lately. I've been so wrapped up in my problems I didn't notice. And now...Damn it! It's all my fault."

"Don't be silly, Becky. It's not your fault if she didn't tell you and that car smelt of petrol when you were out here before, it could have gone up any time."

"I suppose so, but now I've lost my only friend and, Oh God, everything's such a mess. I need to go. I have to get to the police or something. It's not just this. I know so much. I have to tell someone what I've found out."

"What are you talking about? What have you found out, Becky?"

"It's complicated. I don't know if I should tell you."

"It can't hurt to tell us, Becky. It's not true that you've lost your only friend. We're your friends aren't we, Peter?"

"Of course we are. Tell us what's going on"

"Well, there's the drugs and the girls at the hospital and the men on the beach and Michael's gun and..."

"Whoa! Becky, stop! Start at the beginning and just take it real slow."

"Sorry, OK. I'll try..." She told them everything; how she'd found out that girls on the island were having illegal abortions and that she suspected Sister Carey of doing them, the photos in her apartment, about Michael and the trips in the plane and finding the drugs in his lounge, and, how she saw Troy and the other man on the beach taking a delivery of drugs.

Josef and Peter hardly said anything. The more she told them the more shocked they looked. They glanced at each other frowning, Peter got up and looked through the window, Josef fiddled with the gold coloured cross he wore around his neck. By the time she'd finished it was dark. Josef had carried Mari to bed. Outside the wind was howling and the rain pattered on the roof.

"Josef, Peter, I'd better go. I should go the police I think."

"You can't go out this time of night, Becky. It's too late. Anyhow you're in danger. You're in real danger, you knows too much. You needs to be careful. You just can't go to the police. Everyone knows they're corrupt. Is there anyone you can trust? Someone with money who can get you out? Maybe to the States, you could go to the cops, or the CIA, or FBI, or something like that there," said Josef.

"Or home. You could just leave and go back to England," said Peter.

Becky felt wistful for a moment. *England - home with her parents and her brothers. She could just forget the whole thing, just say it hadn't worked out here. Return to a comfortable life. Safe and secure.* She thought about what had been done to Teresa and all those other girls and how Michael had deceived her. "No. No I won't go home. I couldn't help Teresa but I'm not going to let this happen to anyone else. As for Michael and Troy I've got a score to settle with them. Anyway in case you've forgotten there's a hurricane coming. Let's face it no-ones going any where."

"There must be someone who can help you. Someone who's lived here a long time, someone with money. A person who can protect you, who you can trust."

"I don't think I know anyone like that."

"Think, Becky. There must be someone. What about the doctors? Surely there's one you can trust? Someone who can help, who will know what to do."

"There's Stefano...but no... I'm not sure about him. I don't think there's anyone... God it's such a mess."

"Look, it's late now. You can't go back to your flat. You don't want to risk Michael coming round, he could be suspicious and you might let the cat outa the bag. With you disappearing, he may have guessed that the game's up."

"So he could be trying to find me?"

"Becky, I'm sorry but you need to be real careful, you knows all the wrong people."

"Well, thank God I know you two and Mari," Becky said, with a sad smile.

"We're all tired now. Why don't you go sleep with Mari? She won't mind, we'll think of something by the morning. Everything will look better then."

"Are you sure?"

"Yeah. You'll see. Let's all just sleep on it."

After an hour or so Becky crept into Mari, who was by now already asleep.

"Mama," Mari muttered as Becky pulled her close glad of her company and warmth as she snuggled into her. As she drifted off to sleep totally exhausted she thought, *maybe...yes maybe there was someone.*

If she'd pulled back the shutters and looked out she'd have seen a red Alfa Romeo slowly driving past.

Chapter 15

This is radio Grand Bahama. It's the nineteenth of October and I guess you all know what the weather's like! Hurricane Bertha, she's dead on course for us now and we expect her to hit in the next twenty four hours. If you haven't got your supplies of food, water and torches in, you'd best go get them straight away. Don't forget to put sellotape across your windows so that if they gets blown in they won't break all over the floor. Keep listening to radio Grand Bahama - your sunshine station.

Isabella woke to find she'd fallen asleep and spent the night in her hard upright chair. Her face was more gaunt than before and her hands trembled as she pushed them through her long unkempt hair. She'd seen the car fire and explosions yesterday and she knew that it was somehow connected with THE MAN. THE GIRL too was here with Josef and Mari. Isabella sensed that the danger was close, starting to engulf them. She was no longer sure if she could stop it.

Going out into the yard the wind whipped at her hair and the rain stung her face. Taking out a sharp knife from her pocket she cut the herbs she needed. Back inside she ground them up with a pestle and mortar. The chanting was starting in her head as she added them to the chalice.

She opened the drawer and took out the figure and the fifth pin. She started to chant aloud. The howling of the wind outside obliterated the sound.

Becky woke early with a start sitting bolt upright on the hard mattress on the floor. Mari slept beside her, her arms spread wide a cherubic smile on her face. She looked beautiful. Her dark eyelashes were impossibly long and her hair had been braided with brightly coloured beads. Becky gently kissed her sleeping head and pulled her close.

The horror of the last few days started to come back to her in a jolting slide show of images, each one worse than the one before - being on the beach and realising smugglers had arrived, hiding under the boat. Seeing Troy. Finding the drugs in Michael's flat. Hearing his car draw up, having to play the devoted girlfriend. Josef's phone call. Running to Teresa's car. The explosion. Flames and glass. Screaming.

Mari stirred. Becky found she was gripping her tightly as tears silently pouring down her face. As she loosened her grip more memories slid their innocuous way into her mind. Going into the staff room that very first time - Teresa turning around to greet her. Teresa's red hair falling out of its grips, a smile splitting her face. "What's your name? Where are you from? Have you got a boyfriend?" Teresa's bubbly laugh and that first trip to the beach for snorkelling.

If only she hadn't gone to the bar that night. If only she hadn't had that lift and gone to the beach with Troy. She might not have met Michael; Michael who she'd thought was so wonderful, who turned out to be a drug smuggler. For God's sake he'd even used her as a cover on his trips to pick the drugs up.

He'd deceived her. What else had he done that she didn't know about? She thought back over their times together, on the beach, at his apartment, the trip on the launch. A thought hit her then. *Where was he when she saw the man downstairs having oral sex with Suzy? The man with blond hair. No, it wasn't possible - was it?* She remembered then, that when she'd gone up on deck, he was nowhere to be seen, he'd said he'd gone to get them a drink...

How stupid she'd been. How in love. For all she knew he could be working with Troy. God what a mess!

And Teresa, poor Teresa. Why hadn't they done something about that petrol leak? Had Teresa really been having an abortion here in Eight Mile Rock? Thinking back, Becky realised that Teresa had been quiet lately, *she should have asked her what was wrong. She'd failed her.*

She felt determined now to sort it all out, she was certain that it was Sister Carey doing the abortions. *She would expose her, and Troy and Michael. There was no way that she was going to just slink back to England. She'd show them that she wasn't just a silly naive girl who'd messed up.*

The rain was drumming hard on the roof and she shivered. There was a leak in one corner and rain dribbled down a dreary white washed wall. There were no toys for Mari, except for the tatty woollen doll which she clutched to her even in her sleep. Becky realised how little she knew of the lives of the people working and living around her, and she felt ashamed.

In her mind she kept going over and over the people she knew, wondering who could help her. There was only one person she could think of. She didn't really have any choice.

Gently she disentangled herself from Mari and quickly got dressed. Going through into the next room, she found Josef making coffee on a tiny oil stove.

"Becky! How you doin'? You, sleep OK?" A big smile broke across his face. "You, want some coffee?"

"Yes, and yes please. Where's Peter?"

"He go get some water an stuff. They say this hurricane's headed straight for us."

Becky looked worried. "Will you be OK?" She looked around the flimsy house.

"Yeah, don't you worry none 'bout us. We's all off to the Bethel Baptist church. They say it stood through the last tropical storm. Anyways, might as well be close to the Lord when it hits eh?" he laughed, a chuckling warm sound. "You too, Becky you needs to come with us."

"Thanks, Josef but there's something I have to do first. I know who to go to now and I need to go while the phone lines are still up." She drank the coffee that Josef had made. "Damn it! I've hardly got any gas in the car."

"I think you should stay here anyway, Becky till after the storm."

"Thanks, Josef don't worry about me, I'll be fine. If I can get some gas, I'll return. Or I can take shelter at the hospital, I might be needed to help out."

"OK. You needn't worry about the gas. Peter keeps a little out the back for lighting fires and things. We guessed you were going to insist on going, so he's put some in for you - not much. You sure you have to go?"

"Yes, I'm very sure. We can't let these people get away with what they're doing."

"Tell you what, I'll come with you, Becky. You ain't safe."

"No. You've done enough. I don't want you to get involved. Mari needs you here." Becky looked around the room, at the sagging threadbare sofa, two hard wooden chairs, a table, a stove and a picture of Christ on the cross. "I'll be back, Josef I promise. Back to see you and Peter and little Mari. Back to help."

She went across and kissed him on the cheek. A deep blush spread under his dark skin. Becky hesitated. *It was safe here.* She thought of Troy, turned quickly and opened the door.

"Take care, Becky! Take care!" Josef shouted after her.

She opened the door and the wind slammed it backwards out of her grasp. Josef came and grabbed it, looked at her anxiously and managed to pull it to behind her. It was difficult to catch her breath against the strength of the wind and she fought her way to the car through driving rain. The sky was black with clouds and she thought that Grand Bahama had never looked as threatening as it did that morning.

She drove away from Eight Mile Rock across the island to an altogether different area. Hibiscus grew down the central reservation of a tarmacked road and individual large white houses could just be glimpsed at the bottom of drives fringed by oleanders. Behind high walls and through the security gates, you could see green lawns, fountains, sculptures and huge swimming pools.

Becky finally reached the house she wanted and drew up outside its security gates. Its high white washed walls were topped off with a sprinkling of jagged glass embedded into the concrete. Large notices abounded warning of cameras and guard dogs. She sat in the car for several minutes and noticed her hands were trembling. *No, they're not going to get away with this,* she thought, and got out of the car and rang the bell in the security entrance system.

Three massive Rottweilers came racing through the grounds, barking and snarling, jumping up at the gates trying to reach her. Becky took two steps back in alarm. A disembodied woman's voice came from a speaker, "Mr Silver's residence. How may we assist you?"

"Can you tell him it's, Becky, Becky Lewis, please. From the hospital. Err... I need to speak to him urgently."

"Wait one moment please."

The minutes passed. Becky looked back down the road twirling her hair nervously, it wouldn't do for Michael to turn up and ask her what she was doing. At last she heard a whistle being blown and the salivating dogs turned away and with one last snarl ran off back towards the house. The voice said, "Please drive up to the house, Mr Silver will see you."

The doors swung silently open. Becky drove up to a large two storied white house, its porch supported by marble pillars. Immaculate lawns framed a pool with a thatched bar next to it. As she drew up the huge oak door was opened by a maid in a navy uniform and a white apron. Becky looked around to check the dogs had gone and she got out.

"Come in Ma'am. Mr Silver will see you in the lounge." Becky's feet sank into a deep cream coloured carpet in the entrance hall. As she was looking around at the guilt framed oil paintings of landscapes that lined the walls, Suzy came down the mahogany staircase.

A vast amount of leg showed from under a red silk dressing gown. Her blonde hair was tangled and mascara stained underneath her eyes.

"Hiya, honey. I know, you, don't I? You coming to the party with us?"

"Party? Err... No."

"That's a shame. We're going to the Anchor Inn for the hurricane party. Everyone's going. Should be a real laugh."

"No, I just wanted a quick word with your husband."

"I recognise you now. You're the one with the cute boyfriend. What's his name? Micky. That's it isn't it? He's something else, he..."

"Suzy! Shouldn't you be getting changed?" Mr Silver's voice boomed out as he came into the hall. "Daisy, go and make sure all the windows are shuttered," he motioned to the maid. Turning to Becky he smiled, "Well, this is an unexpected pleasure, would you like a drink?"

"That's a real good idea," said Suzy. Mr Silver ignored her.

"No, No. I'm sorry to have bothered you, maybe I shouldn't have come."

"No, don't be silly. It's always a pleasure to see a work colleague." He moved to Becky and took her arm. "Suzy, go and put some clothes on while I have a word with this young lady. You can drink at the pub."

"Gee, you're such a drag."

"Suzy, they won't serve you dressed like that." She shrugged and turned and went back upstairs.

"Come on, come into the lounge."

"Well, if you're sure."

They went into an enormous lounge with huge French windows, now shuttered, that normally would have overlooked the pool. A vase of fresh flowers sat on a white grand piano, a mahogany desk was next to a display of fine china.

"Sit down, Becky. Make yourself at home." Mr Silver, gestured to an antique looking chaise- lounge, two enormous leather settees and four chairs. Becky hesitated and then gratefully sank into a huge armchair.

"Thanks."

"Are you certain you don't want a drink? If you don't mind me saying you look as if you could do with one."

"No thanks, really." Becky became horribly aware that she was still wearing the track suit she'd put on yesterday, that she hadn't washed and her hair was uncombed.

"You don't mind if I do?"

"No, of course not."

He went across to a decanter and poured himself a scotch.

"What's the problem then, Becky?"

"I don't know where to start."

"Come on, we're friends surely, not just work colleagues. Why don't you try the beginning?" he gave a short laugh and smiled at her encouragingly.

Becky took a deep breath. She was here now. What else could she do?

"OK. I guess it started when I first arrived here. When I met Troy and Michael..."

She told him everything. Mr Silver walked up and down looking concerned and shaking his head, occasionally muttering, "Disgusting," or "Dear, dear."

"You poor girl. Thank goodness you've come to me."

"I'm sorry, I didn't want to bother you, but I couldn't think who else to go to."

"No, you were right to come. Your friends were quite correct, we need to get you somewhere safe. Let me think." He frowned for a moment and then smiled, "Don't worry, I know just the person. He can look after you until this damn hurricane's passed over and then we'll get you out on the first flight to Miami. I know the chief of police there personally. We'll get you safe and nail these bastards."

Becky felt so relieved it was wonderful to have told someone who understood and who could help. "Thank you, thanks so much."

"That's OK, it's my pleasure. You've been really brave, it's a delight to meet someone who's not afraid to stand up for what's right. These drugs are a curse. Damn things are flooding the island. These men sound like nasty pieces of work all of them. As for Sister Carey - I never did get on with her. We'll get her sorted out once this hurricane's passed, don't you worry. Meantime you go back to your apartment whilst I get in touch with Luther."

"Luther?"

"Luther Clarkson, he's a sergeant in the police here. I'd trust him with my life."

"Yes, I know him. He came into the Emergency Room after trying to arrest some drug dealers. He was lucky not to have been killed."

"Yes, he's a good chap to have around. It's great that you know him, Becky. You'll recognise him. But listen whatever you do don't answer the door to anyone else. These guys will stop at nothing. Your Michael's obviously heavily involved and who knows who else as well."

"Tony, are we going or what? Come on we're going to miss all the fun." Suzy tottered into the room on high heels wearing a boob tube and mini skirt. "You too, honey. We don't want to be stuck here in this weather."

Mr Silver looked her up and down and sighed. "It may have escaped your notice, sweet-heart, but there's a hurricane coming."

"Well don't I just know it? I was booked in to have a manicure this morning. Are you sure you don't want to come with us, honey? We could talk girly things..."

"Sorry, Suzy but I've got to go. Thanks, Mr Silver. Thanks a lot."

"Don't forget. No-one but Luther."

Michael drove slowly past the supermarket frowning, his face pale and set. Some men were nailing boards over the windows. It seemed that no one on the island had really believed that a hurricane was coming up until now. He'd come here yesterday looking for Becky and noticed that there were still plenty of supplies of food and drinking water. He'd quickly picked up a few things himself whilst he was there. He knew too well from living in Miami what damage a hurricane could do. His problem was that he was much more worried about the damage that Becky could do.

Michael had tried to find her yesterday but she seemed to have vanished into thin air. Margaret told him she'd borrowed her car and driven off in a hurry. As soon as he'd got up this morning he'd gone to her flat, but there was still no sign of her or Margaret's car and the flat looked to be empty. *God damn it! It was a small island where could she be? She knew way too much and he had to find her.*

The woman in Eight Mile Rock put both her hands to the small of her back and stretched. *Carrying out abortions was hard on the body,* she reflected - *all that bending over; she reckoned they were lucky these girls to have someone like her doin' a social service. Ah well, in spite of the coming storm she reckoned she could fit a couple in today. Soon she'd have made enough for a retirement in Florida, where no-one would ask inconvenient questions about the source of her wealth.*

There was a hesitant knock on the door. A girl aged about sixteen stood there shivering in a thin cotton frock.

"I'm Rose - my daddy sent me."

"Come on in, girl. Lord knows it's dangerous out there today!" She chuckled and took the girl through to the kitchen.

Becky arrived back at the flat exhausted but buoyed up by the thought that soon she would be safe and she could get Michael and Troy arrested. *Thank goodness it looked as if Margaret and Alex weren't in. They must have decided to go to a hotel after all to sit the hurricane out.* Becky didn't fancy trying to explain what she'd been doing in Margaret's car for the last twenty four hours, or why it was covered in mud from the deteriorating state of the island's roads.

She ran upstairs and locked the door behind her leaning back on it she sighed heavily. Walking into the lounge she pondered - *was it really only yesterday that she'd left? It seemed as though she'd been a different person then.* She thought of Michael and bit her lip, *she'd really loved him, how could he....how could he be a drug smuggler...maybe he'd even been having sex with Suzy, whilst she was sleeping just above them on the launch...*a tear slid down her face. *It felt like something out of a book. As for poor Teresa, why hadn't she told her what was going on? God, what a mess it all was.*

Going into the bathroom she was shocked when she saw her reflection in the mirror. Hair wet and clinging to her face, no make-up, her clothes bedraggled. She'd physically aged so much in the last three days. She drank some water straight from the tap. *Stop feeling sorry for yourself and pull yourself together. Luther will probably be here any minute.* She splashed her face with hot water and dried her hair roughly with a towel. She felt cold and changed into a pair of jeans and a jumper. There was a banging on the door and she caught her breath. Going to the small 'spy hole' in the door she saw Luther standing there.

"Thank God! Come on in, Luther."

"Becky, it's great to see you again. This is some mess ain't it?" he said, looking concerned.

"Yes, I'm sorry, I seem to have mucked everything up."

"No, no. Don't you go thinking that. You haven't mucked anything up. We're going to put some evil characters behind bars because of you. I've already got my men out looking for this Troy and Michael. Don't you worry. You've done exactly the right thing." He laughed, "Hell! I might even get a promotion out a this." He walked into the lounge. His eyes were everywhere as he spoke looking around the flat. He went to the French windows and checked the balcony. "We can't be too careful, Becky. Are you ready? We'd best get goin'."

"I'll just get a few clothes and my passport." Becky went into the bedroom and started to put some clothes and her passport into a small bag. Then she heard it. A familiar noise. The sound of an Alfa Romeo engine, followed by a screech of brakes. "Oh my God! I think Michael's just drawn up outside!"

Luther cautiously pulled back the curtain a fraction. "Is that him?"

"Yes. It's him."

"Shit! Do you know - does he carry a gun, Becky?"

"Yes, no, well sometimes, I think."

"I guess we'll have to go out the back way then."

"Back way? What? Back way?"

"This one. Come on." He grabbed Becky by the arm and rushed her through the lounge.

Michael was shouting now from the bottom of the stairs, "Becky! Becky! It's me Michael!" They heard his footsteps pounding up the stairs.

Luther unlocked the French windows and went onto the balcony. "Quick get out here."

"What now?"

"This'll do. You got a head for heights?"

"What!"

He'd taken the key from the inside of the door and was quickly locking it from the outside. "It's easy, Becky. You just need to climb from this balcony, across the gap, to next door. We'll get in there and hide 'til he's gone. I don't want a show-down while you're in my care. Come on let's go!" He took Becky's bag and threw it across the one foot gap.

"I'm not sure if I can do it," she said looking at the gap and the twenty foot drop below them.

"Becky you have to! Or we're both gonna be dead meat!"

"Oh, My God! OK .OK."

"Get up here." He helped her and held her steady as she half knelt on her rail whilst grasping the drain pipe in her hands. She got one leg over the rail of the next balcony. "That's it you can do it, girl."

Bang! Bang! Bang! Michael was pounding the front door.

"Becky I need to speak to you! Becky I know you're in there!"

Becky looked down at the ground and wobbled. "Oh shit!"

"For Christ sake put your other leg across I've got you. Jesus! You're gonna get us both killed!"

"Becky, answer the God damn door! I know you're in there! I've seen Margaret's car. I can explain. I can explain everything!"

"You bet he can, girl," muttered Luther.

"For Christ's sake! Open the fucking door!" There was a large crash as he tried to break the door down. Becky grabbed out for the other railing and half fell across onto the next door balcony.

Luther quickly followed her and wrapped his hand in a handkerchief. He broke a small pane of glass. The sound of wood splintering could clearly be heard, as Michael succeeded in breaking the door down next door.

Luther reached through and opened the French windows. He pushed Becky inside the empty flat and closed the curtains behind them. He bundled her into the kitchen and whispered, "Shhh, not a word."

Becky stood shaking in the kitchen. She put both hands to her face and rocked slightly to and fro. Michael could be heard rampaging through the flat next door.

"Becky! Becky! Damn! Damn! Damn!" They heard the sound of him shaking the doors of the French windows. "Christ!" he shouted. He strode through the flat and slammed the front door. His footsteps clattered down the stairs. The noise of the Alfa Romeo engine starting up filled the air and with a roar he drove off.

"Thank God!" said Becky. Luther put his arm around her and she cried.

"Come on. Everytin's gonna be all right. I promise, you. Let's go, 'fore he comes back."

"Thanks Luther. Thank you so much. I never thought I could be so scared, especially of Michael. He must have guessed that I found the drugs. God, this is such a mess."

"Don't worry you're safe with me."

"I don't know what I'd have done without you and Mr Silver."

"That's OK. Jus' doin' my job. And Mr Silver, you can rely on him in a crisis." Luther went out first, carefully looking around him, before gesturing to Becky to follow, "Come on. Let's go."

They ran down the steps to Luther's car a yellow blacked out saloon which was parked around the corner. "Get in the back and lie down, Becky."

Becky wrenched open the back door and got in as Luther got in the driver's seat. As she lay down she suddenly realised there was someone else sat in the front passenger seat. She frowned puzzled.

"Luther? You didn't say anyone was with you?"

"Didn't I? I guess I forgot. This man's what you might call a colleague of mine." The man in the passenger seat turned around to look at her.

"Well just looky who we've got here," came a familiar voice. Smiling at her from the front passenger seat was - Troy.

Chapter 16

*This is a special announcement from radio Grand Bahama.
Hurricane Bertha's going to hit us in the next few hours. It has
been upgraded to a category three. We expect winds between one
hundred and eleven and one hundred and thirty miles an hour.
Yeah, you heard right, one hundred and thirty. Wow! This is gonna
be some storm! You all make sure you got a big supply of drinking
water and food. The government urges you to go to a place of
safety. We are going off the air but, God willing we will be back as
soon as possible for more records and reports. This is Virginia
Groves signing off from radio Grand Bahama, the sunshine
station. May the Good Lord protect us all.*

As Becky got into Luther's car, the staff at the hospital,
were wondering why she hadn't turned up for work. In the Royal
as many patients as possible had been sent home. The cook in the
kitchen was busy cooking up fish heads with peas and rice, for the
few remaining staff and patients. Clifford wandered around with a
roll of tape, sticking pieces across the glass of the windows.

"Do you think that's gonna do much good Clifford?" asked
Kathleen, a new and young Nurses Aide.

"Sure thing, honey. If the wind's real hard and the glass
break, it won't all crash in."

"Are we gonna be OK?"

"'Course we will. You got nothing to worry about. I'm
stayin' the whole time."

The nurse smiled and moved off. Clifford thought privately that sticking tape on the windows was a complete waste of time. *The God damn roof was probably gonna blow off anyway, but hell, he wasn't paid to think. Who knows, if Kathleen got real scared maybe she'd like to shelter with him,* he'd got a place staked out - in the linen cupboard at the far end of the corridor.

In the pub most people had arrived early for the hurricane party. The rugby club was in full swing, pints were lined up on the bar; a rendition of 'She'll be coming round the mountain,' replete with actions was threatening to drown out all other conversation.

The people present were mostly ex-pats, they thought that there was no need to move down to the basement as yet, but those not involved in the singing were enthusiastically helping to move bottles and cans of alcohol down there.

Chris, the rugby club member who'd been chatting up Teresa that first time that Becky went there, noticed that Suzy was wandering about on her own.

"Hi, there. Are you all alone in the storm, so to speak?"

"Not exactly, honey. My husband's supposed to be parking the car, but it's sure taking him a while."

"Can I get you a drink while you're waiting?"

"You certainly can, darlin'." Suzy touched his arm lightly and clambered up on the bar stool revealing her long legs. A wave of Chanel Number Five engulfed Chris.

He smiled. It looked as though the party was shaping up nicely.

Back in Luther's car, Becky heard the sound of the central locking device. She sat upright on the seat as Luther started up the engine. "Luther! What the hell is going on? Don't you know who this is?"

"He knows alright, sugar. We're brothers in arms ain't we, Luth'."

"What! What's he talking about? Luther, what's happening?"

Luther looked at her in the rear view mirror. "Girl, you shouldn't have stuck your nose in where it wasn't wanted." He drove the car out of the complex.

Becky's eyes widened. "No! NO. It's not possible. Dear God! Let me out!" she screamed. She frantically started to try to open the car doors and pounded the blacked out windows.

"Heh. Get the little bitch to stop that, she gonna damage my car!"

"I don't bloody..."

She heard a click.

"Shut it, girl!" said Troy, pointing a gun straight at her between the front seats. "If you know what's good for you, you'll sit back and act like a real nice lady."

Troy's face was contorted and angry now. Becky shrank against the seat. "You've been nothing but trouble since you came here. You, with your hoity toity, posh English accent. Looking down on guys like me."

"That's not true. I've never looked down on you. What possible trouble could I be to you? I've never done anything to harm you."

"Oh yeah. Well first of all you were a little prick teaser, next up you're sneaking around on the beach and now you've gone blabbing your mouth off to anyone who'll listen."

"I only went to the beach to clear my head. How was I to know you were going to turn up there?"

"Yeah. You're real fond of the beach aren't, you?"

"Luther why aren't you doing something?"

"Christ, you're thick, Miss High and Mighty! You still haven't worked it out have you?" Troy gave a short laugh.

Becky frowned. "Luther! It was you wasn't it? The other man on the beach. Bringing the drugs ashore the night before last."

"Finally, she gets it," Troy laughed.

"Troy, your mouth flaps too much."

"She isn't going to be telling anyone."

"I don't know what you think you're going to do. You can't get away with this. Luther, you know that I've told Mr Silver all about the whole thing."

Luther looked at her in the rear view mirror again. "Sure do, girl. You still don't understand, do you?"

"Oh my God! Mr Silver, he's involved as well?"

"Involved! He's the main man, honey," said Troy. "You see, your Mr Tony Silver's, had a bit of a name change. He's actually Antonio Da Silva. His family shipped over to America from Sicily in the last century. But you know what? He's got real good links with the old country and an even better cover here. Why, he's the surgeon doing great works for the poor and needy. Right under everyone's noses. How do you think he got that fancy house and trailer trash wife of his?"

"Oh my God! I can't believe it."

"Well you'd better start believing."

Becky noticed that they were driving on minor roads away from the centre of Freeport. The roads were deserted.

"But, Luther you came into the ER. You were knifed by the dealers, how on earth did you get involved?"

"You really want to know?"

"Yes. Yes I really want to know.

"OK then I'll tell you. That stupid arsed Johnson tryin' to get promotion that's how I got myself knifed. He'd almost got it worked out. He knew that information about our patrols was leaking like a sieve outa the station. Being young and keen, he thought he was real clever. He figured it was Woods, on account of him bein' there so long, an' bein' a lazy sod, an' takin bribes an all."

"So?"

"So, he hatches a plan, comes and tells me, his superior officer. 'I got it all worked out,' he says. 'I'm gonna drive on my own, real quiet around the beaches that are most deserted around two a.m. I'm starting tonight at Sunset Cove and then I'm gonna work my way along the shoreline'.

'That ain't a good idea, I tell him. You could get yourself killed.' He's insistent though and he starts giving me a strange look. So I says, 'OK you can't go on your own, boy. I'll come with you.' 'Cause damn it, he's got beginners luck and we got a shipment all fixed up to come in there that very night."

"Oh my God!"

"Like the damn fool he was, he grateful. 'Gee thanks, Luther. Are you sure?'" Luther laughed a bitter laugh. Becky felt her stomach lurch.

"So off we goes to Sunset Cove."

"Jesus," muttered Becky.

"We was walking down a narrow track to the beach, he droning on an' on about that fool wife of his nagging him for promotion and how he dun got her pregnant again. Well, I'd just about had enough of listening to all this garbage so I gets out my knife. I was just about to take him when some damn lizard or somethin' rustled in the bush, he that jumpy he turned straight around to me.

'I hear sometin'!' he says. Then he see it don't he? Sees the knife in my hand and for a fool boy he caught on real quick.

'What the hell you playin' at?' he says. Then it dawn on him. I see the whole thing play right across his face. All he said was, 'It's you, Luther! Christ!'

Well the shit hit the fan then. Damn fool lunged at me and made a grab for the knife. We wrestled on the sand and that bastard was younger and stronger and before I knew it he'd got the knife and done stabbed me."

"Hell, Luth'," said Troy.

"Yeah,well I lay moaning on the sand, 'I'm dyin' I can't get my breath,' I said. Christ, I wasn't lying, it hurt like hell. He had this sort a scared look on his face, muttered, 'Gees, Luther.' I said, 'If you don't go get me some help they'll do you for manslaughter at least. I'm dyin' here.' I took my hand off my chest and it was covered in blood. Well, that did it."

"What happened?"

"'Ok. I'll get an ambulance,' he said, and the fool boy turned and started to run away up the beach..."

"And?" said Becky.

"And! And, what do you think?"

"Oh my God, you shot him!" said Becky her hand went to her mouth.

"Sure thing."

Troy chuckled in the front. "Yep, that's one son of a bitch that isn't gonna bother us again."

"Then, you came in and acted like you were a hero. My God, I helped save your life," said Becky.

"Never said I wasn't grateful, girl, did I?"

Becky felt physically sick. She huddled back in the seat as far away as she could get, thoughts jumbling through her head. *What an idiot she'd been. How easily she'd been taken in. And now, what to do? What to do? Who knew where she was? How could she escape? What were they going to do with her?*

She knew the answer to that question. It was obvious. *If Luther had shot Johnson in cold blood they must be taking her somewhere quiet to do the same thing. Luther had no guilt and Troy - he was loving this. He obviously still harboured a grudge ever since she fought him off on the beach and Michael had turned up. Michael...She couldn't bear to think about his involvement. Maybe he'd known Troy even back then.* None of it made any sense. Troy put the car radio on. The record, 'Brown Girl In The Ring,' was playing. The words mocked her. She was in a ring, wasn't she?

Now that she just lay back in the seat, Troy seemed less alert, half turned around in his own seat to face her. He was smoking holding the cigarette in one hand and the gun in the other. The hand holding the gun rested on the upright of the seat, the gun still pointing at her. She looked from the gun to him. Thought about trying to wrest it off him, but she knew from past experience how strong he was and, there was Luther to contend with as well.

Her eyes lit on the handbrake. She was desperate. *Maybe... maybe it was worth a try.* They went around a sharp bend. She made a sudden lunge for it and pulled it on hard. The car screeched as the back wheels locked up.

"You stupid cow." Troy made a grab for her arm, but missed as the car swung wildly.

"What the fu..."

Skidding on the wet road the car careered off into the bush. Becky screamed as Luther fought with the wheel and a huge palm tree reared up in front of them. With a mighty crash the car hit it head on.

No-one spoke for a few seconds. The bonnet had sprung up and emitted a hissing noise. Luther had banged his head and he started groaning in the front.

"My shoulder," Troy muttered.

The doors were buckled, Becky wrenched hers open. She ran down the road and into the bush. She ran as she'd never run before. Her lungs were bursting and she was sobbing. Bushes caught at her clothes, scratched her face.

"Bitch! The bitch has got away!"

"Follow her!"

It was muddy underfoot and she slipped and skidded as she ran. Her heart was pounding in her ears, her breathing ragged. The rain was a solid screen of grey. Then she fell. Pain shot through her knee. She got up and tried to run. The pain seared through her and her pace slowed. She could hear them just behind. Seeing some bushes she dragged herself in as far as she could.

"Where the fuck is she?" Luther's voice was close at hand.

"She can't be far."

They were crashing through the undergrowth nearby. She could just make out Troy's legs as he strode past the bush. She made herself into as small a ball as she could. Her breathing sounded so loud to her and her heart was banging in her chest. She heard the bushes rustle close by.

"Well, well. Just look what we got here."

Luther's hand grabbed her by the hair and pulled her out. Becky screamed and fought and kicked him, but he was far too strong for her. He got her down onto the ground. Her face hit the hard earth.

"No, Luther, please."

He grunted and grabbing her arms, dragged her hands round behind her and tied them with some rope out of his pocket. Then he pulled her to her feet by one arm.

Troy approached. "You bitch! You're more trouble than you're worth!" He took out his gun and took aim. Becky froze. The world was reduced to the barrel of his gun.

"No! Not here, you bloody fool! We don't want her body lying around for some wild dog to drag out for all the world to see. We'll take her to the beach."

They each took an arm and dragged Becky between them back to the car.

"Please, I won't say anything," she sobbed.

"Just shut it, girl," said Luther.

He opened the boot and threw her in.

It was hot and dark. Suffocating. Becky struggled to breathe. Her knee hurt and she shook from head to foot. She frantically tried to push the boot open with her shoulder but it was no use. She fell back and tried to still her breathing. Tried to quell her panic. Tried to think.

After five or ten minutes the car stopped. She heard the doors open and slam shut and held her breath waiting for them to open the boot. To her surprise they seemed to have moved a little distance away talking, but she couldn't catch what they were saying.

There was a noise and light suddenly flooded in. Rain was pouring down. Luther grabbed her roughly. "This is where you get out, bitch." He dragged her along. She realised she was on the beach at the East End of the island, the romantic spot where Michael had first made love to her. They even passed the place where they'd lain together. The images flashed through her mind, of them laughing, drinking champagne and making love that first magical time.

She was soaking. Through the rain she saw Troy just in front of them. He went to where a jetty was being built and picked up what looked to be an enormously heavy large concrete slab. She watched in horror, unable to comprehend what was happening.

Troy put the slab down and walked the short distance back to them. The rain was driving and his hair was plastered to his face. He looked ugly and wild, his pupils were huge. She realised he was enjoying this.

"You sure we haven't got time to have a bit of fun with her first, Luther?"

"For Christ sake! Stop thinking about your dick! We're already late for a pick up. Jesus! My stomach hurts!"

"Cool it, man! No harm in asking. You OK? You look a bit crap."

"Yeah. Come on. Let's get rid of her."

Troy had produced a length of rope from under his arm and he started tying it to the concrete.

Becky had been looking at her feet as Luther dragged her along. She looked up then and saw it. A matter of three yards away. The Blue Hole.

She looked, from the Blue Hole, to Troy tying the rope. For a few seconds she couldn't take in the enormity of it. What they were going to do with her.

She gasped. "Oh my God! NO!" she screamed, fighting and kicking Luther. He had her down again in an instant. "Help! Help! No! No! NO!" She was still screaming as they tied the rope around her waist. They started to drag her and the concrete towards the hole. The water within it swirled. Deep and dark.

"Thought you liked swimming, Becky," said Troy.

"No! NO!"

They drew closer to the edge.

Suddenly Luther let go of her and fell to the sand. "Christ!" he said and clutched his stomach. He bent double and started vomiting blood. Dark red blood. Splattering his face, his hands, his clothes. Pouring from his mouth in a dark stream. "Arghh!" he gurgled and collapsed. Blood stained the sand. He lay face down. Silent.

"Christ, man! What's wrong?" said Troy.

Becky got to her knees and looked in fascinated horror.

Troy went across to him. Pushed him with his foot. When he rolled over she could see. Luther was dead.

Chapter 17

With the hurricane only a matter of hours away now, Eight Mile Rock was almost deserted. One or two people were refusing to go to a shelter or the church, obstinately saying they were going to stay and protect their property.

Earlier Josef had taken Mari to the local church, Rachel was going there and so were Mari's new friends. He thought it would help to distract her from being frightened.

In one hut a lamp was still lit. A woman moved the kitchen table with the filthy cloth and prised up a floorboard underneath. Reaching in, she fished out an ancient and battered tin, the logo on it long since worn off. She took out some ampoules of pethidine, opened them and emptied them down the sink. The glass she ground up under her feet before sweeping it up and putting it in with her rubbish. "Seems like a waste," she muttered, thinking of the risk she'd run obtaining them at the hospital. However she wouldn't need them anymore and she certainly didn't want customs finding them on her.

Then she smiled as she took out the money. She knew exactly how many hundred dollar bills she had, but she couldn't resist counting them again. It took some time. Then she stuffed them in a bag along with a change of clothes. The wind was screeching around now, the rain loud on the roof and she realised she'd better get herself to the very private shelter that she and her boyfriend had organised.

Becky looked without speaking from Luther's inert body, to Troy. Troy turned back to her a smile on his face. He gave a short laugh, "Well, well, here's a turn up for the book. Look's like our Luther really did have that ulcer he was always whinging on about." He took a cigarette out and lit it in a leisurely fashion cupping it in his hands to shelter it from the wind and rain. He looked Becky up and down and then looked across at the Blue Hole.

"Troy... Please..."

"Yeah, Pretty please," he said mockingly. "I bet you can be real nice when you want to, can't you? I bet you were *real* nice to Michael, weren't you?"

"Troy, look I'm sorry I've been an idiot. I won't tell anyone. Just let me go and we'll call it quits, eh?"

He gave a short laugh. "I'm not thinking of letting you go anywhere, honey."

Becky was still sat next to the slab of concrete and was frantically trying to untie her hands behind her back as she spoke.

"Well if you don't let me go, Michael will guess it's you and come looking for you."

"That piece of shit! Haven't you worked him out yet? He's in on it. I never wanted him in, but we needed a new courier. Mr Silver reckoned he was a good bet, on account of having a job that was the perfect cover for making trips out and about, plus the bastard knew how to fly a plane. Michael needed the money because of his gambling debts and hell, honey, you made the perfect cover. Romantic weekends on the Out Islands, wasn't it?" he laughed.

Becky started to cry.

"So you see we don't have to worry about him too much."

He strolled across and crouched down beside her. "You want a cigarette? Don't you Brits have some cute custom to do with, 'the condemned man and last requests?' Only I guess it's the condemned woman in your case."

"No, no I don't smoke, you know I don't."

"Ah, yes course I should have remembered. It's your little friend that wanted a last cigarette."

"What are you talking about?"

Troy took a cigarette out of the packet in his top pocket. Lit it slowly and blew the smoke in her face. She turned her face away.

He cupped it roughly in his hand and turned it back to face him. "I'm talking about Teresa. Your so-called friend, Teresa."

"What about Teresa?"

"Yeah, well that was an unfortunate mistake. All your doing of course."

"Mistake? My doing? What are you talking about?"

"Well I may as well tell you. You've always been a nosey cow. You see, when I saw her car being driven away that night on the beach. I thought she was the only cunt that drove it. Naturally enough I thought it was her spying on us."

"Oh my God!"

"Yeah. Exactly. So when I found the car and her in it, in that God damn disgusting mess, I'm not a cruel guy, so I let her have a cigarette."

"What!" Becky's eyes were huge and she tried to pull away from him.

"Yeah. Sure was a shame about that petrol leak. Somehow, that cigarette...Well, it ended up on the back seat."

"You! You killed her! You knew that car was full of petrol fumes! Jesus Christ!"

"Well like I said, honey, it was all *your* fault."

"You're sick, Troy. Do you know that?"

"No, I don't think so. Seems to me, it was Luther that was sick. You didn't know that either, did you?"

"No. No I didn't."

"Yeah. You knew sweet FA. Anyways, this must be my lucky day. 'Cause not only has Luther just doubled my cut, it means that you and I can still have some fun," he licked his lips suggestively.

"You bastard!"

He untied the rope that attached Becky to the concrete. "Now that ain't nice is it?" Becky shrank away from him. "You know what, bitch? I could have you right here and now, but hell it's kinda wet out here ain't it? And, I've got a real important pick up on the other side of the island, that I'm already late for on account of you. So I think I'm going to be real good to you and keep you somewhere warm and dry, 'cause I'm sure going to savour a little treat with you later."

"You'll never get away with this."

"I don't see any cavalry coming over the hill, darlin'." He put his hand up Becky's T-shirt and started fondling her breasts.

"You little shit!" Becky spat in his face.

Troy wiped the spittle away slowly. Dragged her to her feet and without a word he drew back his hand. He hit her full across the face with the back of it. Becky staggered and fell back onto the sand. "You want to play rough we can do that too, sweetheart. I like a woman with a bit of spunk."

He grabbed her by the hair and pulled her along by it. She started screaming as clumps came out in his hands. With his other hand he took out his gun again. "I've had just about enough of you. Shut the fuck up, or I'll shut you up right now."

Becky gave a sob and stopped screaming. They'd reached a ramshackle hut at the back of the beach. A wooden door was padlocked and two large pieces of wood rested across the entrance on metal supports, keeping it closed.

Troy shot the padlock off. Becky screamed and staggered back. "I'll be back to have some fun with you, sweetheart! You'd better think about being nice to me. Real nice." He moved the wood, opened the door and threw her onto the floor inside.

"No, Troy! Please!"

He shut the door and she heard him putting the wood back across. Then he was gone. She lay crying on the floor. As her eyes got used to the dark she peered around the hut. She felt the sandy floor where she was sitting. She stood up with difficulty and barged into some tins, half a dozen plastic chairs that were sat on top of one another collapsed and sprawled over the floor, scratching her leg as they fell. She reached the back of the hut where there seemed to be three or four plastic tables.

She almost slipped on a plastic bag. *Maybe it held something that would help her get out.* It was difficult to get down onto the floor near it, she had to roll backwards and eventually she managed to grab it. Holding it in one hand she felt inside it with the other. Her hand touched a decaying mess of stinking sandwiches. She sat and cried - tears of frustration and fear. Then she rolled forwards onto her knees, wincing as she did so, and tried to stand, putting her weight on her good leg. She tried feeling around for objects with the other foot.

Her foot touched something metal. She got down onto the filthy floor again and felt the objects. They seemed to be heavy tins - probably paint. She tried to grab the plastic handle of one. It slipped from her grip. Getting hold of it again she scrambled to her feet and tried to bang it against the sides of the hut. It was hopeless. She let it fall from her hands.

She screamed, "Is anybody out there? Help! Help me! I'm in the hut!" There was nothing but the noise of the storm.

She peered into every corner. Frantic. Every nook and cranny. Every filthy edge of the hut. Felt under every table and chair. Straining her eyes. Crying and talking to herself. "Come on! Come on! There must be something! There must be!" And she realised that the light was worsening as the time passed and the noise of the storm outside was increasing. An hour must have gone by. Fighting nausea and breathlessness, she started to cry uncontrollably.

Suddenly there was a bang! The branch of a palm tree must have fallen onto the roof. She thought of Troy's inevitable return and was filled with panic. Taking deep breaths she sat on the floor and tried desperately to distract herself. Tried to remember what it was like when she first arrived in the Bahamas...

Time passed and the noise of the storm was building. Suddenly there was a loud, ripping, tearing noise followed by an enormous crash. The whole hut shook. Bricks and timber cascaded around Becky. She screamed and tried to protect her head with her hands. A piece of timber hit her left shoulder. The dust cleared and light filled the hut and Becky saw that a palm tree had crashed into the far end.

She got herself up onto her knees in the debris and then stood swaying and shocked for a minute, oblivious to the howling wind and rain. It suddenly hit her. *My chance, this is my chance!* Scrabbling through the debris, she tried to kick away the rotten wood and bricks with her good leg as she walked.

She emerged onto the sands. The wind whipped at her hair and the rain poured down. Her head was filled with the noise of the pounding waves. Looking around her quickly, she saw that the beach was empty of all life, even the birds seemed to have fled. She started to hobble along the beach breathless with the effort. Her injured knee was slowing her down and, it was hard to push against the wind with her hands tied behind her back.

Her eyes scanned the flotsam and jetsam on the beach. Going across to where the wind had piled up some rubbish she saw in amongst it a glint of glass. "Yes!" she shouted aloud as she saw the broken remains of a Becks beer bottle. She sat down clumsily next to it and managed to pick it up in her hands behind her back. She started to try to walk and cut the rope binding her hands at the same time, but she dropped the bottle. "Damn! Damn! Damn!" she swore aloud to herself. "Sit down and calm down. You can do this!" Easing herself back down onto the sand she reached for the broken glass, and managed to grab it. "Ow!" It had sliced her hand as she picked it up.

Looking back for any sign of Troy, she stood up and limped further along and to the back of the beach. She sat down and started to try to saw through the rope. Time was passing far too quickly. In spite of the wind and rain and being soaking wet she was sweating, her face was contorted with effort. "Come on. Come on! For Christ's sake! How can it be so difficult!" She glanced along the beach biting her lip and screwing up her eyes to see, as the sand flew around. At last! The rope frayed. "Thank God!" Her hands were free.

She looked up and between the palm trees at the back of the beach. There was a flash of a mirror and a glimpse of yellow. "Oh my God!" - Troy drove a yellow car.

She made her way as quickly as she could along the beach but the pain in her knee meant that her progress was slow. Far too slow. Any minute now he would reach the hut and find she'd gone.

Then she saw it. At the back of the beach under some trees - a small dinghy, its sails furled up next to it. *Someone must have left in one hell of a hurry.* She looked at the waves. They were almost five foot high and the sound of the surf was loud in her ears. The wind was blowing hard, at least force eight or nine she estimated but the hurricane hadn't yet arrived. She'd sailed some rough seas in her time. Once with her father they'd almost capsized when a sudden gale got up, but she'd never sailed in anything as fierce as this.

She looked back at the hut. Something moved. A speck of a figure was walking around. It had to be Troy. She got hold of the dinghy and began dragging it with a strength she didn't know she possessed down to the water's edge. The figure moved away from the hut to the bushes at the back. *Had he seen her yet*? Getting the sails, she made a massive effort and lifted them into place still furled.

The figure started to run in her direction. She pushed the boat into the water uncaring of the pain in her knee or the waves crashing around her. The boat surged back out again and she saw Troy clearly enough to recognise his green T-shirt.

Sobbing and grunting with the effort she pushed and heaved the boat back into the waves. Swung it around in the shallows and scrambled in. Struggling to keep her balance she pushed down the dagger board. There was a loud bang! Something whistled passed her head. She ducked instinctively. *Christ! He's shooting at me!* Taking hold of the tiller in one hand and the sheet for the sail in the other, she let the reefed sail out a fraction.

She looked back. Troy was only a matter of ten feet away now. She could see his white, grim set face, his snarling mouth. Feel his eyes boring into her, the depths of his hatred. He raised his gun and never taking his eyes off Becky's terrified face, took aim.

A massive wave reared up. Troy vanished underneath it. It almost engulfed the boat too but Becky struggled to control it and somehow they stayed upright. The wind filled the small amount of sail she'd let out and the boat took off. The beach blurred and the wind lashed Becky, as she strained with all her might to keep the sail in tight. She tacked from side to side as gusts of wind hit the tiny dinghy. The boat tipped at a forty five degree angle and she struggled to get her feet into the foot straps as she lay horizontally on the massive waves which threatened to swamp the dinghy.

She glanced back. Troy had disappeared. Gasping and panting she returned to the fearsome task of trying to keep the boat upright.

The waves were huge now and Becky glanced at the horizon continually. The sky was black and the clouds were low. A water spout suddenly erupted only feet away from her, "Shit!" she cried out, as the sea was siphoned up into the cloud like a mini typhoon of water. The sky, the sea and the rain merged into a grey wall. She knew from recent weather warnings, that near the eye wall of the hurricane, waves from all directions converged creating erratic crests. These could build on each other creating rogue waves which could reach one hundred and thirty feet. She needed to land and soon.

Through the waves and all engulfing greyness she glimpsed a low building on the shore. She headed for it, fighting to hold the sheet and sail in towards the shore. As she got closer, she realised it was Harry's Bar, which had a small jetty projecting into the water. She'd often been there to watch the sun set over a tranquil sea, whilst sipping one of the drinks so appropriately called Harry's Hurricanes.

She tried desperately now to tack her way towards the jetty. Gybing too early, the boat overshot it. She tried again. She was just feet from it, when suddenly a gust from a different direction took the boat out again. She was panting and sobbing.

Looking up she saw it. Coming straight at her. A wave ten feet high. It hit, hard and instantly. She was swept out of the boat and under the water, struggling and fighting, completely at its mercy. Tossed and turned by it, she was engulfed in a place of blackness.

Her head broke the surface and a massive jolt went through her body as she slammed into the jetty. She reached out and grabbed a metal strut hanging on to it as the wave receded and tried to pull her back out to sea. Somehow she hung on, gasping and gulping in air, to her burning lungs. Hauling herself upright she clung to the jetty supports and stumbled towards the shore. She fell in the surging water. Finally, she crawled on her hands and knees, as the waves broke over her and tried to suck her back into their grasp. At last she reached the beach. Looking behind her she saw the little dinghy crash into the jetty and disintegrate, as though it was a balsa wood model.

She lay down. Panting, soaking wet and shivering oblivious to the rain and wind for some ten minutes. She felt completely numb. Then she remembered. *Had Troy also made it to the shore? Was he dead or searching for her right now? And Michael - he must still be on the island somewhere. Still hunting her.* She hauled herself up into a sitting position. The closed up bar was just a few feet away. Staggering to her feet she wove an uneven path to it and sat leaning against a pillar just under the porch roof at the entrance, where there was a little shelter from the elements. With her hands clamped around her knees, she shook and wondered what to do next.

The building was creaking. A huge oleander bush suddenly flew past in front of her, as though it was a tiny twig. Bags, cardboard, branches all manner of things blew past in swirling, biting sand. After about ten minutes there was an enormous bang. She turned and looked behind her. Part of the thatched roof of the bar flew completely off. It was as though it was a plastic toy, vanishing as if it had never existed. Becky's eyes widened, her mouth literally dropped open. There was a massive rumble and a great crash. The far wall caved in. Choking dust filled the air. "Not safe. Not safe here," Becky mumbled.

Even if the bar wasn't collapsing around her, a still functioning distant part of her brain was telling her that she was far too close to the beach. The TV programmes she'd seen had told her of the massive waves that could occur at sea close to the eye of the storm; they had also talked of storm surges - waves of between ten and thirty feet high that swept inland, and of winds that could reach as high as one hundred and thirty miles an hour.

She had to find safety, forcing her brain to work she remembered where the bar was and realised that she was very close to Eight Mile Rock. Maybe she could reach Josef and stay with him and Peter. She dragged herself up and limped away from the bar. A massive noise enveloped her. Greater even than the howling wind. The bar had totally collapsed. The porch had disappeared and lay somewhere under a pile of debris. She swallowed hard. Turned and pushed onwards, fighting the wind that threatened to blow her into the bush. Sand and shingle pounded her like hail, excoriating her skin.

Eventually she found herself on one of the dirt tracks that led into Eight Mile Rock. Her knee was swollen, she could hardly walk. The noise of the wind filled her head, she was cold and shivering, unable to think straight. Eight Mile Rock was deserted. Bins and branches from trees rolled around or were tossed up into the air. Not even the dogs roamed. *Where was everyone?* She saw a small house ahead of her. A light shone through some net curtains where the shutters were broken. She staggered up the tiny rubbish strewn path and hammered on the green painted wooden door. She leant on it for support.

Minutes past. She felt as though she would be leaning on the door until she was an old woman. Suddenly it opened. Becky stumbled over the step and almost fell. She was caught up by an indistinct figure in the gloom inside.

"Lord above! Look what the storm dun blow in! Now what have we got here!" said a familiar woman's voice.

Chapter 18

Becky looked up at the woman half holding her. It was Sister Carey! They looked at each other in astonishment. Sister Carey's mouth literally dropped open and her eyes widened. Becky groaned softly. She glanced around the tiny room. *It was so weird. The walls and furniture seemed to be breathing. They moved in and out, and up and down, it was like being on board a ship at sea. The furniture blurred at the edges, somewhere in the distance another person was speaking but the ship gave an almighty roll -* Becky was enveloped by a blissful darkness and calm.

She'd no idea how much time had gone by. Becky thought she must be lying in her bed. *God, she'd had such a bad dream. Something about being chased and a Blue Hole. A storm and waves. She'd been scared, really scared.* Moving her legs a pain shot up through her left knee. Awake in an instant, she found she was lying on a bed in a tiny room. A chest of drawers squashed up against one wall with a crucifix nailed up above it. A vase of yellow plastic daffodils sat on what looked suspiciously like a commode.

Becky's head swam, "Where am I? Where am I?" she shouted.

Sister Carey walked in, "Heh, girl, calm down, you's OK." She bent over her looking concerned. "You're with me and my Mum."

Becky struggled to sit up, "Got to go! Got to go! They want to kill me!"

"Calm down! You's OK. You's here with us. No-one gonna hurt you here."

"Is the girl OK, Geraldine?" an old lady's voice came from the next room.

"Geraldine!" said Becky.

"You tell anyone at work, I'll kill you myself," Sister Carey said, but with an unexpected grin. "You best call me, Gerry like everyone else round here."

"I need to get away, they're looking for me."

"Look here, Lewis," she hesitated. "It's Becky isn't it?"

"Yes."

"OK, Becky. We all needs to get away. In case you hadn't noticed we got a category three hurricane about to hit. I don't know what you got yourself into, God knows you always causing trouble and sneaking about..."

"Geraldine, if you gonna push me all the way to the church we need to go right now," the elderly woman's voice came from the next room.

"OK, Mum. She's right. Explanations can wait. If we don't get to the church and outa this house the whole lot's gonna tumble down around us. Here you best put some of my sister Rosie's clothes on." She turned and put a bundle of clothes on the bed.

Becky tried to get her thoughts in order. *This must be the house she'd seen Sister Carey go into. The house where she thought she was carrying out abortions. Dear God,* she thought, *it had turned out to be the home of Sister Carey's elderly mother.* "I'm sorry, Sister, I've been an idiot."

"It's Gerry here and don't waste time telling me stuff I already know!"

Becky put her head in her hands.

"Come on, Becky," Gerry said gently, "We can sort all this out later. Meantime if you don't want to be in no house with no roof, we need to get a move on."

When Becky had dressed she went through into the other room where an old lady was sat in a wheelchair with a small bag hanging over the back and her face almost obscured by a larger bag on her lap.

"How do you do? I'm, Gerry's Mum. You can call me Elsa if you like, child."

Her face was lined and creased with age, her hair thinning and white but her smile was warm and comforting.

"Thank-you, Elsa. This is really kind of you."

"No. The Lord tells us to help one another, child."

"Hell, I'm hoping you can help me push her up the road to the church, Becky. You better put these things on as well. " Gerry gave her a huge coat and woollen hat. Becky looked startled. "It ain't gonna be no picnic out there. Come on! We need to go. You got everything, Mum?"

"Sure thing. We got the torch, some water, some tinned sausages and some real nice peas and rice in this here plastic box. We won't starve," She chuckled to herself.

Becky put the coat and hat on and they opened the door. The noise was incredible. The wind was screeching now and the rain hammered down.

"Here lean on the chair and help me push," screamed Gerry, into Becky's ear. Sand and shingle carried by the howling wind stung their faces and its force threatened to over topple them all. The old woman's lips moved in soundless prayer. Becky used all her might to push the chair along the dirt tracks flowing with six inches of water, she was no longer aware of the pain in her knee.

The whole world had taken on a surreal black and white intensity. The black sky seemed to be coming down right onto them. A palm tree suddenly crashed down right beside them, just missing them and Gerry yelled, "Jesus!"

"No need for blasphemy, girl," shouted her mother.

Gerry raised her eyebrows at Becky. Bins, rubbish, pieces of wood, cardboard and corrugated iron sheets were blowing around. Every now and then there was a massive crash as the wooden or tin roof of a house lifted off.

At last the church appeared through the grey curtain of rain and spray. As Gerry struggled with the door, Becky looked around her. She saw a tiny house lift up from its foundations. "Jesus Christ! Gerry! Look!" To Becky's astonishment the house was air born for several seconds. She was still struggling to comprehend the sight when it crashed down. As the corners of the house hit the ground the walls fell out. The whole house exploded into fragments. It had transformed from house to rubble in a matter of minutes.

Gerry's eyes widened. She grabbed Becky, "Come on, girl we've got some praying to do." Becky pushed open the door of the tiny brick built church and Gerry wheeled her Mum in. Becky was greeted by the sound of music - it was as though she'd entered a parallel universe. The tiny church was filled with the joyous noise of a hundred or more people, praising the Lord and singing gospel hymns. It was like leaving an inferno and entering a religious pop concert. Becky shook her head and looked around her in amazement. People helped them in through the door, concerned and kind.

"You OK, child?"

"Gerry, bring Elsa and the child over here."

"Heh, come sit by us."

An old man looked at Becky's face. "You don't need to worry, dear. We's in the Lords house. You safe here." He gave a huge reassuring smile showing up a lot of missing teeth, and even in the dim candle light Becky could see the kindness in his rheumy eyes.

As her own eyes adjusted to the light she looked around the tiny church. People sat in wooden pews on either side of a small aisle. Underneath their coats, you could just glimpse that many of the women were wearing smart dresses; some had large elaborate hats floating in feathers and organza. Becky smiled to herself for a moment wondering how they'd managed to keep hold of them in the hurricane.

On a small dais at the front behind a lectern stood a pastor dressed in long white robes conducting a choir of young people slightly to the side of him. The scent of hair unguent mingled with that of the guttering candles. The children were enthusiastically joining in, all looking freshly scrubbed and as if they were wearing their 'Sunday Best.' Many had their hair prettily plaited with coloured beads.

People gestured to Becky to go in first, to a remaining empty pew, which was near the back up against the far wall. Then two of the men physically carried Elsa out of her wheelchair and with considerable difficulty wedged her into the pew next to Becky. She turned to Becky, "I hates being stuck out in the aisle like I'm different. I like to worship with everyone around me, like I always done before I got this arthritis thing." She patted Becky's hand, "Don't you worry. Whatever's troubling you the Lord will provide."

Becky smiled, "Thanks, Elsa." Gerry sat next to her mother and two large ladies came across from the pew opposite and started laughing and chatting to Gerry. Becky realised that Josef and Mari were sitting two rows in front of her and asked the people in front to tap Josef's shoulder. He turned and looked surprised and then overjoyed to see Becky. He crossed himself, gave her a huge smile and mouthed, "I'll see you afterwards."

Smiling back at him Becky started to relax and feel that she was safe, that she was with friends and good people. The music rose and fell around them and Elsa began clapping in time. Gerry and the two women next to her got to their feet and started singing and swaying with the hymns. The music buoyed Becky up and she even found herself swaying in her seat as well. For a few precious minutes, she forgot where she was and what had brought her to this place. When the music stopped the people cried out around the church.

"Hallelujah!"

"Praise the Lord!"

"Jesus! Jesus!"

"Jesus saved me I know it!"

It fell quiet in the church. The noise of the hurricane could be heard clearly then. The wind screaming, the rain hammering on the tin roof, great crashes were happening outside. Small children started to cry and the mood inside the church shifted. The pastor turned and prayed in a mighty voice that drowned out the storm. He raised his arms and in his booming voice, he talked of salvation and sin, of sacrifice and the soul. The congregation quietened, murmuring their assent. Becky started to drift. She felt exhausted, almost trance like in the thrall of his hypnotic sermon. No-one heard the door open just to the side of the dais behind a screen at the front of the church.

The pastor finished his sermon. People stood up, giving witness to the works of the Lord in their lives, the congregation lending their support.

"You know it true, sister!"

"He healed me too!"

"Hallelujah!"

Then the pastor took up his baton and the choir started to sing another gospel song. On the dais sat great candles and the congregation clutched their own smaller ones which flickered and spluttered in the draughts.

A figure moved behind the choir and Becky suddenly felt alert. A shiver ran down her spine. Shifting uneasily she looked around her. Nothing had changed. She shrugged. Then she saw him.

He stood half behind the screen, next to the choir who were singing at the side of the preacher who faced the congregation. She saw his blond hair. Michael was up there. Watching.

No-one else seemed to notice. She couldn't breath. Couldn't speak. For a moment, she couldn't move. The music swirled and cavorted around her. People were lost in its power. Many stood, one arm stretched palm raised heavenward, swaying and singing in time, their eyes closed, engulfed, in the very presence of their Lord. They clutched their bibles, prayed, chanted and sang-they were a living breathing single organism. All seemed to be transported, far away from the present time.

Becky turned towards Gerry, frantically trying to gain her attention, but she was engrossed in the gospel song. Her eyes, like so many others, were half closed, one arm raised to the ceiling. Becky couldn't reach past Elsa, to touch Gerry. Elsa looked up at her concerned, as Becky tried to get out of the pew, but she was wedged, completely trapped in by Elsa.

She turned back to face Michael. Their eyes met for a fraction of a second. He looked as though he too was in another place. He seemed to look straight through her. The Michael she thought she knew had vanished. This was a man who was totally focused. In the light of the guttering candles she saw him move to where he had a clearer view of her. He reached inside his jacket.

She shouted, "Josef! Help me! Josef. He's here!"

The choir and congregation drowned her out, "Jesus is our life, our one salvation."

"Josef! JOSEF!"

Josef half heard and struggled to turn around in the small pew to look at Becky. She looked back at Michael. Saw him take aim. Saw his outstretched arm. Saw the gun glint in the light.

Josef stared at Becky, puzzled, concerned. Becky pointed back frantically at Michael as she tried to clamber over the pew in front of her.

"It's Michael! Look!" she yelled.

Josef turned back to see who she was pointing at. The music swelled to a crescendo. "Hallelujah, Hallelujah! Christ is Lord! Christ is King". The pastor put down his baton. Becky was transfixed. She held her breath. Place and time dissolved around her. The only reality was the glinting black gun barrel.

Two shots rang out. Becky felt something hit her hard. It felt like a massive punch from a giant hand. She saw Gerry turn and look along at her, saw the horror on her face. The strangest feeling spread though Becky's body, as though ice had been poured into her veins. The ice spread throughout her. Far and wide, numbing her deeper and deeper. She heard someone scream, then she slumped forwards. She toppled into a night of deepest purple and total silence.

Pandemonium broke out in the church. Screaming and shouting. People diving under the pews, yelling for their kids, colliding with one another. Michael sprinted down the aisle, shoving people out of the way, shouting and waving his gun, his eyes wild, his face menacing. He reached the door, shoved it open and ran out into the howling wind and rain.

Josef turned to the woman next to him. "Look after Mari for me!"   He leapt over the pews and ran after Michael.

Mari's screams of "Papa! Papa!" echoed in his head as he ran.

When Michael got outside the wind almost took him off his feet, but he ignored it trying to focus on the figure just ahead of him. Troy was running back to his car clutching his thigh. Troy had entered the back of the church seeking shelter from the hurricane. It was in one of the few places still standing intact and he'd arrived, a short while after Michael.

Michael raised his gun and tried to stand steady in the wind that was threatening to overpower him. He had Troy in his sights. He squeezed the trigger. Suddenly he was tackled from behind. His legs taken out from under him, his face hit the dirt and the shot went wild.

Michael rolled over and Josef smashed his fist into Michael's face. Josef was small but he'd been brought up having to fight to survive in Port Au Prince. They rolled over, Michael punched Josef on the jaw yelling, "For Christ's sake! He's getting away!"

"Fuck you, man!"

"He's getting away! For God's sake!"

"Who's getting away!"

"Troy!"

"Who?"

Josef got a punch under Michael's diaphragm winding him.

"Just let me explain!"

"I'll let you fucking explain back at the police station! You done shot Becky, you bastard!"

Michael got Josef by the throat, "Listen to me!"

A bullet whizzed past their heads.

"Shit! What was that?"

"That was a bullet, you idiot! It's what I'm trying to tell you. It's Troy, trying to kill us both!"

"You piece of shit! You tried to kill Becky!"

"No, no. You've got it all wrong." They rolled over again and a bullet pinged into the sand beside them. "Christ! Let's at least take cover if you want a bloody discussion!"

They both rolled rapidly across to where the remnants of a house provided some cover. Troy's car started up. He moved off. Michael knelt up and aimed a shot which went through the rear window. Troy appeared to duck, the car careered to one side and then vanished down the dirt track.

Michael went to move. A hand swiftly went around his neck from behind and he felt a knife at his throat.

"Drop the gun, you bastard! 'Bout time we had that little discussion don't you think?"

Just a short distance away Isabella came to with a start. She was still in her flimsy home, in the room with the curtains drawn. She'd fallen into a deep sleep after the trance. She was unsure what had happened. The power had taken her over and all became black as THE MAN'S face had crumpled and disintegrated in her mind.

The sixth and final pin was embedded in the figure.

It should be finished but something was wrong. She searched in the shadowy recesses of her mind. Then she heard it. THE GIRL IN WHITE had cried out. There was another man who would destroy her if he could.

She wasn't sure if she was strong enough but she would have to try. Would have to go back... into the darkness...

Michael threw his gun to one side. Josef reached down carefully, picked it up with one hand and put it in his pocket. He kept the point of the knife digging into Michael's neck. "You'd better talk fast, man. You'd be dead right now but for I recognise that son of a bitch you was shooting at. He's the bastard that got my wife killed. This wouldn't be the first time I've used this knife. I might have put my previous life behind me now, but Becky saved my daughter's life. I know all about you and the drugs. You're just a small time, no good smuggler of filth and if I find you're in it with him..."

"You're wrong, Josef. Let me show you." Michael reached inside his jacket.

Josef pulled Michael tighter against him, "Don't you fuck with me, man!"

"OK! Ok!" Michael dropped his hand. "Feel in my inside jacket pocket. I've got I.D. there."

Josef carefully felt inside Michael's pocket still holding the knife at his throat. He brought out a wallet stuffed with dollar bills and rifled through it with one hand.

"For your sake you better not be tryin' to bribe me, man."

"No! I swear! Look!"

An American Express, gold card fell out. Josef gave a derisory laugh, "So you're a big spender, man," His face darkened. "This ain't one of them occasions when that'll do nicely, like the ad. say!"

"Not that card! For Christ's sake! I'm C.I.A.!"

"What! No shit!"

"Yeah. No shit. Look, there, it's that card there."

Josef held up the card the others blowing away in the howling wind. He moved the knife slowly from Michael's throat. "Jesus!" he whistled slowly. "C.I. fucking A. Who'd a believed it. I'll be watching you. Take more than this to convince me."

"I didn't shoot Becky, it was Troy. I saw him aiming for her. He was stood at the back of the church. I think I winged the bastard. Let's get back inside, Josef. Explanations can wait. We need to see if Becky's OK"

"OK, man. Don't forget your gun's in my pocket."

"Come on. Becky could be...God Damn it! Let's go!"

They fought their way against the wind back to the church. It was so strong now it threatened to blow them both over, and they had to hold on to one another to prevent themselves being swept away by it.

When they reached the church Becky was laid down on the dais, covered by a red blanket.

"Oh my God!" said Michael quietly, his face drained of all colour. The rain drummed on the roof and the wind was howling and whistling like an enraged devil. In spite of this he felt a strange stillness in the church. Some people were on their knees praying. Others held up one hand in supplication, their lips moving silently. A child cried. Michael felt a terrible sense of dread. He rushed down the aisle to Becky. Josef went to check on Mari who was by now sat on Elsa's lap. Then he followed Michael to where Becky lay.

She was unmoving and white as death itself. Gerry was on her knees beside her along with Nurse Rolle. Gerry was frowning and feeling for a pulse at Becky's neck.

"Is she...Is she..." Michael faltered.

"No, man. She's alive but something ain't right. At first I thought she'd just fainted but it's more than that. Here, Pam, let's get a good look at her." They pulled the blanket off her. Becky moaned softly. Her lips were tinged with blue. The front of her T-shirt was covered in blood. It was spreading from the top of her arm just underneath her shoulder. "She's been shot."

The church suddenly went silent. The wind and rain stopped. "It's the eye of the hurricane," said the pastor who stood nearby looking worried. People started to go towards the door. "No!" he shouted in a mighty voice. "No-one is to go outside. It hasn't gone. This is the most dangerous time. It will come back stronger and harder. We need to sit and pray for our daughter."

The congregation went back to their seats and all started to pray. Different voices, chanting different prayers, rose from all sides of the church. Michael was astounded. It should have been discordant but it was strangely soothing.

Gerry was pulling up Becky's T-shirt. "I need scissors, water, cloths and something to make a bandage."

Michael took off his jacket and started to tear his shirt up. Josef went to get a bottle of water. Becky groaned and opened her eyes.

"You's OK, girl."

"What happened?"

"You jus got yerself shot that's all."

"I'm sorry," she muttered.

"Don't you worry none. I knews you was gonna be trouble the minute I set eyes on you," Gerry smiled softly at her.

"Am I going to die, Gerry?"

"Hell no! What you think I can't look after a little problem like you. All the years I worked at The Royal, pouf! I just needs to pad you up a bit, then we'll get you into The Royal. Get you fixed up proper."

Becky tried to give her a smile but she could feel the blackness coming back for her again. She fought it off, but it was no good. She sank back into where it didn't hurt anymore. Back into nothingness.

Gerry put a pad of cloth where the bullet had entered the top of Becky's arm and pressed on it firmly. Becky's breathing was rapid and shallow and her colour was worsening.

"Is she gonna be OK, Sister?" asked Josef quietly.

Gerry shook her head and said softly, "I sure hope so. She's bleeding really bad. It's bright red so it must be an artery. I need to stop it." She looked around the church. "Ask the pastor if I can have his baton."

It crossed Michael's mind that this determined woman was going to conduct them all in a prayer of some sort, but he went and asked the pastor for it all the same. He took it back to Gerry.

"Right". She'd put a pad of cloth where Becky was bleeding from. "Give me one of them strips of cloth."

"What are you doing?"

"I'm making a tourniquet." She wound the strip over the pad around Becky's arm, put the baton in and tightened it.

"What can I do?" asked Michael.

"Write down the time and tell me when every fifteen minutes has passed." "Why?"

"So I can loosen this off every fifteen minutes."

"What will happen otherwise?"

"Otherwise. Otherwise she's gonna get gangrene and loose her arm from lack of blood." Gerry looked him in the eyes. "Sometin' else you can do too."

"What? What else can I do?"

"You can pray, honey. That's what you can do."

Troy drove away from Michael and Josef swearing. "Son of a bitch. I always knew he was trouble. Right from when he took that little cow out from under my nose. He's going to get what's coming to him!" When Troy had quietly entered the back of the church he'd been looking for somewhere to sit out the storm. Anywhere that was still standing in fact. He couldn't believe his luck when he'd seen Becky sitting wedged in at the back. He wasn't sure now if he'd got the bitch or not with that damn fool Michael shooting at him.

He struggled to control the car as wind and sand lashed it. The rain was a solid wall. A great bolt of lightning illuminated a scene from hell. Raging torrents of water ran down the dirt tracks. The entire landscape seemed to have changed. Some houses were almost buried under the sand that had been carried inland from the beach. Troy pressed on his leg and his hand came away covered in blood.

"Shit, the bastard grazed me!" He drove on into a dark world. The windscreen wipers were all but defeated by the rain, the car lurched and tilted. He gripped the steering wheel and gritted his teeth, cursing the pain in his leg. He peered out through the windscreen.

He'd gone about five miles when suddenly the world changed. The rain stopped. The wipers screeched on the windscreen. The wind dropped. He stopped the car and got out. It was completely silent apart from the noise of the waves on the nearby beach. It seemed that the hurricane had blown itself out.

He hunted in his car and found an old t-shirt. Looking down at his leg he could see he was still bleeding from the bullet he'd taken. He tore the t-shirt up into strips and fixed them as best he could around his leg. He took his hip flask of whisky out of his pocket and took a great slug. He was astounded by the silence that engulfed him, he lay back and shut his eyes. He didn't know how long had passed when he came to.

"I need to take a leak," he muttered and limped across the road to between some palm trees from where he could clearly see the sea. Great waves continued to pound the shore but everything else was silent. He felt uneasy. "Something wrong here." He decided he'd try to get to see Mr Silver, he'd know what to do next. He started to limp back to the car.

A great blast of wind blew him off his feet and three foot into the air as the hurricane screeched back into life. The eye of the storm had passed over and now it returned in all its fury. The rain and winds were driving in from the opposite direction to before and the hurricane hit as if reborn. More ferocious than ever.

"Jesus Christ!" Troy screamed as the wind carried him several hundred yards before depositing him on the ground. He screamed again as his leg hit the soil hard. Then the wind took him again. It lifted him from the ground and tossed him around like one of the grains of sand and shingle that were tearing into his body. He was still screaming as It dropped him heavily with his injured leg twisted underneath him. He lay on the beach gasping and choking. He looked up. Then he saw it. A massive grey wall of roaring water, foaming, curling on its crest. Twenty foot high and half a mile across. The storm surge. He didn't get the chance to run. He lay transfixed, his eyes widened in horror. His mouth opened to scream. The wave engulfed him and Troy Murchinson was no more.

Isabella's chanting rose to a frenzy. Blackness rose up all around her. There was a wild screeching in her head. She fought the blackness but it engulfed her. She lay in a place of great darkness.

Chapter 19

When the hurricane had finally moved on the congregation hesitantly went outside. Many just stood and looked, shaking their heads, unable to comprehend the changed landscape around them. Most of the flimsier dwellings had simply blown away, sand was piled up half burying others and palm trees and branches littered the roads, power lines were down.

Inside the church, Becky's condition had worsened. Her lips were a darker shade of blue and she was ghostly white. Her pulse was rapid and feeble. Sister Carey had positioned Becky so that she was half sitting, to try to help her breathing. Becky's eyes were closed and she was icy cold and semi-conscious. She moaned softly.

"Jesus, she looks bad, Gerry," said Michael.

"Yeah we need to get her to the hospital quick. There won't be no ambulances they'll be too busy. Go get a car and we'll take her ourselves."

"Ourselves!"

"Yeah. Who else? And if you want her to live get a move on!"

Michael shot out of the church. Mari stood near Becky with Josef. "Is Becky going to be alright, Papa?"

"Yeah, course she is, sweetheart."

"We won't lose her like we lost Maman will we?"

Josef gave her an agonised look. Rachel came across to them.

"Why don't we all go and say a little prayer for her eh, poppet?"

"Yeah, Rachel, that's a good idea." Josef smiled at her.

"Then we'd best go see what's happened to our houses eh?" said Rachel.

"Yeah. You're right." He turned to Gerry, "I'll come in to the hospital later, see how she's doin'. Come on, Mari," said Josef. They went to a pew and said a prayer together and then they all left together.

When Michael got outside his car had vanished. Probably like so many it had been picked up and blown away by the winds. He ran around frantically and found an old Ford Escort wedged up against a building. No-one was around so he quickly hot wired it to get it started. Explanations to owners could wait until later. He drove back to the church and ran inside.

"How is she?"

Gerry's lips were pursed and she was frowning. "No time to waste. Let's go. I need you and two other men to carry her to the car."

"OK."

Michael and two other men quickly lifted Becky under Gerry's instructions.

"Watch that tourniquet for God's sake!"

It was difficult to get Becky onto the back seat, Gerry making sure that the tourniquet didn't move. Becky moaned but she didn't open her eyes. Gerry wedged herself in next to Becky.

"OK, Gerry?"

"Yeah, drive."

Michael started driving down the road at about fifty miles an hour.

"Slow down! Slow down! It's too bumpy back here," yelled Gerry. The car screeched to a halt. Gerry struggled to keep herself and Becky on the seat. "What the hell are you playing at?"

"Look!" Michael pointed at the tangle of trees and power lines draped across the road making it impassable..

"OK, reverse, Michael. I know another way."

Michael reversed back down the road.

"Turn right here."

He drove down the next road as carefully and quickly as he could. The road was littered with overturned cars, bits of roof, old bins and containers. It seemed that anything that hadn't been physically tied down had been swept up by the hurricane and deposited at will.

"Turn left here."

They drove past some ground that Michael didn't recognise but then everything was so changed by the hurricane.

"Jesus save us!" screeched Gerry from the back seat.

"What ! What's wrong?"

"Look!"

"Shit!" said Michael and swerved almost crashing the car. "What the hell is that?"

It was starting to get dark. Michael switched on the headlights. They illuminated a scene from a horror film. Gerry with one hand over her mouth pointed silently to the ground on their right. Skeletons and decaying bodies lay there, some still with fabric from their garments attached, others seemed to leer down at them from where they hung in the trees, they were spread-eagled over bushes, their grinning skulls mocking them. Worse still, were the bones and body parts scattered at random across the ground.

Gerry laughed nervously and crossed herself. "Lord have mercy! Don't worry we ain't in hell yet. It is, or should I say was, the cemetery. The storm surge must have done washed them all outa their graves. Lord what a sight." She crossed herself again though and, in spite of her laughter, she looked almost as pale as Becky.

Michael felt the bile rise up in his throat. For a few seconds he sat transfixed. Then Becky moaned quietly. He put his foot down on the accelerator. "Let's get out of here!"

He drove like a man possessed the rest of the way. At last they reached the hospital.

"Jesus!" said Michael, looking at the car park which was illuminated by the street lights and car headlamps. It overflowed with cars, trucks, prams and even supermarket trolleys which people were using to carry patients. Other people milled around, calling for family members, laughing, crying and hugging one another.

"Don't bother going for no stretcher, you won't find one," said Gerry.

"Yep." Michael grim faced picked Becky up and carried her. Gerry parted the people, like Moses parting the Red Sea. She was a big woman, imperious and intimidating.

"Can't you people see this girl's sick. Get outa the way. I'm the Sister In Charge of this here hospital. Move it." People recognised her she was evidently well known and not just in the hospital.

"Sorry, Sister."

"Yes, Sister."

"Sure thing."

They glanced at each other sullenly but all moved out of the way. Michael and Gerry ran through the entrance hall and pushed their way past the people who crowded the narrow corridor that led to Emergency Room. Eventually they shoved their way in. Michael was panting and sweating from the effort. Becky lay in his arms not moving her eyes closed.

Stefano was there along with three local G.P.'s who'd come in to help.

"Oh! Jesus Christ! It's Becky! What's wrong with her?" he said, looking horrified.

"She been shot. Michael get her up onto the couch. I think she's bleeding from the brachial artery. We needs to get her to surgery."

"Impossible, Gerry. Theatres are full and no - one can find Mr Silver."

"Well you gotta do something. I got a tourniquet on her but she's been bleeding for more than an hour now."

"Shit! OK, we'll sort her here. Go get me a cut down set, stitches, and some plasma, until we can get her blood grouped and cross matched."

"Michael, go wait outside. Ain't nothing you can do now."

"But..." he faltered and passed his hand over is face.

"Don't worry we'll sort her out. She's a whole lot tougher than she looks." Gerry started pulling equipment out of cupboards. Stefano took a plastic cannula out of his pocket, wrapped a tourniquet around her other forearm and started tapping her hand trying to raise a vein so he could insert the cannula.

Gerry looked at the patient a few feet away who was having oxygen, his lips were blue and he was moaning and clutching his chest. "God damn it," she muttered. She ran to the door where Michael was standing white faced. "Michael, go round to the ward. Tell Nurse Robbins, that I sent you and that you have to have an oxygen cylinder. Tell her, I don't care who's having it, we got to give it to Becky."

Michael fought his way through crowds of people throqging the corridor to the ward. Some were crying, others were chatting excitedly and laughing, a family were sitting on the floor eating peas and rice. They cursed him as he pushed his way past. At last he reached the ward and found a harassed nurse bandaging a woman's bleeding head. He told her what he needed.

"I don't know about that. I don't think..."

"God damnit. Where the fuck is it!"

"Ain't no need to take that tone with me..."

Michael ran out and down the ward looking in every room for the oxygen. Eventually he found it. A very old man lay back on the pillows looking exhausted and wheezing slightly. Michael stopped in his tracks. He looked at him. The man opened his eyes. "Can I do something for you, young man?" he wheezed.

Becky's face came into Michael's mind. "Yes, sorry, yes you can, Sir. I need your oxygen."

"What?"

He went up to the man and took off his mask.

"What you doin? You can't take that."

"Sorry. Sorry. I'll bring it back."

"But I can't ..."

Michael gave him an agonised look. Tilted the oxygen trolley so it would wheel and hurried back shouting at people as he went.

When he reached the emergency room they'd got an infusion running into Becky's vein and Stefano was probing her arm for the bullet. Gerry quickly put the oxygen on Becky.

"Let me stay. Please."

Stefano looked at Michael. "Yeah, OK. Don't get in the way."

The couch was soaked with blood. Stefano muttered to himself as he probed for the bullet and Gerry's lips were moving silently as though in prayer, as she passed Stefano the instruments he needed.

"Got it!" he suddenly cried in triumph and there it was clamped in his artery forceps-a silver bullet. Gerry sighed with relief and Stefano gave a big grin as he started to stitch up the artery and then the wound. As they put up another infusion this time a mixture of dextrose and saline Becky's colour improved. They attached her to a monitor, she was in sinus tachycardia. It showed that her heart was beating rapidly but normally. Gerry and Stefano smiled across at each other.

Chapter 20

October twenty first, eleven a.m.

When Becky opened her eyes everything hurt. She'd been having such terrible dreams. She looked around her; she was in a small whitewashed room with no decoration of any kind, there was a grubby window with a blind half down on her right, a half open door seemed to lead into a corridor. Then she heard the 'canned' music. *Good God! She was in a bed in The Royal!* Struggling to sit up pain shot through her and she found she had a large dressing around her arm and shoulder and an intra-venous infusion in her hand.

She tried to call out but her mouth was too dry and then the room swam before her eyes and she sank back into a blissful darkness.

Further down the corridor Stefano was looking in on another woman who had also just regained consciousness. "How are you feeling now?"

"I'm fine. I need to get home."

"Well we'd like to keep you in for a couple of days and run some tests. Do you mind if I call you, Isabella?"

"No, 'course not. What sort of tests?"

"The neighbours found you unconscious in your home and you didn't seem to have been knocked out by anything falling. In fact, your house is apparently miraculously untouched, but there you were completely unconscious in the chair."

"Really?" said Isabella with an impassive face.

"Yes, really. Look, Isabella, your neighbours seem to think that you had some, shall we say, interesting plants growing out the back."

"Do they?"

"Yeah. My only interest is your health, but if you've been taking some...some...herbal medicines, I think you should stop. A lot of them are pretty toxic. They can lead to seizures, hallucinations and loss of consciousness. You were very weak when you came in.

"I don't know what you're talking about, Doctor. Tell me, do you have a white nurse working here, blonde hair, very pretty?"

"Yeah we do. Becky. Why?"

"Is she OK?"

"I guess someone's told you about the shooting, so I may as well tell you, yeah she's OK. Why do you ask?"

"I just wondered that's all." Isabella lay back on the pillows smiling.

"OK. Anyway I understand that although your house is still standing, a surge of water went right through your land and pretty well destroyed everything growing there."

"Don't worry. I don't think I'll need to grow anything but sweet potatoes and peppers when I go back." She gave Stefano a strange smile.

"That's good, Isabella. I'd better get on we're pretty hectic here just now. I'll be back later to do those tests."

"Thanks, Doctor, you're very kind."

When a Nurses Aide looked in the room half an hour later, Isabella had gone.

Michael was in the office talking to Gerry. "Is she going to be alright?"

"Yeah she's gonna make it. She lost a lot of blood while we waited out the storm but now that's been replaced she'll be just fine."

"Thank God and thank-you so much. I can't bear to think what would have happened if you hadn't treated her in that church."

"Wow, that was some trip we had in that car wasn't it?"

"Yeah. That's a ride I'm never going to forget. What about the old man that I took the oxygen from?"

"He's OK, though I guess you ain't his favourite person," Gerry laughed heartily. "We often has to switch the oxygen around a bit, we've only got about four cylinders and they ain't always full." She laughed again.

Stefano had come into the office. "Anyhows it ain't me you gotta thank, it's this doctor here."

"Hi, it's, Michael isn't it? Didn't we meet one time before on Mr Silver's boat?"

"Oh yeah, that's right. God, that all seems like a lifetime ago."

"Mr Silver, he ain't no-where to be seen now," said Sister Carey. "It like he vanished into thin air. Sure hope he wasn't hurt in the hurricane."

"Ah yes. Mr Silver," said Michael his eyes narrowed and his face angry.

Later that same afternoon Tony Silver arrived at the airport. With him was a plump Bahamian woman - Sister Della Patterson. They both carried two heavy looking bags.

Mr Silver had been holed up in a secret hideaway that he'd had built some time ago for just such a time as this. His light aircraft was waiting for them on the runway.

"You never thought you was gonna leave me here to face all that shit did you?" Sister Patterson said.

"'Course not, darling'."

"I hear that cow was admitted to The Royal. She knows far too much and God knows what that idiot Troy told her."

"Yeah, if they'd just followed my instructions, everything would have been OK. You know I always meant to bring you anyway, honey," Tony Silver said with a smile that came nowhere near his eyes.

"I knew she was trouble the minute I laid eyes on her. I really thought she'd leave after I left her that little message in her bathroom."

"Yeah, for a quiet little thing she was a real pain in the arse."

"It's a God damn shame. We was a good team. Any of them girls that couldn't pay you, got sent to me, an' we was on, win win. If they didn't have it legal they could pay me a whole lot less to do it. I reckon it worked pretty good for all concerned. A lot of girls are gonna be really stuck now."

Mr Silver looked at her and smiled. *God damn it! To hear Della speak any one would think she was performing a public service. He wasn't sure how much she knew about his drugs and immigrant operations, but she certainly knew far too much to just leave her on the island and have her blabbing her mouth off. He reckoned that once he got her to Miami, The Family could discreetly dispose of her.*

They got in and fastened their safety belts. Mr Silver started the pre take off checks and a disembodied voice came over the radio from the Control Tower.

"ZR162, You are cleared for take off."

The sound of the engines filled their ears and Mr Silver taxied down the runway.

Watching them from the Control Tower was Michael. Woods who'd now been promoted to sergeant was by Michael's side. He turned to Michael and said, "I still think we should have arrested the bastard here and now."

"Well that sure would have given me a lot of pleasure too, but by letting him go he may well implicate his Mafia boss in Miami. He's the one that's really pulling our Mr Silver or should I say Antonio Da Silva's strings."

"Who?"

"Antonio Da Silva. That's his real name. His family came over from Sicily in the last century, and like so many Americanised their name. They've been working for the Mafia for decades. The Mafia probably paid for him to train as a surgeon, got him a job here and heh presto - a real respectable surgeon, running all their covert operations in Grand Bahama."

"It's Incredible! He was the last guy we would have looked at. He'd worked here for years"

"Yeah, it was a really good cover and of course Luther Clarkson was in on it too. He was feeding you all misinformation, making sure you were always on the wrong beach when drugs or immigrants were coming in."

"That bastard! Bent cops like that get the rest of us a real bad name."

"I was trying to find out who was running it here. In the end it was Becky who found out. We should recruit her to the C.I.A. Hell she was like a ferret with a rat, where I was concerned! I thought we could have a relationship, without her suspecting what I was doing. I never thought for a moment that she'd get involved, Jeez I really underestimated her." There was a roar of engines and the plane took off.

"That's him gone, man" said Woods.

"Yeah. He made a stack of money out of drug and immigrant smuggling. And that bitch Sister Patterson did untold harm with her abortions. Now they think they've got away, along with a small fortune tucked into those bags I shouldn't wonder."

"I sure hope he gets what's coming to him."

"Don't worry about that." Michael gave a tight smile. "He'll get his due."

Becky woke again later that day feeling stronger. She looked around her and pressed the call button. Gerry came in. "Well, well, you back in the land of the living girl. 'Bout time too."

"Gerry, I don't understand anything. What happened in the church? How did I get here? Why have I got a drip up?"

"Whoah, one at a time, girl. You sure you feel well enough to listen?"

"Yeah. I'm a bit tired but I want to know, please."

"You jus lay back then, girl. But 'fore I start to tell you, I think I should say sorry for how I was with you before."

"No, don't be ridiculous."

"There you go again. Will you just be quiet and listen for once!"

"Sorry, Sister."

"It's, Gerry," she said with a smile. "Where was I. Yeah, You English nurses we've had a stack of them. Most takes one look at the facilities, the lack of staff, no air con. an' all and you can see it on their faces – they ain't stayin'. It makes us feel bad.

We only been self governing since sixty five, just before you come we got independence. We're just getting on our feet. I got fed up of showing all them nurses around, them looking down their noses at us and then gettin' on the first plane outta here."

"Yes, I can understand that."

"You were different though - you stuck it out. Then you dun followed me home that time, it sort of threw me you know."

"I'm sorry about that. I jumped to the wrong conclusions."

"Don't you worry, you got there in the end. Now then let me explain to you just what was going on. I got a stack of stuff to tell you starting off with that boyfriend of yours."

" Michael? He tried to kill me!"

"Like I said I got a stack of stuff to tell you, so you jus lie back and if you feels up to it I'll fill you in. Firstly, your Michael's not what you thought..."

Tony Da Silva hummed to himself as he saw the turquoise waters around Grand Bahama beneath the aircraft. Leaning over he squeezed Della's hand and heaved a small sigh of relief. "That's us then. Off to a new life."

"Yeah. No more working in that stinking hospital and going to that hut all hours of the day and night," she smiled contentedly. "What did the boss say when you told him your cover was blown?"

"You don't want to know. He was mad as hell, but I smoothed him over. After all I've just spent the last thirty years organising everything here for them."

"Yeah, aint that what you best at, well, that an' other things," she said with a throaty laugh.

He smiled across at her, *God! The sooner he made the arrangements for her disposal the better,* he thought. "I can't believe how I misjudged that bastard Michael. And as for that girl I should have taken her out when I had the chance instead of leaving it to those two idiots."

"Yeah, ain't that the truth."

She was pretty too, he mused to himself, *If only I'd had my drugs to hand when she came to the house. It would have been so simple to have put one in her drink.*

He'd enjoyed the sex that last time on the yacht, with that other stupid nurse, so much that he'd left his supply on board by mistake. He was certain he'd be able to obtain more in Miami, even if Della wasn't working with him. After all a surgeon's like a God at work. No-one ever questions what they're doing and they've always got access to drugs.

The engine missed. "Damn."

"Something wrong, honey?"

"No, it's just the crap fuel they've put in it."

"I just realised, I've left the spare set of keys to the ward drug cupboard in my locker, at the hospital. Do you think they'll find them?"

"Doesn't matter if they do. They'll never trace us."

"Yeah."

Then there was a splutter. "Shit" he yelled. The gauges went crazy. The plane continued to splutter.

"What's wrong, Tony? What the fuck is going on?"

"The engine... Christ!"

The plane went into a nose dive, its screaming obliterating the screams from the cock pit. A massive explosion rent the air. The flames lit up the sky until it plunged into the ocean. Within three minutes, it had vanished from the face of the earth. Only the contents of their bags fluttered on the breeze. Sharks started to arrive and circle the site where it had gone down. It seemed that Tony Da Silva was expendable after all.

In Eight Mile Rock people were going about their daily business. Many homes had been completely destroyed by the hurricane. A hard life for the poorest of the poor had been made a lot harder. Most of the flimsiest dwellings had simply vanished into the air, the wreckage spread right across the island. Lots of people were having to get by living with their families. It made life pretty cramped in the tiny houses and shacks that had been crammed to the brim with people even before the hurricane had struck. Many others had got on with the job of collecting timber and tin, cardboard and sacking, and were trying to construct some sort of new shelter for themselves and their families.

Josef was just getting ready for his shift at the supermarket when he heard screaming outside.

"What now," he said to himself, rushing out into the road. He frowned. *What the hell was going on here?* People were behaving strangely. Laughing and shouting, jumping up and down, catching pieces of paper. Josef scratched his head puzzled. Then he saw the Pastor doing the same thing.

A piece of paper floated past Josef. He reached out his hand. It was a hundred dollar bill. "Holy shit!" he screamed. He shouted to Peter "Quick! Come quick! It's raining money! All our troubles are over!"

The pastor smiled benevolently looking at his church. Seeing where the plaster was coming off in chunks and at the tin roof which had somehow withstood the hurricane. He fell to his knees clutching a handful of bills. "The ways of the Lord are truly wondrous. Hallelujah! "

The phone rang in the police station, "Call for you Sarge'"

"Thanks," Woods took the phone.

"Have you sorted it?" said, an anonymous voice, with a Sicilian accent.

"Yeah. It's cool. There won't be any more fuck ups at this end."

"There better not be. We'll be in touch."

"Sure thing."

Woods put the phone down and smiled to himself. "Right, boys, let's take a look at these beach patrols."

Becky's doorbell rang. Clifford stood there. "Seems like a long time don't it, Nurse since, you done arrived."

"Yes it surely does, Clifford." She looked around the apartment. "I'm going to miss all this."

"We're gonna miss you too, Nurse."

"Thanks, Clifford."

"You sure you wants to go?"

"Well my parents and my ex-boyfriend are all waiting for me."

"Yeah, I guess after all that's happened you wouldn't want to stay here."

"Come on, Clifford we're going to be late."

Michael was waiting for her at the airport. He looked good enough to eat as usual she thought, but even though he'd explained how he was just 'a plant' by the C.I.A, that he didn't gamble, that he certainly wasn't a drug smuggler, she felt let down. He should have trusted her.

"Hi. Michael."

He looked at her sadly, "You're really going then."

"Yes. I'm really going."

"Just like that?"

"Yes, Michael. I told you, I'm not the compliant little girl that you met any more. I can't love someone whose life is secret. I'd never know what you were doing or where you were - it wouldn't work."

Michael looked sad. Then he smiled at Becky, "We were great though, weren't we?"

A million memories flashed through her mind - the beach, snorkelling, Bimini... "Yes, I wouldn't have missed it for anything." She reached up and kissed him gently on the cheek. Turned and walked into the departure lounge.

Sister Carey was cursing, "Oh for the love of God. The damn fan!" A fan, perched precariously on the cluttered desk, had blown the little pieces of paper with the patient's names on them out from underneath around twenty individual medicine pots.

Nurse Rolle came in, "There's a new nurse here. Jus' come from England."

"Yeah ,Yeah." She carried on sorting out the pieces of paper.

"Name of Rebecah."

Gerry looked up with a start. Becky stood there. She wore a well fitting uniform that just skimmed the knee and on her fingers were a hint of pink nail polish.

Sister Carey almost smiled. "Rebecah, eh?"

"Yes. Rebecah."

"Hope you're gonna be better than the last tom fool nurse we had out from England ."

"I'm certainly going to try, Sister."

Gerry turned back to giving out the medicines. "You can call me Gerry, if you likes - when we're not on duty that is."

Becky smiled, "Thanks. Maybe you and the other girls would like to come round for some jerk chicken, and peas and rice at the week-end."

"Yeah, why not? Meantime you'd best get round to the ER. There's plenty of work to be had."

Becky walked round to the Emergency Room. Stefano's mouth dropped open when he saw her. He rushed forward and enveloped her in a hug, "I thought you'd left, Becky!"

"It's not Becky anymore. It's Rebecah. And yes, I did almost leave but then I thought, the Bahamas is the land of seven hundred islands. I've only seen two of them, it might be interesting to see the rest."

"I don't suppose you'd let me show you them?"

"Well you know, Stefano, before, I was worried about your wife."

"Wife! What wife?"

"Yes, I know now. Gerry - Sister Carey that is, told me that Teresa was lying to me. I don't blame her really. Teresa was worried that you'd want to take me out." Becky's face grew sad.

"She was a lovely girl. I'm sorry for all that happened. What about Michael?"

"Michael deceived me. I couldn't live with someone who carries a gun in his pocket and has three different passports in his safe. I've changed since I met him but not that much!" she laughed.

"I'm not what you thought either, Becky. All that stuff with the tourists. I was trying to make you jealous."

"You were?"

"Yeah. I swear to God. When Gerry brought you in from the church, I thought I'd lost you. I was so scared."

"Well I guess I owe you. Maybe we could go for a drink." She smiled, "Take it from there. Slowly."

Stefano grinned from ear to ear.

"How much longer am I gonna wait here? I could bleed to death waiting on you two love birds!" A man stood in front of them with a blood covered rag on his hand.

"Looks like we've got work to do, Stefano."

"Yeah. Let's get started."

" We've got lots of time, time to get to know each other, time to get to know the land of seven hundred islands."

Cathy Zelenka lived and worked in the Bahamas for two years. Her experiences there provided the inspiration for this book. She wrote her first book aged eleven but her various lives as Sister in Intensive Care, Nurse Teacher, TV Meter Collector, B&B Landlady and Reflexologist interfered with her pursuance of writing. She has had many short stories published and was chosen to read one at the Cheltenham Festival of Literature.

She has also written a romantic thriller set in the Spanish Civil War – 'The Hungry Years', and a collection of short stories set in Spain, both of which will be published shortly.

50% of the profit from this book will be donated to the Sue Ryder charity (reg.1052076).